WARRIORS

THE UNTOLD
STORIES

WARRIORS

EXPLORE THE
WARRIORS
WORLD

Also by Erin Hunter

SEEKERS

RETURN TO THE WILD

MANGA

SURVIVORS

WARRIORS
THE UNTOLD STORIES

INCLUDES
Hollyleaf's Story
Mistystar's Omen
Cloudstar's Journey

ERIN HUNTER

HARPER
An Imprint of HarperCollinsPublishers

Special thanks to Victoria Holmes

The Untold Stories
Hollyleaf's Story, Mistystar's Omen, Cloudstar's Journey
Copyright © 2012, 2013 by Working Partners Limited
Series created by Working Partners Limited

Library of Congress catalog card number: 2013934257
ISBN 978-0-06-223292-2

Typography by Hilary Zarycky
13 14 15 16 17   LP/OPM   10 9 8 7 6 5 4
❖
First Edition

CONTENTS

WARRIORS

HOLLYLEAF'S STORY

ALLEGIANCES

THUNDERCLAN

LEADER   **FIRESTAR**—ginger tom with a flame-colored pelt

DEPUTY   **BRAMBLECLAW**—dark brown tabby tom with amber eyes

MEDICINE CAT   **LEAFPOOL**—light brown tabby she-cat with amber eyes

         APPRENTICE, JAYFEATHER

WARRIORS   (toms and she-cats without kits)

         SQUIRRELFLIGHT—dark ginger she-cat with green eyes

         DUSTPELT—dark brown tabby tom

         SANDSTORM—pale ginger she-cat with green eyes

         CLOUDTAIL—long-haired white tom with blue eyes

         BRACKENFUR—golden brown tabby tom

         SORRELTAIL—tortoiseshell-and-white she-cat with amber eyes

         THORNCLAW—golden brown tabby tom

         BRIGHTHEART—white she-cat with ginger patches

         SPIDERLEG—long-limbed black tom with brown underbelly and amber eyes

         BIRCHFALL—light brown tabby tom

         GRAYSTRIPE—long-haired gray tom

         BERRYNOSE—cream-colored tom

         HAZELTAIL—small gray-and-white she-cat

         MOUSEWHISKER—gray-and-white tom

         CINDERHEART—gray tabby she-cat

HONEYFERN—light brown tabby she-cat

POPPYFROST—tortoiseshell she-cat

LIONBLAZE—golden tabby tom with amber eyes

HOLLYLEAF—black she-cat with green eyes

APPRENTICES

(more than six moons old, in training to become warriors)

FOXPAW—reddish tabby tom

ICEPAW—white she-cat

QUEENS

(she-cats expecting or nursing kits)

FERNCLOUD—pale gray (with darker flecks) she-cat with green eyes

DAISY—cream long-furred cat from the horseplace, mother of Spiderleg's kits: Rosekit (dark cream she-cat) and Toadkit (black-and-white tom)

MILLIE—striped gray tabby she-cat, former kittypet, mother of Graystripe's kits: Briarkit (dark brown she-cat), Bumblekit (very pale gray tom with black stripes), and Blossomkit (pale brown she-cat with a dark stripe along her spine)

WHITEWING—white she-cat with green eyes, mother of Birchfall's kits: Dovekit (gray she-cat) and Ivykit (white tabby she-cat)

ELDERS

(former warriors and queens, now retired)

LONGTAIL—pale tabby tom with dark black stripes, retired early due to failing sight

MOUSEFUR—small dusky brown she-cat

SHADOWCLAN

LEADER   **BLACKSTAR**—large white tom with huge jet-black paws

DEPUTY   **RUSSETFUR**—dark ginger she-cat

MEDICINE CAT   **LITTLECLOUD**—very small tabby tom
       APPRENTICE, FLAMEPAW (ginger tom)

WARRIORS   **OAKFUR**—small brown tom
       APPRENTICE, TIGERPAW (dark brown tabby tom)

       ROWANCLAW—ginger tom

       SMOKEFOOT—black tom
       APPRENTICE, OWLPAW (light brown tabby tom)

       IVYTAIL—black, white, and tortoiseshell she-cat
       APPRENTICE, DAWNPAW (cream-furred she-cat)

       TOADFOOT—dark brown tom

       CROWFROST—black-and-white tom
       APPRENTICE, OLIVEPAW (tortoiseshell she-cat)

       KINKFUR—tabby she-cat, with long fur that sticks out at all angles

       RATSCAR—brown tom with long scar across his back
       APPRENTICE, SHREWPAW (gray she-cat with black feet)

SNAKETAIL—dark brown tom with tabby-striped tail

APPRENTICE, SCORCHPAW (dark gray tom)

WHITEWATER—white she-cat with long fur, blind in one eye

APPRENTICE, REDPAW (mottled brown and ginger tom)

TAWNYPELT—tortoiseshell she-cat with green eyes

QUEENS   **SNOWBIRD**—pure-white she-cat

ELDERS   **CEDARHEART**—dark gray tom

TALLPOPPY—long-legged light brown tabby she-cat

WINDCLAN

LEADER   **ONESTAR**—brown tabby tom

DEPUTY   **ASHFOOT**—gray she-cat

MEDICINE CAT   **BARKFACE**—short-tailed brown tom

APPRENTICE, KESTRELPAW (mottled gray tom)

WARRIORS   **TORNEAR**—tabby tom

CROWFEATHER—dark gray tom

OWLWHISKER—light brown tabby tom

WHITETAIL—small white she-cat

NIGHTCLOUD—black she-cat

GORSETAIL—very pale gray-and-white cat with blue eyes

WEASELFUR—ginger tom with white paws

HARESPRING—brown-and-white tom

LEAFTAIL—dark tabby tom with amber eyes
APPRENTICE, THISTLEPAW (long-haired white tom)

DEWSPOTS—spotted gray tabby she-cat
APPRENTICE, SEDGEPAW (light brown tabby she-cat)

WILLOWCLAW—gray she-cat
APPRENTICE, SWALLOWPAW (dark gray she-cat)

ANTPELT—brown tom with one black ear

EMBERFOOT—gray tom with two dark paws
APPRENTICE, SUNPAW (tortoiseshell she-cat with large white mark on her forehead)

HEATHERTAIL—light brown tabby she-cat with blue eyes

BREEZEPELT—black tom with amber eyes

ELDERS
MORNINGFLOWER—very old tortoiseshell queen

WEBFOOT—dark gray tabby tom

RIVERCLAN

LEADER
LEOPARDSTAR—unusually spotted golden tabby she-cat

DEPUTY
MISTYFOOT—gray she-cat with blue eyes

MEDICINE CAT
MOTHWING—dappled golden she-cat
APPRENTICE, WILLOWSHINE (gray tabby she-cat)

WARRIORS

BLACKCLAW—smoky black tom

VOLETOOTH—small brown tabby tom
APPRENTICE, MINNOWPAW (dark gray she-cat)

REEDWHISKER—black tom

MOSSPELT—tortoiseshell she-cat with blue eyes
APPRENTICE, PEBBLEPAW (mottled gray tom)

BEECHFUR—light brown tom

RIPPLETAIL—dark gray tabby tom
APPRENTICE, MALLOWPAW (light brown tabby tom)

GRAYMIST—pale gray tabby

DAWNFLOWER—pale gray she-cat

DAPPLENOSE—mottled gray she-cat

POUNCETAIL—ginger-and-white tom

MINTFUR—light gray tabby tom
APPRENTICE, NETTLEPAW (dark brown tabby tom)

OTTERHEART—dark brown she-cat
APPRENTICE, SNEEZEPAW (gray-and-white tom)

PINEFUR—very short-haired tabby she-cat
APPRENTICE, ROBINPAW (tortoiseshell-and-white tom)

RAINSTORM—mottled gray-blue tom

DUSKFUR—brown tabby she-cat
APPRENTICE, COPPERPAW (dark ginger she-cat)

CATS OUTSIDE CLANS

OTHER ANIMALS

WARRIORS

HOLLYLEAF'S
STORY

Hareview Campsite

Sanctuary
Cottage

Sadler Woods

Littlepine Road

Littlepine
Sailing
Center

Littlepine
Island

River Alba

Whitchurch Road

Abandoned
Workman's
House

Quarry Road [disused]

Crystal Pool

Quarry

Hare Hill
Woods

Hare
Hill

ctuary
e

Knight's
Copse

Hare Hill
Riding Stables

Hare Hill Road

Deciduous Woodland

Pine Forest

Marsh

Lake

Footpaths

NORTH

CHAPTER 1

❧

Thunder crashed, louder than anything Hollyleaf had heard before. There was a ripple overhead and a strange cracking sound. *The sky is falling!* And then it was all around her, sharper and harder than Hollyleaf expected, throwing her to the ground and crushing her bones. *I can't breathe!* She struggled frantically, feeling her claws rip, but the sky was too heavy, too cold, and she let the endless dark sweep her away.

Hollyleaf was standing on the edge of a cliff. Behind her, the hollow yawned like a hungry mouth. Flames, hissing and orange, filled the air with smoke and bitter ash. Hollyleaf's littermates, Lionblaze and Jayfeather, crouched beside her; she could feel them trembling against her fur. In front of them, Ashfur stood at the end of a branch that would lead them through the fire. Squirrelflight stood next to him, fury blazing in her eyes. Hollyleaf stared at her mother, waiting for her to move Ashfur out of the way.

"Enough, Ashfur," Squirrelflight hissed. "Your quarrel is with me. These young cats have done nothing to hurt you. Do what you like with me, but let them out of the fire."

Ashfur looked at her in surprise. "You don't understand. This is the only way to make you feel the same pain that you caused me. You tore my heart out when you chose Brambleclaw over me. Anything I did to you would never hurt as much. But your kits . . . If you watch them die, then you'll know the pain I felt."

Squirrelflight met his gaze. "Kill them, then. You won't hurt me that way." She took a step away from him, then looked back over her shoulder. "If you really want to hurt me, you'll have to find a better way than that. They are not my kits."

The ground lurched beneath Hollyleaf's paws. Squirrelflight is not my mother? Hollyleaf was Clanless, codeless. She could be a rogue, even a kittypet. There was no way Hollyleaf could let Ashfur tell the four Clans about Squirrelflight's confession. She and her littermates would be driven out! Everything they had done up till now, all their loyalty to the warrior code, would count for nothing.

The silence was deafening, pressing more heavily on Hollyleaf's ears than the stones that pinned her to the cold floor. Dust filled her mouth and nose, and pain stabbed through one of her legs. *I've been buried alive!* Hollyleaf thrashed and bucked against the weight of the rocks. Her head broke free with a shower of small stones. There wasn't a sliver of light from the mouth of the tunnel. She was trapped in the dark.

"Help! Help me! I'm stuck!"

She stopped. Who was she calling to? She had no Clanmates now. She had left that life behind—on the other side of the rocks, as far away as if it were the moon. Her brothers and Leafpool knew that she had killed Ashfur. And now Jayfeather and Lionblaze probably thought she had died in the rockfall. *Maybe it's better that way. At least they won't come looking for me.* Hollyleaf closed her eyes again.

Hollyleaf had followed Ashfur to the WindClan border. She had stalked him like she would a piece of prey, treading softly, claws sheathed to keep them from catching in brambles or scratching on stone. When he reached the bank of the stream, with the water foaming far below, Hollyleaf sprang on him, twisted his head to one side, sank her teeth into his fur and skin, telling herself over and over: This is the only way! *Ashfur dropped to his belly and Hollyleaf jumped back as he rolled into the stream. She washed the blood from her paws, letting the cold water chill her legs, her flanks, all the way to her heart.* I did it for my Clan!

Hollyleaf forced the images from her mind with a shudder. Taking a deep breath, she wriggled her front paws free and pushed away the stones that were pressing against her chest. Then she reached out as far as she could and started to haul herself out. She hissed when one of her hind legs moved. It was so painful, her leg felt as if it might be broken. Hollyleaf pictured the well-stocked medicine den, with comfrey to mend the bone and poppy seeds to help her sleep through the worst of the discomfort. *As far away as the moon,* she reminded herself. Gritting her teeth, she dragged the rest of her body out of the stones. Her wounded leg bounced agonizingly onto the floor.

"Great StarClan, that hurts!" Hollyleaf growled. Speaking aloud seemed to help, so she carried on. "I've been down here before. I know there are other ways out. I just need to follow this tunnel until I find a source of light. Come on, one paw in front of the other." In spite of her fear, in spite of the pain in her leg, the memories kept flooding back. . . .

"I am your mother, Hollyleaf," Leafpool had whispered. Hollyleaf shook her head. That was impossible. How could she be the daughter of a medicine cat, when medicine cats were forbidden to have kits? Worse than being a rogue or a kittypet, her own birth had broken the code of the Clans.

Hollyleaf unsheathed her claws to give her a better grip on the stone. To her dismay, several of them had already broken off in her struggle to get out, and the tips of her pads felt wet and sticky. She smelled blood and pictured the trail she was leaving as she crawled along the tunnel. If Lionblaze and Jayfeather dug through the rockfall, they'd know she'd survived and would follow the trail to find her. Suddenly her front paws thudded into stone. She yelped with pain and swiveled sideways to follow the curve of the wall. It was so dark, she couldn't even tell if her eyes were open. *If I can just find some light. If, if, if . . .*

Jayfeather had figured out who their father was. "It's Crowfeather."

Hollyleaf stared at him in disbelief. "But . . . Crowfeather's from Wind-Clan! I'm a ThunderClan cat!"

"Yellowfang came to me in a dream," Jayfeather insisted. "She told me it was time we knew the truth."

For Hollyleaf, there was nothing left. Half-Clan? She stood in the mouth of the tunnel and felt the scent of stone smooth her ruffled fur. She could disappear down here and emerge somewhere far from the Clans. She could begin a new life, away from all these lies and broken promises.

Hollyleaf turned and ran into the tunnel. She heard Jayfeather calling to her—and then the thunder came, and the sky fell in, and she was swallowed up by the dizzying black.

Hollyleaf kept going. *Breathe, scrape, haul.* Over and over. She longed to stop, to sleep, to wait for a StarClan warrior to come for her. But did StarClan even know she was here? Her birth had broken the warrior code. She had killed another cat. And she had given up her place in ThunderClan. No ancestors would be watching over her. Had they been watching when Hollyleaf spilled all her Clan's secrets at the Gathering?

"Wait!" Hollyleaf leaped to her paws. "There's something that I have to say that all the Clans should hear." There had been too many lies, too much damage done to the warrior code, for her to keep quiet any longer.

The clearing was so quiet that Hollyleaf could hear a mouse scuttering among the dead leaves under the Great Oak. "You think you know me," she began. "And my brothers, Lionblaze and Jayfeather of ThunderClan. You think you know us, but everything you have been told about us is a lie! We are not the kits of Brambleclaw and Squirrelflight."

"What?" Brambleclaw shot to his paws from where he sat with the other deputies among the roots of the Great Oak. "Squirrelflight, why is she talking such nonsense?"

"I'm sorry, Brambleclaw, but it's true. I'm not their mother, and you are not their father."

The Clan deputy stared at her. "Then who is?"

Squirrelflight turned her sad green gaze on the cat she had always claimed as her daughter. "Tell them, Hollyleaf. I kept the secret for seasons; I'm not going to reveal it now."

"Coward!" Hollyleaf flashed at her. Her gaze swept around the clearing, seeing the eyes of every single cat trained on her. "I'm not afraid of the truth! Leafpool is our mother, and Crowfeather—yes, Crowfeather of Wind-Clan—is our father."

Yowls of shock greeted her words, but Hollyleaf shouted over them. "These cats were so ashamed of us that they gave us away and lied to every single one of you to hide the fact that they had broken the warrior code. It's all her fault." She whipped her tail around to point at Leafpool. "How can the Clans survive when there are cowards and liars at the very heart of them?"

Her words seemed to echo from the walls of the tunnel. Hollyleaf wished she could go back to the start of the Gathering, take back the terrible truth she had spilled, spare her Clanmates the pain and shock she had seen in their faces. *What have I done?*

The constant dark was making her eyes ache. She had been searching for a chink of light for so long that she imagined one had appeared up ahead. The faintest line of something paler than black, like the first hint of milky dawn above the trees. Hollyleaf blinked and shook her head, trying to clear her vision. But the gray stripe was still there. Maybe it *was* light? She limped faster, ignoring the burn in her hind leg. The light grew stronger. It was seeping from a gap in the wall: another, smaller tunnel leading off. Hollyleaf dragged herself around the corner. Was it her imagination, or could she see the walls of a cave opening out ahead? In her excitement, she tried to stand up. Her hind leg buckled beneath her and stars exploded in her head. The last thing she saw was the stone floor rushing up to meet her.

CHAPTER 2

❧

Leafpool! Leafpool, I'm thirsty!

Hollyleaf was burning up. Her throat felt parched and her tongue was stuck to the roof of her mouth. She must be in the medicine den with a fever. Where was the soaked moss that Leafpool always left close to her patients? She twisted her head, and her muzzle bumped into something soft and wet and green-smelling. Hollyleaf sucked at the tendrils of moss, trying not to wince as she swallowed the precious water. Nothing had ever tasted better.

Suddenly she realized she wasn't alone. There was a cat bending over her, pushing something beneath her injured leg. Hollyleaf hissed in pain, and the cat apologized softly. "It's just some feathers, to make you more comfortable. Lie still now."

Hollyleaf stiffened. She didn't recognize this cat's voice or scent. "Who are you? Where am I?" She started to flail her front paws. "Let me go!"

A small, cool foot was placed on her shoulder, gently pushing her back down. Strong-smelling leaves were moved close to her muzzle. "Hush, it's all right. You're safe. Eat these, then go back to sleep."

Hollyleaf allowed herself to be nudged back onto the floor. She swallowed the herbs—comfrey, from the scent of it—and two tiny poppy seeds. The feathers felt soft and warm against her wounded leg. With a small sigh, Hollyleaf closed her eyes and sleep dragged her away once more.

When she woke next, her head felt clearer and the pain in her leg had dulled to a nagging ache. Hollyleaf lay still for a moment, letting her eyes adjust to the near-darkness. This definitely wasn't the ThunderClan medicine den. She was lying on a thin bed of feathers over cold stone. *I'm still in the tunnels!* Hollyleaf felt a jolt of relief, then alarm. Who was down here with her? Hollyleaf tried to recall the scent of the cat who had told her to go back to sleep, but her belly rumbled and suddenly all she could think about was how hungry she was. When had she last eaten? She tried to stand up but her hind leg crumpled and she flopped onto her side, frustrated.

"You're awake!" A face loomed from the shadows. "How is your leg?"

Hollyleaf opened her eyes wide until she could make out ginger-and-white patches on the cat's pelt. He smelled of stone and water and moss. "Who are you?" she asked, her voice hoarse from lack of use.

The cat ignored her. Instead, he pushed something toward her with one paw. "You must be starving. Here, eat."

Fresh-kill! Hollyleaf bent her head, ready to dive in, then pulled back. A small, slimy minnow lay in front of her. "I don't like fish," she mewed.

The cat twitched his ears. "Down here, you don't always have a choice." His tone was mild, but Hollyleaf felt embarrassed. Her belly let out a loud growl as if it would be happy with anything, even crow-food. Holding her breath, Hollyleaf bit into the fish. *Plump, tasty mouse,* she told herself. *Pine-scented squirrel. The first pigeon of newleaf.*

She swallowed the last mouthful and drank from the moss beside her. The ginger-and-white cat watched her expectantly. "Thank you," Hollyleaf meowed. "I . . . I guess it didn't taste too bad."

The tom was still studying her. "You're Hollypaw, aren't you?"

She blinked. "Hollyleaf, actually. How did you know? I've never seen you before, have I?"

The cat shook his head and his eyes clouded. "No, you've never seen me. But I saw you with your littermates when you came to rescue those kits, just before the river flooded."

Hollyleaf stared at him. She would never forget the desperate search for the lost WindClan kits with Jayfeather and Lionblaze. They had been washed out of the tunnels and into the lake when the underground river overflowed. It had been a lucky escape for all of them. Now this cat was telling her that he had been here! "Who *are* you?" she mewed.

The ginger-and-white tom busied himself with the feathers underneath her injured leg, rearranging them so that they were spread evenly. "My name is Fallen Leaves," he meowed quietly.

"You're not from the Clans, are you?" Hollyleaf pressed. "Where do you live?"

Fallen Leaves padded over to a small bundle of herbs and started dividing them up. "Once I lived in the hills above the lake, but this is my home now." He turned, pushing some herbs toward Hollyleaf. "Eat this comfrey; it'll help your leg. I won't give you any more poppy seeds unless you have trouble sleeping."

Hollyleaf obediently chewed the fragrant leaves. "Were you a medicine cat?" she asked.

Fallen Leaves tipped his head to one side. "I don't know what that is. We all learned about herbs and injuries so we could help one another. Is that what you mean?"

"Kind of." Hollyleaf propped herself up on her front legs, feeling her heart beat faster. "Who were the other cats? Were you part of a Clan?" Was there another group of cats living near here, one that the Clans didn't know about?

"No more questions," Fallen Leaves ordered. "You need to rest. You haven't broken your leg, just wrenched it. You'll mend soon enough, and then I suppose you'll want to go back to your friends."

"No!" Hollyleaf yelped. "I can't go back! Not ever!"

Fallen Leaves just shrugged. "That's up to you. Lie down and stop wriggling. I'll bring you something to eat later." He picked up the scraps of fish bones and walked away.

Hollyleaf stared after him until the shadows swallowed him up. The walls of the tunnel seemed paler, as if more light

was filtering in. When she'd been speaking, she'd heard her
voice echoing from far away, which suggested that her first
impression had been right and she was lying at the entrance to
a cave. She couldn't hear any water, so it wasn't the cave with
the river. Hollyleaf rested her chin on her paws and closed her
eyes. She was lost and injured, but somehow a cat had found
her and kept her alive with food and water, and herbs for her
leg. Had he been sent by StarClan? Or was she just very, very
lucky? Either way, she figured that she was safe, at least for
now.

She woke from a doze to find another little fish beside her,
as well as freshly soaked moss and some more comfrey. It was
harder to see the walls of the cave, which meant it must have
gotten darker outside. Was it night? Hollyleaf wondered how
many days she had been down here. It had been a full moon
when she . . . left. Perhaps Fallen Leaves could tell her what
the moon was now. After eating her fish and masking the
taste with the comfrey, Hollyleaf tried to stay awake, hoping
that Fallen Leaves would come back. The cave grew darker
until she couldn't see a thing. Hollyleaf gave up waiting for
her strange companion. He would come again in the morning,
she was sure.

This time she was awake and half-sitting up to wash her
chest when Fallen Leaves arrived. He was carrying something
bulkier and fluffier-looking than a fish. Hollyleaf paused
between licks. "Hey! You caught a mouse!"

Fallen Leaves deposited the fresh-kill at her paws. He

looked flushed with triumph. "I heard it creeping into one of the tunnels," he explained. "I hoped you'd like it."

"I do!" Hollyleaf meowed. "Thanks!" She leaned forward to take a bite, then looked up. "There's plenty here. Would you like some?"

Fallen Leaves shook his head. "No, it's all yours." While Hollyleaf continued eating, he gently prodded her injured leg. "Is it mending, do you think?"

Hollyleaf nodded with her mouth full. "Definitely," she mumbled. "I can bend it now, and it doesn't hurt so much when I move."

"You can try walking on it when you've finished eating," Fallen Leaves decided. "Not too far, but you need to start exercising it before the muscles waste away."

Hollyleaf twitched her ears with surprise. Fallen Leaves sounded just like a medicine cat. He *must* have come from a Clan! Or something very close to a Clan—like the Tribe of Rushing Water. She swallowed and mewed, "Are you a Tribe cat? Did you come from the mountains?"

Fallen Leaves stared blankly at her. "This is my home now," he replied. "There is nowhere else."

Hollyleaf shivered as if a cold claw had run down her spine. There was something about Fallen Leaves's voice that made her feel more alone and desperate than she could imagine. She straightened up and nudged away the scraps of mouse ears and tail. "Where should I walk?" she asked.

"Don't get too excited," Fallen Leaves warned. "Just a few steps today, that's all."

Hollyleaf used her front legs to push herself to her paws. A stab of pain ran up her injured leg, but she took a deep breath and kept her paw on the ground. Hesitantly, she took one step forward. Her hind leg held, though it felt weak and not quite connected to the rest of her. Hollyleaf limped toward the place where the light grew stronger. The walls of the tunnel opened out on either side into a small cave, about six fox-lengths wide. A tiny hole in the roof blazed with light, so bright that Hollyleaf had to screw up her eyes to look at it. "The sun is shining today," Fallen Leaves commented as he came to stand by her shoulder.

Hollyleaf turned to face him. "Do you ever go outside? How can you live here all the time?"

Fallen Leaves looked away. "This is my home," he repeated. "Now, can you make it back to your nest?"

Hollyleaf started to walk back along the tunnel, frustrated that she hadn't gone farther. But by the time she reached the dented pile of feathers her leg was aching badly, and she sank down with relief. "You can try again tomorrow," Fallen Leaves meowed as if he could tell she was in pain. "Rest now."

He turned to leave but Hollyleaf reached out with one paw. "Wait! I'm bored of being on my own. Can't you stay and talk to me?"

Fallen Leaves viewed her with somber blue eyes. "Rest," he mewed. "That way your leg will heal faster. I'll see you again later."

He padded away and Hollyleaf slumped down on the

feathers. She willed her leg to get better soon. She'd wanted to escape from ThunderClan, but a life in the dark, dependent on another cat for food and water, was not what she had imagined.

CHAPTER 3
❧

The slim beam of sunlight felt warm on her fur as Hollyleaf marched across the cave and back again on all four paws. "See?" she challenged Fallen Leaves, who was sitting at the entrance. "Good as new!"

It felt like whole seasons had passed before Hollyleaf had been able to walk all the way across the cave without limping, but Fallen Leaves assured her the moon wasn't full again yet. He had insisted that she stay within the cave to exercise, walking in circles until she felt dizzy. He still left her on her own for most of the day and all night, but Hollyleaf didn't want to start roaming the caves without him. She had been lucky once; she couldn't rely on Fallen Leaves finding her again.

Fallen Leaves came over and sniffed her leg. "If you're telling the truth about not being in pain, then it must have healed."

"Of course I'm telling the truth!" Hollyleaf protested. How dare he suggest she was lying? The truth was the only thing that mattered, ever. *But it didn't feel like that when I spilled my Clan's secrets at the Gathering.*

Hollyleaf pushed the image of Squirrelflight's horrified

face out of her mind. "Can we explore now?" she asked.

Fallen Leaves traced a line in the stone dust with his paw. "You mean, you want me to show you the way out."

"No!" Hollyleaf exclaimed. "I want you to show me around your home. Where is the cave with the river? How far do the tunnels reach?"

The ginger-and-white cat looked at her in surprise. "You really want to know? Most cats want to get straight out of here."

There was such pain in his eyes that Hollyleaf felt a rush of sympathy. "I have nowhere else to go," she mewed softly. "You've been a good friend to me, Fallen Leaves. Why would I want to leave you now?"

Fallen Leaves led Hollyleaf down a narrow tunnel on the far side of the cave, into darkness so thick that it seemed to lap at Hollyleaf's fur like water. The floor felt smooth and cold under her paws, and she was only aware of the walls on either side when the tips of her whiskers brushed against them. At first she reacted too much and lurched into the opposite wall with a crash, but soon she learned to move her head just the tiniest amount when her whiskers tingled.

"The tunnel opens out down here," Fallen Leaves called back over his shoulder. He must have heard her stumbling from side to side.

Hollyleaf realized she could see her companion's outline against a paler shade of gray. The sound of water echoed down the tunnel, not exactly splashing but a soft liquid murmur that could only be the underground river. Hollyleaf broke into a trot, squeezing past Fallen Leaves and bursting into the huge cavern. It was filled with dusky light and to Hollyleaf, after being trapped in the dark for so long, it seemed as familiar and welcoming as her den in the hollow. In front of her was the river, tame and quiet between its shallow stone banks, and there was the ledge high up on the wall where Lionblaze had boasted of standing.

"Your brother and the she-cat played up there," Fallen Leaves remarked, coming to stand alongside her.

He means Lionblaze and Heathertail. Hollyleaf felt a stir of discomfort. Was Fallen Leaves's impression of the Clans based on cats hiding out of sight and breaking the warrior code? To change the subject, she nodded toward a tunnel on the far side of the river. "That leads to outside, doesn't it?" It was strange to think that a short walk would take her back into the heart of ThunderClan.

"It used to," Fallen Leaves meowed, "but it's blocked by mud now. Do you remember that tunnel over there? That's where you found the kits."

Hollyleaf looked at the yawning black mouth, close to the edge of the river. She shivered as she recalled the desperate search for the lost WindClan cats, while far above them Onestar and Firestar prepared to wage war over their disappearance.

"The tunnels aren't scary once you get used to them," Fallen Leaves reassured her. "I'll show you, but first you should eat." He padded to the edge of the river and paused for a moment, his gaze fixed on the black water sliding past. Suddenly one of his front paws shot out and scooped a trembling silver fish onto the rock. It flapped madly until Fallen Leaves killed it with a single strike. "Here," he meowed, pushing it toward Hollyleaf.

"Er, don't you want to eat, too?" Hollyleaf suggested, hanging back from yet another fishy meal. If she'd been born in RiverClan, she would have chosen to starve by now!

Fallen Leaves shook his head. "No, this one's for you. Eat it up; then we can explore."

Grudgingly, Hollyleaf gulped down the fish. It didn't taste too bad this time, and when she drank from the river, the cool, sharp tang of the water was refreshing. Fallen Leaves was waiting for her at the mouth of the darkest tunnel. He beckoned to her with his tail before trotting into the shadows. Hollyleaf followed more slowly, taking one last glance back at the half-lit cave before surrendering to the blackness.

She could hear paw steps ahead, ringing confidently on the stone. "It'll get lighter soon," Fallen Leaves called back to her. Hollyleaf broke into a trot, glad to get some warmth into her bones. Suddenly her nose brushed something soft, and she slowed down to avoid crashing into Fallen Leaves's haunches. She sniffed, trying to get a fix on his scent, but all she could smell was cold, damp stone. Had Fallen Leaves been in the tunnels for so long that he'd taken on the scent of his surroundings?

Fallen Leaves put on a burst of speed and Hollyleaf ran to keep up with him. The walls of the tunnel emerged from the shadows and she could see the outline of the cat in front of her. Hollyleaf couldn't tell where the light was coming from, and for once she didn't instantly look down to check where she was putting her paws. She knew the floor was smooth and level here—no loose pebbles had tripped her up so far, and there hadn't been any sharp inclines.

Fallen Leaves turned to look at her, his eyes gleaming in the semidarkness. "Okay to go a bit faster?" he meowed. There was a hint of challenge in his voice.

"Of course!" Hollyleaf replied. Her injured leg wasn't aching in the slightest, and she was ready to use muscles that had been kept still for too long.

She hardly had time to take a breath before Fallen Leaves raced away. His ginger-and-white pelt was almost instantly swallowed up by the shadows beyond the reach of the pale light. This time Hollyleaf didn't think twice about following him. Her whiskers quivered with the effort of feeling for the walls on either side, and she kept her weight low over her paws so that she could adjust to changes in the floor of the tunnel. It started to slope down steeply, so Hollyleaf rocked backward until her front paws were doing little more than feeling the way, keeping her balanced on her haunches. After a while her hind leg began to hurt, but then the tunnel flattened out and Hollyleaf was able to run at full-pelt again. She could hear Fallen Leaves ahead of her, and she was starting to know when the tunnel curved or hit an incline from the sound of his paws.

When they burst into a small cave that was filled with sunlight from a crack in the roof, Hollyleaf was almost disappointed. The cats stopped for a moment, panting.

"That was fun!" Hollyleaf gasped.

"You're doing really well!" Fallen Leaves purred admiringly.

"Thanks!" Hollyleaf looked around. "Where are we? I mean, in relation to outside?"

"We've come to the other side of the hills," Fallen Leaves explained. "That tunnel over there"—he nodded to a gap in the wall—"leads out if you follow the scent of trees when you reach the fork."

Hollyleaf tipped back her head and stared at the ceiling. Pointed stone blades hung down, ringed with delicate lines. A drip of water clung to each tip. She didn't know the territory above them, not if it was beyond Clan boundaries. But it was weird to think that caves like this, and long winding tunnels, had been beneath her paws all the time.

"We should head back," Fallen Leaves meowed. "You don't want to hurt your leg. Come on, let's go a different way."

Before Hollyleaf could protest that her leg was fine, he darted into a side tunnel. "Wait for me!" Hollyleaf squeaked playfully. She raced into the darkness, stretching her neck until her muzzle bumped against cold fur. "Caught you!" she teased.

Fallen Leaves chirped with amusement. "We'll see about that!" He lengthened his stride and pulled ahead.

Hollyleaf leaped forward, but her toe caught on a loose stone and she stumbled. Regaining her balance, she stopped to listen. Fallen Leaves's paws sounded faintly somewhere down the tunnel. Hollyleaf set off, but almost at once she crashed into the wall because she was so busy straining her ears for footsteps. She paused and shook her head. *Focus!* She straightened her whiskers with a flick of her paw and started trotting down the tunnel. She could definitely hear Fallen Leaves ahead of her. A breeze on her face revealed a tunnel leading off to one side. Hollyleaf instinctively turned her head to look but it was so dark she couldn't see any change in the shadows around her. She fought down a pulse of alarm and sniffed the empty space where the side tunnel began. There was no trace of warmth or fur, no sign that Fallen Leaves had gone this way. Had he kept to the main tunnel, then? Hollyleaf pricked her ears. The silence pressed around her, heavy as water filling her ears. She forced herself to walk forward, and jumped as she heard the faintest sound of paw steps. She stopped, straining to listen. The footsteps had stopped. Hollyleaf looked down at her paws, even though she couldn't see them. *Mouse-brain!* She'd been listening to the echo of her own steps. She was completely alone in the darkness.

A wail rose in her throat and she swallowed to keep it down. Her pelt stood on end and she felt her paws start to tremble. Surely Fallen Leaves would notice she wasn't behind him? Or would he assume she'd found a different way back? She'd been running so confidently after him. Hollyleaf took a step forward and her head thudded against rock. Reeling, she jumped sideways and hit her shoulder against the opposite wall. Had the tunnel shrunk? Were the walls closing in on her, slowly crushing her to nothing?

"Hollyleaf!" A whisper beside her made Hollyleaf almost jump out of her skin. "Are you okay?" Fallen Leaves asked, coming closer until his muzzle touched her ears. "What happened?"

"I didn't know where you were!" Hollyleaf burst out. "It was so dark, and I thought I could hear you but it was only my own paw steps! Then I hit the walls and I thought you'd lost me!"

"I'll never do that, I promise," Fallen Leaves murmured into her ear. "You will never be lost down here, because you have me. Come on, I'll take you back."

With his head close to hers, he led Hollyleaf along the tunnel, slowing his pace as she limped beside him. They emerged into the cavern, waded through the river, and headed back into the tunnel where Hollyleaf's nest lay. She collapsed into the feathers, feeling grateful for their warmth against her chilled fur. Her leg throbbed and Fallen Leaves pushed some poppy seeds toward her.

"Eat these—they'll help you sleep," he prompted. He turned to leave but Hollyleaf lifted her head.

"Can . . . can you stay here tonight?" she mewed. "I don't want to be alone in the dark again. There's room in my nest if I shift over."

Fallen Leaves hesitated, then stepped into the circle of feathers. "Okay, just for one night," he meowed. He curled next to her somewhat awkwardly, and Hollyleaf wriggled to give him more room. The poppy seeds were working and her eyelids felt heavy. She uncurled until her spine was pressed against Fallen Leaves's flank. For a moment it was like being back in the hollow, sharing her nest with Cinderheart. Hollyleaf breathed deeply and started to drift into sleep. But just before the limpid blackness filled her mind, she flinched. *Why am I so cold?* There was no warmth coming from Fallen Leaves's pelt at all. Had living underground chilled him right to the bone?

CHAPTER 4

♣

"Hey! Wake up! It's time for the morning patrol!"

Hollyleaf rolled over and rubbed a paw over her eyes. Fallen Leaves was looking down at her, his tail curled high over his back.

"Come on, sleepy slug!" he teased.

Hollyleaf scrambled up. She had been dreaming that she was back in ThunderClan, chasing a squirrel that got tinier and tinier the closer she came. Just as she reached out to grab it, the squirrel had vanished completely.

She peered past Fallen Leaves to look at the pale yellow light slanting into the tunnel. The angle between the beam of light and the roof was narrower today, which meant the sun was lower in the sky. Hollyleaf tipped her head to one side. She'd been here . . . how many moons? Three or four, at least. Leaf-fall must be creeping into the woods outside, turning the trees gold and scarlet. Hollyleaf wondered if it would get colder in the tunnels. She prodded her nest with her foot. She'd need to find more feathers.

Fallen Leaves was trotting away from her. "I'll take the moor-tunnel today," he called over his shoulder. "And you can check the woods-tunnel."

He had come up with names for the two main exit tunnels that didn't lead back into ThunderClan territory. They never went into those tunnels; without saying anything out loud, Hollyleaf knew that Fallen Leaves was trying to keep her distracted from her former home. She had chosen to stay with him, so that must be what she wanted, right? When she had told him about daily life in the Clans, with border and hunting patrols and ceremonies for apprentices and warriors, he had suggested doing the same down here. Now each day started with a patrol of the exit tunnels—not that they ever found anything in the empty stone pathways—followed by fishing in the underground river. Hollyleaf had learned to hook minnows with her paw almost as smoothly as Fallen Leaves, and she had grown used to the strong, watery taste. She could run through the dark confidently now, detecting the faintest breezes on her whiskers and picking up the tiniest echoes of flowing water from the river to locate where she was. When she was patrolling an exit tunnel, she only went as far as the light that spilled in from the mouth, hanging back as if it would burn her paws. She belonged in the shadows now, hiding from daylight and the sound of the wind in the trees.

Hollyleaf shivered. She had shelter, food, and company. Wasn't that more than she deserved, after what she had done? Fallen Leaves was much less demanding than her old Clanmates; he let her eat all the fish they caught together, and he never spent so long with her that she grew tired of his company.

In fact, he often left her alone, especially at night. Hollyleaf wondered where he slept; she thought she'd explored all the tunnels by now, but she'd never seen signs of another nest.

"Come on!" Fallen Leaves's voice echoed down the tunnel, and Hollyleaf broke into a run. She caught up with him in the river-cave and they stood side by side, looking down at the water. It was flowing more quickly today, and little waves spilled over the edges of the stone gully.

"It rained last night," Fallen Leaves explained.

Hollyleaf felt a flash of alarm. "Is the river going to flood?"

Fallen Leaves shook his head. "Not yet." He walked over to a corner and came back rolling a large flat stone with his muzzle. He nudged it to the edge of the wet line left by splashing waves. "We'll use this as a marker to see if the river rises any more."

Hollyleaf ran her paw over the stone. It felt smooth, like an egg. "That's a good idea," she commented.

"It's what the sharpclaws told me to do," Fallen Leaves meowed. "Before I came down here for my initiation."

Hollyleaf looked up at him sharply. Fallen Leaves had mentioned once before that he had gotten lost in the tunnels while training to be a sharpclaw, which seemed to be the same as a Clan warrior. He wouldn't tell her anything else about his Clan, or Tribe, or whatever his kin had called themselves.

"If you went back now," she mewed gently, "you'd be one of the greatest sharpclaws ever. You may have gotten lost once, but you know these tunnels better than any cat! If finding your way through the tunnels is supposed to teach you to be strong, brave, and independent, you are all of those things! You'd be a hero!"

Fallen Leaves stared at her as if she'd lost her mind. "Go back?" he hissed. "I can't go back! Don't you understand? It's too late!" Shaking with distress, he whirled around and raced into the tunnel that led to WindClan, the one they called the moor-tunnel.

"Wait!" Hollyleaf called, running after him. But she stopped when she reached the edge of the river-cave. All she had were questions for Fallen Leaves, and she didn't want to make him more upset. The thought flashed in her mind that she might not be the only one fleeing from a terrible secret. She had never told Fallen Leaves what had happened with Ashfur; perhaps she had more in common with her new companion than she realized.

She turned and padded back across the cave. The entrance to the woods-tunnel was on the far side of the river, and today it took a much bigger leap to clear the gully. Hollyleaf yelped as her hind paws splashed into the edge of the water and showered her belly fur with icy droplets. As she entered the tunnel she broke into a run to warm herself up.

The rough gray walls on each side emerged from the darkness as she neared the entrance. The wind was blowing directly into the tunnel, filling Hollyleaf's mouth with scents of drying leaves and brittle grass. She padded closer until the light spilled over her paws. She lifted up one and looked at her pad in surprise. It was pale and tough from moons of running on stone. Suddenly Hollyleaf longed to feel soft, green grass under her feet, and to see the sky, vast and full of light, above her. She felt herself pulled toward the mouth of the tunnel as if she were a twig on a river. *Outside!*

The light grew stronger and Hollyleaf screwed up her eyes. It wasn't sunshine—this light was cool and gray—but it was brighter than anything she'd seen in a long while. The entrance to the tunnel was a circle of dazzling white, too painful to look at directly. Suddenly there was a crashing noise beyond the brightness, the sound of branches cracking beneath heavy paws. Then a volley of barking, mixed with a high-pitched yipping. Hollyleaf winced as the noise hit her ears; she was used to the heavy silence of the tunnels. She shrank back against the wall, too startled to know which way to run. There was an explosion of paw steps at the entrance and a huge dark shape burst through the light. At the same time a wave of stench hit Hollyleaf's nose. *Fox!*

Fear rooted her paws to the ground. The intruder crashed into her, bounced off the opposite wall, then turned and stared back the way it had come, taking no notice of Hollyleaf cowering in the corner. A head was thrust through the circle of light at the mouth of the tunnel. A long pink tongue hung from dripping jaws, and huge ears flopped down on either side of mean yellow eyes. The fox let out a yelp and scrabbled backward, squashing Hollyleaf against the wall of the tunnel. She held her breath, dizzy with terror. The dog at the entrance growled and took a step toward them. It blocked out the light so that its features vanished and all Hollyleaf could see was the faint outline of its massive shoulders. The fox crouched down, filling Hollyleaf's nose with soft, tickly fur. She longed to sneeze but couldn't risk being discovered.

There was a shout from outside—a deep Twoleg voice, raised in anger—and the dog's ears twitched. A moment later it jerked backward, and Hollyleaf squinted into the glare to see the Twoleg holding the dog's collar with one fat, pink paw. The dog whined as it was dragged away. The fox relaxed, giving Hollyleaf just enough room to slide gently back. It was only a cub, no taller than she was, and its fur smelled of milk and earth from its den.

Suddenly Hollyleaf heard a fierce whisper. "What's happening? Are you all right?" Fallen Leaves was standing just around the curve in the tunnel. She ran toward him. His eyes gleamed like moons in the half light.

"Look out!" Hollyleaf hissed. "There's a fox behind me! Run!"

CHAPTER 5

❧

Hollyleaf tucked her nose under her tail and tried to shut out the noise that drifted down the tunnels to her nest. The fox cub was still somewhere underground, whimpering in the dark. Why hadn't it left? Was it afraid that the dog was waiting for it? Hollyleaf sniffed and wriggled deeper into the feathers. The high-pitched whine broke through, niggling her like thorns.

Hollyleaf sat up. *For StarClan's sake, shut up!* There was no way she could sleep through this noise. She hopped out of her nest and padded along the tunnel to the river-cave. It was filled with a pale gray wash of starlight. Fallen Leaves was sitting at the edge of the water.

"Can you hear the fox?" Hollyleaf asked irritably.

Fallen Leaves shrugged. "It'll find its way out eventually."

"But it's keeping me awake!" Hollyleaf complained. *Doesn't Fallen Leaves need to sleep too?*

The fox let out a loud yelp, as if it could hear them talking. Hollyleaf felt a rush of pity. She knew what it felt like to be lost and frightened in the dark. "Maybe I should go find it," she murmured.

Fallen Leaves stared at her in surprise. "But it's a fox!"

"It's a baby," she countered. "You wouldn't leave a kit down here, would you?"

"A kit wouldn't try to eat me," Fallen Leaves pointed out.

"I'm too much of a mouthful for this cub," Hollyleaf assured him, hoping that was true. The fox had smelled strongly of milk, which meant it probably wasn't eating fresh-kill yet. And it certainly hadn't noticed it was sitting on top of prey when the dog chased it into the hole. She shook out her fur and started toward the woods-tunnel.

"You're not really going to look for it, are you?" Fallen Leaves sounded astonished.

"Yes, if it means I can get some sleep," meowed Hollyleaf. "If I'm not back by dawn, come and fetch me, okay?" she added, only half-joking.

"Of course," Fallen Leaves replied somberly.

The darkness felt even more solid than usual, and Hollyleaf struggled against the urge to turn tail and flee back to the river-cave. The fox cub's whimpering echoed off the walls, confusing her senses and disorienting her. She paused when she felt cold air blowing on one side of her head. There was an opening to another tunnel here; had the cub gone this way? She listened for a moment. There was a tiny scraping noise, as if soft pads were shuffling against the stone. If the fox really had gone down here, it would be truly stuck, because this particular tunnel got narrower and narrower until it ended abruptly in a rockfall. Which meant that if Hollyleaf followed the cub, she could get trapped in a dead end. . . .

Hollyleaf took a deep breath and stepped into the tunnel. Almost at once, the fox let out a shriek as if it had heard her approaching. "It's all right, I'm not going to hurt you!" Hollyleaf called into the darkness. There was a fast scrabbling sound, and a wave of fox-scented fear rolled down the passage toward her. Hollyleaf reminded herself that this was just a lost and scared youngster, so she wasn't in any danger. She padded closer. "Hush, don't be frightened," she murmured.

The scrabbling stopped, and Hollyleaf guessed the fox was pressed against the rockfall with nowhere else to go. It let out the tiniest whine. "Poor little scrap," Hollyleaf mewed, as if she were comforting a kit. "Did you get lost?"

She took another step forward, and her muzzle bumped against soft, strong-smelling fur. Trying not to gag, Hollyleaf gave it a lick. The fox tensed, rigid as a rock, then relaxed as she kept licking. Feeling bolder, Hollyleaf moved closer to where she guessed the cub's head was. Her nose touched the tip of a feather-soft ear. "It's all right, you're safe now," she whispered between licks.

The cub's head drooped until it rested against Hollyleaf's chest. She felt the faint tickle of its whiskers as it tucked its chin under its front paws. Hollyleaf wriggled closer until her body was curled around as much of the fox as she could reach. She could feel its breath slowing and becoming steadier. She stopped licking and rested her head on the fox's neck. "Sleep, little one," she murmured. She pressed close to the cold fur beside her, hoping that some of her warmth would seep in. It crossed her mind that none of her former Clanmates would ever believe she had slept next to a fox. But she wasn't in the Clan anymore, and this cub needed her, just as a kit needed its mother. Hollyleaf shifted her head into a more comfortable position and closed her eyes.

She was woken by something pinching her front leg. Was Fallen Leaves getting her attention by *biting* her? Hollyleaf opened her eyes to a faint gray light. A shape loomed over her, and when she looked down at her leg she saw tiny white teeth sinking into her fur. "Ow!" she yelped, scrambling free.

The fox cub tipped its head to one side and looked at her. "*Yip!*"

Hollyleaf backed away. The cub was bigger than she remembered, twice as broad as her across its shoulders, and its teeth were small but definitely sharp. "Okaaay," she mewed, taking another step until she was safely out of reach. "Let's get you out of these tunnels."

The fox bounced to its feet, filling the space. Hollyleaf braced herself. There was no sign that the cub thought she was prey; in fact, it looked as if it wanted to play. It let out another high-pitched bark and bounced on its front feet. Hollyleaf turned and looked back over her shoulder. It went against all her instincts to have the fox behind her, because now she felt as if she was being chased. *Not chased—followed,* she told herself firmly. "Come on!" she meowed.

She took a few steps forward. The fox ran after her, then stopped and whined. Hollyleaf looked at the tunnel ahead.

It vanished into blackness, compared with the pale light that filled this section. "It's okay," she told the cub. "This is the way out, I promise." She padded into the shadows, but the fox stayed where it was. There was a soft thump, and Hollyleaf realized it had sat down. Sighing, she turned back and squeezed in beside it. "Get up," she urged, nudging the cub's flank with her muzzle. "You can't stay here!"

She jabbed its haunches with her paw and the fox jumped up with a yelp. Hollyleaf gave it another shove with her nose. "Come on, I'll be right beside you." The cub took a cautious step and Hollyleaf stayed close, pressing against its flank. "That's right!" she mewed.

Slowly, they inched their way along the tunnel. The fox stopped dead when they reached the junction with the woods-tunnel, but Hollyleaf nudged and shoved and encouraged it around the corner until they could feel the breeze from outside on their faces. The fox let out a cheerful-sounding yelp and broke into a trot. Overconfident, it crashed into the opposite wall and sat down with a bump, whimpering. Hollyleaf ran forward and licked the fox's muzzle. She couldn't taste any blood, so it wasn't seriously hurt. "You silly thing," she scolded. "Stay beside me until you can see, okay?"

She knew the fox couldn't understand what she was saying, but it still walked more slowly as they rounded the curve in the tunnel. Gray light spilled in ahead of them, painfully bright like before. The fox blinked and whined, rubbing its eyes with a front paw.

"It's because you've been in the dark for a while," Hollyleaf explained. "Keep going; you're nearly there!" She reached up and licked the cub's ears, and a picture of Squirrelflight doing the same to her burst into her mind. She'd fallen into a puddle and her mother had whisked her back to the nursery to dry her off. *Her mother.* Suddenly Hollyleaf missed Squirrelflight with a physical pain.

The fox jumped up and trotted on. It picked up speed as its eyes grew used to the light, and Hollyleaf hung back, resisting the urge to stay pressed against its warm fur. The cub didn't belong here. It needed to be back with its mother, in their den in the woods. Suddenly the cub stopped, right at the entrance. It looked back at Hollyleaf and let out a questioning bark.

Hollyleaf shook her head. "I can't come with you, little one," she meowed. "This is my home." The words caught in her throat like a gristly piece of fresh-kill.

There was a loud yelp from beyond the mouth of the tunnel. The cub's head whipped around, its ears pricked. It let out a yip, and there was another bark, confident and joyous. "That's your mother, isn't it?" Hollyleaf whispered.

The cub bounded forward and vanished into the circle of whiteness. Hollyleaf crept along the tunnel until she could see the trees outside. The tunnel opened into a wood much like ThunderClan territory, with a mix of trees and dense undergrowth. The light crashed into Hollyleaf's eyes and she narrowed them as much as she could. Her ears rang with the sound of leaves rustling, birds singing, and the thunder of paws as cub and mother fox raced toward each other. Blinking, Hollyleaf watched as they collided in a tumble of russet fur. The cub let out a volley of excited yelps as its mother bundled it over, sniffing every part of its fur.

"You're safe now," Hollyleaf murmured, trying to ignore the lump of sadness in her chest. "You're back where you belong." The sight of the cub butting his mother's belly for milk mixed with images of Hollyleaf squirming with her littermates in the Clan nursery, bathed in comforting scents of food. *I was happy then, before I knew the truth,* she thought. *But that life is over now.*

CHAPTER 6

❦

Leaf-fall had settled over the woods and the ground was covered in a layer of brittle red-and-orange leaves. As Hollyleaf watched from the mouth of the tunnel, the breeze snatched another flurry of leaves from a beech tree and dangled them in the air before letting them float down to the floor. A voice behind made her jump.

"Are you looking for the cub?"

Hollyleaf spun around, her fur pricking with guilt. "Fallen Leaves! How long have you been there?"

"Long enough to see how much you want to be out there," meowed the ginger-and-white tom.

Hollyleaf stood to the side, leaving room for him to join her at the entrance, but Fallen Leaves stayed where he was, with his paws hidden in shadow.

"Are you hoping the cub will come back?" Fallen Leaves teased, but his voice sounded hollow in the echoing tunnel.

"Of course not," Hollyleaf meowed. "I know he belongs out there, in the woods, with his mother."

"And what about you?" Fallen Leaves pressed softly. "Do you belong out there, with your family?"

Hollyleaf turned her face away. "I have no family," she growled.

"We all have family," sighed Fallen Leaves.

"Really? Then where are your kin?" Hollyleaf challenged. "You say you came from a large group of cats, but what happened to them? We've never seen any traces of other cats living near here."

Fallen Leaves looked down at his paws. "They left," he whispered.

"Then let's go look for them!" Hollyleaf declared. "There must be some signs of where they've gone."

To her surprise, Fallen Leaves's eyes stretched wide with horror. "No! I must stay here! If I leave, how will my mother know where to find me? She'll come for me one day. I know she will."

Hollyleaf fought down a spurt of impatience. "But we could find her first! Come with me. I'll look after you."

"I don't need looking after," Fallen Leaves hissed. "I just need to stay here. You go if you want. I can't leave." He turned and stalked into the darkness. Hollyleaf stared after him, feeling wretched. So many things he said didn't make sense. Why hadn't his mother come looking for him before? She must have watched him go into the tunnels, so why didn't she start searching for him as soon as he didn't come out? But Fallen Leaves never gave a straight answer. He seemed determined to be as mysterious as possible, and sometimes Hollyleaf wondered if he even wanted company in his underground home. *Well, I don't have to stay here with him.* She lifted her head and let the scents of the forest drift over her muzzle: earth, leaves, squirrel, and the musky scent of a vole hiding among some pine logs. . . . What was she doing, lurking in the tunnels when she could be living outside, where she belonged?

Hollyleaf raced after Fallen Leaves. When she burst into the river-cave, he was curled beneath the rocky ledge with his nose tucked under his tail. He wasn't asleep, though; his eyes were wide open, gleaming in the pale gray light.

"You saved my life," Hollyleaf blurted out, skidding to a halt in front of him. "And I will always be grateful for that. But you're right. I need to be outside, eating squirrels and mice instead of fish, where I can see the sky and feel the wind in my fur—"

"Then go," Fallen Leaves interrupted her. "No one said you had to stay here."

Hollyleaf stared at him. Did he care so little about her that he wouldn't even try to make her stay? Well, she didn't need him either! "Good," she snapped. "I just thought I'd let you know that I'm going in case you wonder where I am."

Fallen Leaves shrugged and flicked the end of his tail over his nose again. Hollyleaf had the distinct feeling that she'd been dismissed. Trying not to feel wounded, she turned and padded back into the woods-tunnel. She walked slowly at first, half-expecting Fallen Leaves to come racing after her, begging her to change her mind. But the shadows behind her stayed obstinately silent.

* * *

The wind was colder than Hollyleaf remembered, pricking her fur even though she tried to stay in the shelter of the widest trunks. The light was fading and shadows spread from the base of every tree, but somehow this darkness was less comfortable than being in the tunnels and Hollyleaf found herself tripping over every fallen twig and clump of moss. Gritting her teeth, she picked her way into a dense thicket of brambles. Had thorns always dragged her fur like this? And were the leafless trees always so noisy as they clattered their branches together? Hollyleaf's ears were too full to pick up the movements of any prey, and her eyesight was oddly fuzzy when she tried to look farther than a fox-length. She kept telling herself that this was just the same as ThunderClan territory, but it wasn't at all, really: There were no familiar scent markers or paths through the bushes, no sign that cats had ever been here before.

Hollyleaf battled her way to the middle of the brambles and turned in circles beside the knot of trunks until she had cleared a small, roughly circular space. She clawed at the dry grass to make a nest to lie on, then curled up and tucked her muzzle under her tail. Her belly growled, reminding her that she hadn't eaten since her morning "hunt" in the underground river, but there was no chance of catching any prey tonight. Hollyleaf pressed her spine against the clutch of bramble trunks, wishing it were Fallen Leaves beside her. Even though he never gave off any warmth, he had been oddly companionable on the rare nights he'd shared her nest. *Is he sorry that he let me go?*

Hollyleaf woke before dawn, too hungry to sleep any longer. She crawled out of the brambles and sniffed the air. The scent of rain was carried on the wind and she shivered. Her prickly den wouldn't be completely waterproof, so she'd need to find some big leaves to weave into the stems immediately above her head. But first she had to hunt. Milky light was filtering down through the branches, just enough to reveal a tiny trail of footprints across the leaf mulch beneath a beech tree. Hollyleaf dropped into the hunter's crouch, her muscles stiff and protesting after moons of not being used. She stalked forward, stepping lightly as she strained to hear the faint telltale rustle of prey. At the base of the trunk, a leaf moved and the tip of a smooth brown tail peeped out. Hollyleaf sprang and landed squarely on the back of the mouse, killing it with a swift bite to the neck.

It tasted like fresh-kill fit for StarClan. Hollyleaf ate where she crouched, relishing each mouthful. Her belly rumbled in appreciation—and almost at once clenched with pain. Hollyleaf hissed through her teeth. It had been a long time since she'd eaten this much. Perhaps she should have saved half the mouse for later, in her own fresh-kill pile. She lifted her head, looking around for the best place to store her catches. Then she shrugged. If she was only feeding herself, what was the point of storing prey? She'd hunt and eat when she was hungry, that's all. Like a rogue would . . .

Hollyleaf stood up and trotted briskly through the trees. She wasn't a rogue, was she? She was a Clan cat with no Clan, that's all. Not a rogue, or a loner, or, StarClan forbid, a kittypet. None of those. *A murderer,* whispered a tiny voice inside her head, but Hollyleaf flattened her ears and ignored it, pushing on as the ground sloped upward. With her head down, she wasn't aware of the woods thinning out until her fur was suddenly blasted by the wind. Startled, she looked up to see that she was nearly at the top of the ridge. Just a few paces more would take her to the peak, and she would be able to look down on the lake, and her old home.

Her paws stayed rooted to the grass. Hollyleaf felt her ears strain for any sound of cats: her former Clanmates on a border patrol, perhaps, or WindClan cats in pursuit of a rabbit. She heard nothing but the wind whistling over the crest and swooping down to rattle the trees below her. Almost without thinking, Hollyleaf started to back away. Part of her longed to hear the distinctive sounds of ThunderClan cats, and race over the ridge to join them; another part feared they might be looking for her to punish her for Ashfur's death. Would Leafpool or Lionblaze and Jayfeather have revealed the truth by now? There was no way she would ever know, because she could never go back. Turning away, Hollyleaf raced down the slope and plunged into the sheltering trees.

A few days later, the first snowfall arrived. Hollyleaf opened her eyes to find her bramble den filled with a strange cloudy light. She pushed her way out and squeaked as a clump of sparkling frost fell onto her neck. She shook it off crossly and jumped clear of the remaining branches. Her paws sank into soft white snow and instantly chilled to the bone.

Hollyleaf hissed under her breath as she bounded to the nearest fallen branch, where only a dusting of flakes had settled. The moss was slimy under her paws but at least she was able to shake them clear of the clinging white stuff. She'd be lucky to catch anything to eat today; all the prey would be burrowed far under a warm layer of leaves. In the Clan, Firestar would have stocked up fresh-kill in a hole outside the hollow, where the cold earth would keep it fresh. Hollyleaf's belly rumbled at the thought, and she curled her lip, annoyed with herself for not being better prepared.

She was about to jump down from the branch and attempt to find something to eat when she noticed a trail of paw prints leading away between the trees. They were bigger than hers, but small for a passing dog. The hair prickled on the back of Hollyleaf's neck. With a hiss of displeasure, she plunged her feet back into the snow and went to take a closer look. More than the size and shape of the prints, the distinctive smell told her who had walked this way: a fox! A young fox, judging by its small paws, and was it just her imagination, or did Hollyleaf recognize the lingering scent?

Yes!

It was the cub she had rescued!

Hollyleaf's heart started to beat faster. At that moment, the prospect of seeing the little cub again filled her with more excitement than the idea of finding food. She followed the trail, leaping carefully alongside the tracks so as not to smudge them. They wound through the trees, heading along the shoulder of the ridge before swerving downward into a dense copse of pine trees. Hollyleaf's legs were aching from jumping through the snow, and it got deeper the farther down the hill she went, but she wasn't going to give up now. The scent of the cub had gotten stronger and the tracks were even clearer, as if it had only just walked this way.

The pine trees opened out in a little clearing where the snow was scuffed and heaped up amid deep claw marks and scarlet-stained feathers. Hollyleaf wrinkled her nose as the scent of blood filled the air. The fox must have killed a pigeon here, she decided, studying the broad gray feathers. She felt a flash of pride, as if she'd mentored the cub herself.

There was a noise behind her and the sharp smell washed over her more strongly than ever. Hollyleaf turned, a purr rising in her throat. The cub was standing at the edge of the clearing, watching her. Its ears were pricked and the tip of its bushy tail brushed the snow. This was definitely her fox! He was growing into a handsome male, his fur standing out against the snow almost as scarlet as the pigeon's blood.

"Hello!" Hollyleaf meowed. "Do you remember me?"

With a snarl, the fox leaped at her. Yellow teeth snapped at the air where Hollyleaf's neck had been, a heartbeat after she scrambled backward. She crashed into a pine tree and spun around to claw her way up the trunk, with the creature snapping barely a whisker's length from her paws. The tree was circled with moss halfway up and Hollyleaf's claws lost their grip; she slithered down, feeling branches jab her ribs and flanks, and the cub jumped up, yelping with hunger and excitement. Hollyleaf dug her claws into the bark and managed to stop her fall just as teeth closed on the fur at the end of her tail. She tore herself free and scrambled to the topmost branches, fear propelling her upward. Below her, the cub snarled in frustration.

Hollyleaf huddled on a thin branch that swayed beneath her weight. She peered down through the dark green pine needles and watched the fox circling far below. *Of course he doesn't remember me. I'm nothing more than prey!* Hollyleaf sank her claws into the branch, closed her eyes, and waited for her heart to stop trying to punch its way out of her chest.

When she opened her eyes again, it was dark. Fear and flight must have exhausted her enough to sleep on her uncomfortable perch. The woods were silent, and all she could smell was snow and the stinging scent of pinesap. The cub was long gone. Above the trees, a full silver moon floated in the sky, surrounded by dazzling stars. The forest was bathed in crisp white light, and Hollyleaf could see all the way to the top of the ridge. On the other side, the four Clans would be meeting on the island for the Gathering. Would her name be mentioned? Did any cat ever wonder what had happened to her? Hollyleaf felt a wave of misery so intense she almost lost her grip on the branch. When it dipped alarmingly beneath her, she came to her senses and eased herself down the trunk to the snowy ground.

There was a sharp pain in her belly, and as Hollyleaf trekked back through the trees she paused by a clump of yarrow that had been sheltered from the snow to eat a few leaves. But the ache inside her persisted, and Hollyleaf knew it was more than hunger: It was loneliness, and regret, and sadness. There was only one place she could go. Fluffing up her pelt against the bitter cold, Hollyleaf began to trudge up the slope.

Dawn was breaking by the time she arrived, lightening the shadows cast by the trees in the moonlight and rousing a few birds into song. Hollyleaf staggered the last few paces and paused at the entrance, gasping for breath. The tunnel yawned ahead of her, warm and dark and welcoming.

"Fallen Leaves!" she called as she plunged inside. "Fallen Leaves, are you there?"

CHAPTER 7

Hollyleaf slept for two whole days after her return. Fallen Leaves brought her fish to eat when she briefly stirred, and some herbs that she didn't recognize for the niggling cough that developed as soon as she was out of the constant wind. Her nest was where she had left it, but softer and deeper than she remembered.

"I added more feathers," Fallen Leaves admitted shyly. "In case you came back." Then he climbed delicately alongside her, and curled his cold body around hers while she drifted back to sleep.

Finally she woke with a clearer head, feeling hungry and restless. Yellow light seeped into the tunnel, hinting at sunshine outside. Hollyleaf was alone in her nest but Fallen Leaves appeared almost at once, carrying a minnow.

"Here, eat this," he urged, dropping it beside her.

It didn't taste as good as the mice and squirrels in the woods—nothing would taste that good again, Hollyleaf suspected—but she swallowed it obediently, feeling strength flow back into her legs. Fallen Leaves sat beside her nest and watched.

"I saw the fox cub again," Hollyleaf announced as she cleaned the last traces of fish from her whiskers.

Fallen Leaves looked surprised. "Are you sure it was the same one?"

"Definitely. I knew its scent right away."

"Did it recognize you?" Fallen Leaves asked.

Hollyleaf looked down at her paws and shook her head. She felt stupid and embarrassed to admit what she had done, but she hoped Fallen Leaves wouldn't judge her too harshly. "It saw me as a juicy piece of prey," she mewed quietly. "I only just got away."

She felt something soft on her ear as Fallen Leaves touched her with the tip of his tail. "I'm so sorry. You save his life, and he repays you like that? Honestly, some animals have no gratitude!"

There was a note of barely suppressed amusement in his voice and Hollyleaf looked up to see his eyes shining with humor. "I guess it was kind of mouse-brained to think he'd remember me," she admitted.

"Just a bit!" Fallen Leaves exploded. "What did you think would happen? That he'd take you to his den to meet his mother?"

Hollyleaf shrugged. "I was so lonely," she murmured. "I just wanted a friend."

In an instant Fallen Leaves was crouched beside her, pressing his fur against hers. "And you have a friend," he insisted. "Right here. Now, I've been awfully lazy about doing patrols while you were away. Should we start with a check of the tunnels—just in case that cub thinks about following you—and then see if you can remember how to catch a fish?"

Later, when the holes in the roof were dark and Hollyleaf's paws were aching from running on stone, she lay in her nest of feathers and felt the pain of loneliness ease. She let out a purr, and Fallen Leaves stirred beside her.

"What are you thinking about?" he murmured.

"How glad I am that I came back," Hollyleaf answered honestly. "I'm not cut out to live alone, I guess."

Fallen Leaves licked her ear. "I'm glad you came back, too."

. Hollyleaf swiveled around to face him. "Do you ever think about the cats you left behind?"

"All the time," Fallen Leaves meowed softly. "But it's been so long, I don't remember that much."

Hollyleaf blinked. She'd been away from ThunderClan for several moons but she hadn't forgotten a thing. "How many seasons have you been in the tunnels?"

Fallen Leaves shrugged and turned his face away. "More than I can count. But it's too late to change anything now."

Hollyleaf knew better than to suggest he go looking for his old community again. Instead, she settled herself more comfortably against his flank and prompted, "Tell me about your family. You must remember them."

"My mother was called Broken Shadow. She was very kind and beautiful. She . . . she didn't want me to go into the tunnels. I think she knew something bad would happen."

"Couldn't she stop you?" Hollyleaf asked.

"Not if I was going to be a sharpclaw," Fallen Leaves replied. "That's what I wanted, more than anything." He trailed off, sounding achingly sad. Then he shook himself. "That's all a long way in the past. What about your mother? Did you tell her you were leaving the Clan?"

Hollyleaf started slicing one of the feathers with her claw. "Not exactly," she muttered.

Fallen Leaves stiffened. "You mean, she has no idea where you are? What if she thinks you're dead?"

"It's probably best if she does," Hollyleaf whispered. As she spoke, she wondered which cat she was referring to: Leafpool, her real mother; or Squirrelflight, the cat who had raised her. "It's complicated," she confessed. "I . . . I have two mothers."

Behind her, she sensed Fallen Leaves prick up his ears. "Two?"

"My real mother, Leafpool, is a medicine cat. She's not supposed to have kits but she ran away with Crowfeather from WindClan, and when she came back, she gave birth to me and my brothers. To hide what she'd done, she gave us to her sister, Squirrelflight, who pretended we were her kits. Even Squirrelflight's mate, Brambleclaw, thought he was our father!"

Fallen Leaves was quiet for a moment. Then he asked, "Do you think Squirrelflight loved you?"

"Oh yes," Hollyleaf mewed. "I mean, she fussed over us all the time, just like the other queens in the nursery. But she lied to us! She only told us the truth when another cat forced her to."

"What about . . . Leafpool, is it? How did she act toward you?"

Hollyleaf sighed. "She always took an interest in us, but I thought it was because Squirrelflight was her sister. I was her apprentice for a while, in the medicine den, but then I decided to train as a warrior instead. I liked working with her; it just wasn't what I wanted to do for the rest of my life."

"And Leafpool knows that you found out the truth?" Fallen Leaves asked.

"Yes," meowed Hollyleaf, wincing as she recalled her final, furious confrontation with the ThunderClan medicine cat. "I . . . I told her she deserved to die for what she had done, but she said the worst pain of all was having to live with it." Hollyleaf stopped talking and looked down at the splinters of feather at her feet.

"It seems to me," Fallen Leaves began carefully, "that both of these cats loved you very much. Surely two mothers are better than none? And whatever you did before you came here, they must both hope that you are alive and safe."

"I guess," Hollyleaf admitted. She shoved the feather splinters out of the nest. "But how can they live with all these secrets? The truth is all that matters!"

"Not always," mewed Fallen Leaves. "Perhaps those cats believed they were doing the right thing for you and your brothers. You can't punish them for loving you too much, Hollyleaf."

He patted her shoulder with his paw, and Hollyleaf lay down again. She couldn't deny that Fallen Leaves was right: Squirrelflight and Leafpool *had* loved her. But everything had been complicated by secrets and lies—and by the fact that

Hollyleaf had killed Ashfur to keep him from telling everyone. *But then I realized it would never stay secret, so I told all the Clans at the Gathering.* Ashfur's death had been for nothing, and Hollyleaf had had no choice but to leave.

Outside, the weather turned even colder. There were fewer fish in the underground river so Hollyleaf made forays into the woods, leaving the tunnels just long enough to catch a mouse or squirrel and once a rather scrawny pigeon. Fallen Leaves never went with her; he had been out a few times, he said, to gather herbs when Hollyleaf first entered the tunnels, but he didn't feel like he belonged there. Hollyleaf's heart always twisted with sadness when she saw her friend's ginger-and-white face peeking from the shadows, watching anxiously as she hunted. Fallen Leaves seemed to view the tunnels as his home and his prison equally. Did he really believe it was too late to find his family?

Hollyleaf always kept an eye out for the fox cub or his mother, but she saw nothing larger than the pigeon among the snowy trees, and only once a trace of snow-filled tracks leading down to the pine copse. She swerved in the opposite direction, using the scent of yarrow to lead her swiftly back to the mouth of the tunnel. There was a little clump growing just outside the entrance, defying the snow with its furry green leaves.

Every time Hollyleaf went outside, she found herself listening for signs of the cats on the other side of the ridge. Were her Clanmates managing to find enough prey in the snow? Were the elders strong and fit? Several times her paws seemed to lead her up to the top of the ridge without her noticing, until she was barely fox-lengths away from the ThunderClan border. But the thought of coming face-to-face with one of her former Clanmates made the blood freeze in her veins, and each time Hollyleaf whirled around at the last moment and ran back down to where Fallen Leaves was waiting for her.

After a quarter moon the snow clouds lifted, leaving a clear sky and crisp, still air. Hollyleaf buried herself in her nest, trying to get warm, but her mind was full of what might be happening in the hollow. She sat up, knowing she wasn't going to sleep now. The tunnel was filled with silvery light, so bright it was almost like sunshine. Hollyleaf stepped out of her nest and trotted along the passage to the river-cave. It was empty, apart from dazzling light that beamed into every corner and turned the river white. Hollyleaf tipped back her head and strained to look through the hole in the roof. Far, far above, a perfect round moon drifted across the sky. It was a cold night for a Gathering. Hollyleaf pictured the cats huddling together in the hollow, steam rising from their muzzles as they listened to each leader speak.

"You miss your Clanmates, don't you?" murmured Fallen Leaves behind her.

Hollyleaf jumped. She hadn't heard him enter the cave. "I just want to know that they're okay," she mewed, feeling a flash of guilt. "Leaf-bare can be so hard in the Clans, and with all this snow, they might not have found enough to eat."

Fallen Leaves held up one paw to stop her. "So go and see them."

"I can't! They have to believe I'm gone forever!"

"Visit them without being seen, if that's what you want," Fallen Leaves suggested. "You can't spend all your time watching the moon, and wondering."

Hollyleaf flinched. Perhaps he was right. She knew her old territory well enough to stay hidden. If she could just make sure ThunderClan was surviving the harsh season, she would be able to sleep again.

CHAPTER 8

♣

Hollyleaf felt as though a swarm of bees were buzzing in each of her paws as soon as she decided to go back to ThunderClan in secret, but she forced herself to wait a quarter moon until the sky was less brightly lit. Just before dawn, when the night was at its darkest point, Fallen Leaves led her to a tunnel that wasn't much wider than a rabbit hole. This was one of the few remaining clear entrances to ThunderClan. Hollyleaf tried to thank him again before she squeezed into the last section, but he turned away before she could say anything and was quickly swallowed up by the shadows.

I'll come back, I promise! Hollyleaf called after him silently.

Hollyleaf crouched down and wriggled into the tiny hole. The roof scraped her ears and for a moment she felt as if she were being buried alive. Her heart sped up in panic and her breath came in shallow gasps, but she kept dragging herself forward with her front paws.

Suddenly fresh air burst onto her face, and the sound of branches whispering in the wind filled her ears. Hollyleaf stood up, drinking in the familiar scents of cats and trails and border markers. She was home!

No! This is not my home now.

Shaking dirt from her fur, Hollyleaf trotted into a patch of ferns and circled a lone oak tree. After checking to make sure there were no cats out on night patrol, she crossed a narrow trail that ran along the top of the cliff. Hollyleaf told herself she was trembling from cold, but she could smell fear on her pelt and she knew she was terrified of being discovered. When an owl flapped noisily from a branch overhead, she nearly fell over with fright. She ducked into a clump of brambles and pushed her way through until she emerged at the very edge of the cliff. She crouched down and peered over.

The hollow was thick with shadows and Hollyleaf couldn't make out any individual dens, but something felt wrong. The noise of the wind echoing off the cliffs was different, and the black shapes below weren't the same as she remembered. It was as if trees had grown inside the camp since she left, full-branched and heavy with brittle leaves. That was impossible!

As she stared, a line of yellow light appeared above the ridge behind her. Dawn was breaking, and it thinned the shadows just enough for Hollyleaf to see a huge tree filling the hollow—not growing, but lying on its side with its roots crumpled in the corner where the medicine den was. Hollyleaf stiffened in horror. If a tree that big had fallen from the top of the cliff, it must have crushed cats beneath it! It was lying directly on top of the warriors' and elders' dens. How could something so terrible have happened to her Clan, yet she had known nothing about it? Couldn't StarClan have told her in a dream?

Perhaps StarClan has disowned me, now that I'm no longer part of a Clan.

Hollyleaf realized she was shaking so much, she was in danger of slipping over the edge. She backed away a little, just as the branches of the fallen tree quivered and two cats stepped gingerly into the cold air. Their breath formed clouds around the muzzles.

"I can go to the dirtplace on my own," Mousefur was grumbling. The air was so still that her voice reached Hollyleaf all the way on top of the cliff.

"I know you can," Purdy rasped. "But there's no harm in having company, is there?"

"I don't seem to have any choice," Mousefur muttered as the old brown tom ushered her across the clearing and into the brambles that filled the entrance to the hollow.

Hollyleaf leaned forward, feeling a thrill of delight. *My Clanmates!*

"Briarlight!" called a voice from the medicine den. "I can bring you something to eat if you're hungry. There's no need to fetch it yourself." It was Jayfeather, sounding as if he'd just woken up.

"I still have two legs that work," came the reply, as a dark brown she-cat emerged from beneath the tangled roots.

Briarkit? Hollyleaf stared in disbelief as the young cat dragged herself over the ground with her front paws, while her hind legs trailed uselessly behind her. Millie burst out of the middle of the fallen branches.

"What are you doing? You only went this far yesterday!

You should be resting!" she scolded.

Briarlight—Jayfeather had used her warrior name, although she clearly wasn't going on any patrols—swerved to avoid her mother. "I'm fine," she hissed between clenched teeth. "You can't do everything for me!"

Millie bent down and licked her daughter's ears. "I wish I could," she murmured.

How had Briarlight been so badly hurt? Had it been when the tree fell? I should have been here! Hollyleaf sank her claws into the crumbling soil at the edge of the cliff. A few tiny stones were dislodged and clattered down into the clearing. Hollyleaf froze.

A familiar dark tabby pelt emerged from the branches. Brambleclaw looked up toward Hollyleaf's hiding place, his eyes narrowing. She shrank back and held her breath. Then she heard him call, "Lionblaze? Cinderheart? Take the border patrol around the top of the hollow, will you? Dovepaw and Ivypaw can go with you."

There was the sound of cats gathering below. Hollyleaf risked one more glance over the edge. Her heart nearly broke when she saw her brother Lionblaze circling around Cinderheart, the tip of his tail tracing her soft gray fur. Dovepaw and Ivypaw—they had been tiny kits when Hollyleaf left, and now they were strong, confident-looking apprentices!—bounced around them looking eager to be out on patrol.

"Did Brambleclaw hear a fox?" Ivypaw asked excitedly.

Dovepaw had tipped her head to one side and was looking thoughtful. "I don't think so," she mewed.

Lionblaze started to lead them toward the barrier of

thorns. Hollyleaf knew she had to leave. She just hoped her pelt still held enough ThunderClan scent that she couldn't be tracked back to the tunnel. Luckily the ferns were soaking wet from frost-melt, which made them less likely to hold traces of her. She pushed her way through, wincing as the cold water pierced through to her skin, then raced for the tunnel. She could hear Lionblaze bringing the patrol up the side of the hollow. Ivypaw was running ahead, reporting back on every bush and bramble that she sniffed.

"Nothing here! No fox came this way!"

Hollyleaf paused for a moment, suddenly wild with hope that they would find her and take her back to the Clan. Surely she was missed in some small way? Then she thought of everything that had happened, the truth that Leafpool, Jayfeather, and Lionblaze had discovered, and she knew the Clan was better off without her. With a tiny sigh, she ducked into the narrow hole and let the shadows engulf her.

"And then I saw Briarkit—well, she's Briarlight now—and she's lost the use of her hind legs! She was dragging herself on her belly across the clearing. Maybe the tree fell on her. I should have been there to help!" Hollyleaf stopped to take a breath, aware that she hadn't stopped talking since she returned.

From his seat beside the river, Fallen Leaves looked at her. It was a gloomy day and there was barely any light filtering into the cave, but Hollyleaf could see his eyes shining faintly. "You couldn't have stopped the tree from falling," he pointed out. "Anyway, you chose to leave, remember?"

Hollyleaf scraped her paw over the stone. "It didn't feel like I had a choice at the time," she murmured. "I . . . I haven't told you everything about what happened. It wasn't just that I found out about Squirrelflight and Leafpool lying to me. Another cat found out as well, a cat called Ashfur. He threatened to tell all the Clans the truth so I . . . so I killed him."

There was a long silence. Hollyleaf risked glancing up at Fallen Leaves. He was staring into the river. "Did the Clan send you away when they found out?" Fallen Leaves asked quietly.

"No! They never knew! Only Leafpool found out, and then I told Jayfeather and Lionblaze. I wanted them to know why I had to leave."

"But you could go back," Fallen Leaves meowed, suddenly lifting his gaze. "Your brothers and Leafpool love you too much to tell the truth about Ashfur. Your secret will still be safe."

"You don't know that!" Hollyleaf wailed.

"I think I do," Fallen Leaves argued. "Everything you've told me proves how important you were to your kin."

"You don't understand," Hollyleaf mewed wretchedly. "Too much has happened. The Clan doesn't need me anymore."

Fallen Leaves turned away. "Your Clan will always need you," he whispered as he padded into the shadows.

Hollyleaf managed to wait for three more quarter moons before going back to her spying place above the hollow. Snow had fallen again, turned to silver sparkles by the harsh frost. Hollyleaf crouched among the brittle grass, shivering, and watched the Clan slowly wake up below her. Brambleclaw sent a patrol of sleepy warriors to check the WindClan border. Hollyleaf was startled by how thin her Clanmates looked. She searched the clearing for any sign of a fresh-kill pile, but there were only a few scraps of fur and feathers beside the tree trunk. Prey must be scarce after such a long spell of harsh weather.

There was a scrabble of movement at the far end of the fallen tree, where the prickly nursery walls were just visible. Poppyfrost's voice rose up, high with frustration.

"Cherrykit! You're not going outside with that cough! Molekit, bring your sister back at once!"

Two tiny, fluffed-up shapes burst out of the brambles and scooted across the clearing. The ginger she-cat in front stopped as her little body was racked with coughs, and her cream-and-brown littermate skidded to a halt beside her. "You can't come out to play today," he mewed. "You know what Poppyfrost said."

A tortoiseshell she-cat slid through the wall of the nursery and bent over the ginger kit. "Come on, little one," Poppyfrost murmured. "Back to the nest with you."

"Can't Jayfeather give me some medicine?" pleaded Cherrykit, gazing up at her mother with huge amber eyes.

"He said he's run out of yarrow," Poppyfrost explained. There was a tense note of worry in her voice, though Hollyleaf could tell she was trying to hide it from the kits. "I'm sure he'll find some today, and then you'll feel much better."

She ushered her kit back to the nursery, leaving Molekit pottering around the clearing on his own. Hollyleaf narrowed her eyes. She knew where there was fresh yarrow growing. She whirled around and ran back to the tunnel. She was used to the tight squeeze now, and hauled herself through without thinking about it. Then she raced through the tunnels, her paws firm and sure-footed on the cool, damp stone. There was no sign of Fallen Leaves as she burst into the river-cave. Leaping over the water, Hollyleaf darted into the woods-tunnel and followed it to the end, plunging out into daylight just as a pale yellow sun broke over the trees.

Thank StarClan!

The clump of yarrow was still growing by the mouth of the tunnel, fresh and green-smelling in spite of the frost. Hollyleaf nipped off as many stalks as she could carry, then headed back into the tunnel, being careful not to step on the trailing leaves. When she emerged from the narrow hole into ThunderClan territory, she put down the yarrow and sniffed the air. A patrol had just passed by, which meant she should have enough time to take the herbs down to the bottom of the cliff. Hollyleaf tried to slow her heart. It was pounding so hard, her paws were shaking in time. It was too early for many cats to be outside the camp, and the patrol was heading in the opposite direction. If she ran fast, and kept to the shadows, there was no reason she would be seen.

She didn't give herself another moment to change her mind. She picked up the yarrow leaves and hared down the trail that led to the bottom of the cliff. Skidding around the corner, she almost crashed into the brambles that shielded the dirtplace.

A voice growled from inside, "Wait your turn!"

Hollyleaf bit back an instinctive apology and darted around the edge of the barrier. There was no cat on guard now that dawn had come. She dropped the herbs close to the well-hidden pathway through the thorns. The next cat to come out would find them. Cherrykit could be treated before the sun rose any higher.

As she heard a cat pushing through the brambles from the other side, Hollyleaf whisked around and raced back up the cliff. Her Clanmates might wonder who had delivered herbs so conveniently, but with luck they'd assume one of the apprentices had collected them unasked. No cat needed to know that Hollyleaf had returned to help them.

Not all secrets were terrible.

CHAPTER 9

❧

"Cherrykit has stopped coughing! Poppyfrost looks so relieved. She was playing with the kits this morning, teaching them how to pounce on a ball of moss. I remember when Squirrelflight showed us our first pounce . . ." Hollyleaf trailed off.

Fallen Leaves, sitting next to her by the edge of the underground river, twitched one ear. "The yarrow leaves worked, then," he meowed.

"They must have!" Hollyleaf jumped to her paws and faced him. "Do you think I should take some more? What about marigold? Or catmint—do you know if there is any growing near the woods-tunnel?"

"No, I don't know," Fallen Leaves answered with a hint of impatience. "I don't need herbs for myself, so why would I go looking for them?"

"But you found comfrey for me, and poppy seeds," Hollyleaf reminded him. "When I'd hurt my leg."

The tip of Fallen Leaves's tail flicked. "That was different," he muttered. "You were right in front of me. I could hardly leave you to suffer, could I?"

"Well, ThunderClan is right above our heads!" Hollyleaf

countered. "The warrior code says we must protect the kits of all Clans, not just our own. If we gather herbs that will help Cherrykit and Molekit through leaf-bare, we are only obeying the code."

"It's not *my* code," Fallen Leaves mewed, turning away. "Good luck hunting for herbs if that's what you want to do." He padded into the tunnel that led back to Hollyleaf's nest.

Hollyleaf watched him vanish into the shadows. He was behaving very oddly. She hadn't seen him at all for several days, and the only creatures she'd had for company were her Clanmates when she spied on them from the top of the cliff. Fallen Leaves never shared her nest now, and never came to watch her hunt from the mouth of the woods-tunnel. Had she done something to upset him?

Perhaps he doesn't like the fact that I spend so much time in Thunder-Clan.

Hollyleaf's pelt prickled with guilt. It was true that she went back almost every day to see what her Clanmates were doing. Poppyfrost's kits were nearly six moons old, so they would be apprenticed soon; Hollyleaf wondered which cats would be chosen as their mentors. If she'd been in the Clan, she would have liked Cherrykit as an apprentice, with her spirit and sense of humor. But she would never be a mentor, not now.

Giving herself a shake, Hollyleaf trotted into the woods-tunnel. She needed to catch something to eat, then she'd scout for fresh herbs. Leaf-bare was at its height, so there were few green leaves anywhere, but she might get lucky in the sheltered spots beneath fallen trees. And maybe she could catch something for Fallen Leaves, to make it up to him for all the time she had spent outside. He had never shared fresh-kill with her before, but perhaps nothing had tempted him. There must be some sort of prey, plump from pinecones and fallen nuts, among these trees that he would be willing to eat.

Hollyleaf caught a squirrel, soft and downy in its pelt of gray fur, but Fallen Leaves was nowhere to be seen when she returned to the tunnels. Hollyleaf ate alone in the river-cave, carefully leaving half for Fallen Leaves before rinsing her muzzle in the icy water. She hadn't found any fresh herbs to take to the Clan, so she headed to her nest, her paws trailing a little from tiredness and disappointment. She curled up on the feathers and tucked her nose under her tail. Tomorrow she'd spend all day with Fallen Leaves—if she could find him—patrolling the tunnels as far as he wanted to go.

She only seemed to have closed her eyes for a moment before Fallen Leaves was nudging her with his paw. "Wake up, Hollyleaf!"

Blearily, Hollyleaf sat up. "Is it dawn already?" she mumbled.

"No!" Fallen Leaves turned a circle, impatience making his fur stand on end. "Two of your Clanmates are in the tunnels!"

Hollyleaf was instantly wide awake. "What? Where? Who is it?"

"I don't know!" Fallen Leaves snapped. "But they can't stay down here. I told them how to get out but they didn't listen and they're still lost. Go and help them, will you?"

"Are they okay?"

"They're well enough to chatter like starlings, so I presume they aren't injured." Fallen Leaves started to walk away. "Just get them back where they belong," he meowed over his shoulder.

Hollyleaf hopped out of her nest and ran to the river-cave. In spite of the river noise, it was the best place to hear if there was anything in the main tunnels. She crouched by the water and strained her ears. High-pitched, nervous chatter echoed down one of the passages. Hollyleaf leaped up and raced toward the sound, swerving confidently around corners without needing to see her way through the dark. Suddenly the voices sounded very close. The cats were just ahead, invisible in the shadows but near enough that their scent washed over Hollyleaf: She recognized Ivypool, the newest warrior, and Graystripe's daughter Blossomfall. She ducked into a crevice at the side of the passage and listened.

"I wish I'd asked that cat his name," Ivypool was muttering. "We could call for him." There was a pause before she added, "I don't suppose he would have come, anyway."

She must mean Fallen Leaves!

A soft scraping noise suggested that one of the cats had flopped to the ground. "I'm sorry," whispered Blossomfall, sounding breathless and scared. "This is all my fault. I was the one who wanted to come down here."

"I could have stopped you," Ivypool argued.

"How? By hanging on to my tail?"

Hollyleaf admired Blossomfall's spirit. She wondered how the cats had found their way into the tunnels. For a moment the urge to reveal herself to them, to be reunited with her Clanmates, was so strong that her legs trembled.

No! You chose to leave! There is no going back, not now.

But she could still help them find their way out. They'd already met one cat down here; as long as they didn't get too close, they would assume he'd come back to help them a second time. Hollyleaf leaned out of her hiding place and called softly, "Come on! What are you waiting for?"

The air crackled as if both cats had tensed with alarm. Hollyleaf heard Ivypool turn to look down the tunnel, but she knew the shadows would keep her dark pelt safely hidden.

"You do want to get out, don't you?" she prompted. "You know you shouldn't be here."

"Oh yes—please help us!" Blossomfall begged.

"Very well. Follow me." Hollyleaf spun around and ran back down the tunnel, judging by the sound of paw steps behind her how fast she needed to go to stay out of sight, but slow enough that the others could follow. She led them on a deliberately confusing route, down side passages and at one stage crossing a tunnel they'd already been through, in order to discourage the cats from coming back. One of the cats—Hollyleaf thought it was Blossomfall—started to walk more slowly and her breathing grew louder.

"Is it much farther?" Ivypool called.

Hollyleaf didn't reply. Around the next corner, the tunnel sloped steeply up to an old fox hole, long abandoned, that opened into one of the less trodden corners of ThunderClan territory. There was nowhere for Hollyleaf to hide inside the tunnel, so she would have to risk going out ahead of the cats and hiding in the undergrowth. She raced the last few paces to the entrance, then darted across the short clearing and pushed her way into a clump of ferns. Turning as quietly as she could, she waited, her heart pounding, as the two cats limped out behind her.

Ivypool stopped and looked around. "Where did it go?" she meowed.

Blossomfall looked too worn out to speak. She dragged herself into the open and collapsed into a patch of sunlight beside an oak stump.

Very slowly, Hollyleaf eased herself farther back into the ferns. She froze when Ivypool's ears twitched and she seemed to look straight at Hollyleaf.

"Thank you!" Ivypool called.

Anything for my Clanmates, Hollyleaf replied silently.

Hollyleaf didn't go back to her former home for many moons. She knew she had hurt Fallen Leaves with her constant visits to spy on the hollow, and he deserved more than that from her. They spent the days patrolling the tunnels for unseen enemies, and lying in wait by the river for minnows to slip past. If they spoke less about what had happened in their pasts, or what lay in the future, Hollyleaf told herself it was because they were more comfortable with silence now, like a pair of elders enjoying a quieter, easier life. She still hunted in the woods when she couldn't stand to eat another fish, but Fallen Leaves didn't watch from the mouth of the tunnel, or comment when she came back smelling of blood and feathers. Hollyleaf never tried to catch something for him again, since he hadn't touched the half squirrel she'd left for him on the night Ivypool and Blossomfall got lost. Fallen Leaves wasn't weak with hunger, so he obviously preferred to eat in private. It was one more reminder that he wasn't a Clan cat, but Hollyleaf had chosen not to live as a warrior, hadn't she? She and Fallen Leaves had more in common than the stone roof over their heads.

Leaf-bare yielded to the determined warmth of new-leaf, and then greenleaf crept into the woods to leave trails of tempting prey scents and damp green smells. Hollyleaf started to spend longer outside, running through the trees with her whiskers quivering from all the fragrances, or lying on the open grassland to let the sun warm her fur. The days grew hotter until she longed to walk beside the lake and let the waves wash over her paws. The upper slopes of the ridge were her favorite place to cool off in the gentle breeze, until one day she strayed too close to the WindClan border and almost ran into a patrol. She raced back over the crest of the hill and dived into the trees, panting with fright.

When her heart had slowed, she made her way back to the woods-tunnel, keeping to the shadows in case any WindClan warriors had come in search of the stranger on their territory. Hollyleaf hoped they wouldn't accuse ThunderClan of trespassing. There had been enough trouble between the two

Clans since they arrived at the lake, even though the elders told of a time when Firestar and Onestar had been good friends across the Clan divide. Hollyleaf wondered how the ThunderClan cats were dealing with the scorching weather. Were the apprentices on full-time moss duty, bringing water up from the lake? Had Brambleclaw ordered dusk hunting patrols to avoid the worst of the heat?

The woods-tunnel appeared in front of her, but Hollyleaf stopped. Stronger than the sun, she burned to know how her Clanmates were. Almost without thinking about it, she swerved around the entrance to the tunnel and headed up the slope. Trees grew all the way to the top of the ridge here and down the other side, providing cover right to the Thunder-Clan border. In fact, Hollyleaf almost missed it completely, until she picked up the faint scent of a border mark on a moss-covered tree stump. The markers would dry fast in the sun, and needed replacing more often than once a day. Checking her pace, she crept through the bracken toward the hollow.

A faint, tempting prey-scent drifted toward her. Hollyleaf parted the stems in front of her with one paw and saw the soft brown outline of a rabbit nibbling at a clump of green plants. Hollyleaf's mouth watered but she knew there was no way she could hunt here. She was about to turn away and leave this plump treat for the next patrol when she recognized the scent of the plants that the rabbit was devouring. *Marigold!* Precious for healing wounds and keeping scratches clean, and rare so close to the hollow. Hollyleaf couldn't let the rabbit eat the entire crop. She leaped forward, hissing and baring her teeth.

The rabbit froze, then scampered away, its bobbing white tail signaling a warning through the trees.

Hollyleaf fought her instinct to chase after it and focused on the marigolds. Nearly all of them had been eaten down to the roots. Hollyleaf couldn't stay here and guard them, and the rabbit would be back to finish them off as soon as she had left. She had to find a way to keep the last plants safe. Looking around, she spotted a deep cleft between the branch and trunk of a nearby tree, not too far from the ground that it couldn't be seen by a passing cat, but too high for a rabbit to reach. She quickly nipped off the remaining flowers as close to the ground as possible. With her mouth full of juicy stalks, she climbed the tree and placed the flowers in the cleft.

She narrowed her eyes, thinking. In this sun, the plants would soon wilt. They needed water to keep them fresh. Hollyleaf jumped down from the tree and paused for a moment to listen for approaching patrols, then set off through the woods toward the border with WindClan. There, she soaked a ball of moss in the stream and carried it carefully back to the marigold patch. When she scrambled up the trunk again, water dribbled onto her chest and belly fur, making her gasp in shock. But the moss held on to enough to fill the cleft with a tiny puddle, which would keep the marigold stems wet until Leafpool or Jayfeather came looking for more supplies.

Hollyleaf leaped down to the ground, paused once to check that the marigolds were safely in their hiding place, and raced back to the tunnel. She may not be a part of ThunderClan anymore, but if she could help them, she would.

All that night, Hollyleaf couldn't sleep for thinking about the marigold plants. Had Leafpool found them? Would the Clan be able to protect the rest of the patch from the rabbit? After two more anxious sunrises, she decided to go back and see if the plants had been taken from the cleft in the tree. She ran along the woods-tunnel, feeling light-headed with nervousness. Beyond the entrance, the trees were quiet and greenleaf-heavy, with only the slightest breeze to stir the leaves. Hollyleaf stayed clear of the trails as she pushed her way through the bracken to the place where the marigold grew. Suddenly she heard voices coming toward her, young and excited.

"Watch this, Molepaw!"

Hollyleaf padded to the edge of the brittle ferns and peeped out. A small ginger she-cat was crouching down with her tail stuck in the air.

"I'm going to attack that stick!" she declared.

"Don't forget you're supposed to close one eye, Cherrypaw," mewed the cream-and-brown tom. "Brightheart said we needed to practice all the moves as if we've been injured."

Hollyleaf let out a purr. She remembered being trained by Brightheart in moves specially designed to cope with the loss of sight on one side. She studied Cherrypaw's position. She wasn't doing too badly, although she needed to shift her weight onto the paws on the side of her good eye to improve her balance.

Suddenly Hollyleaf's nose twitched. A new scent had

filtered into the bracken, above that of warm young apprentices and green leaves. A scent that made Hollyleaf's fur rise and her claws extend: fox! Before she could call a warning, a huge russet shape crashed out of the trees and loomed over the apprentices. Hollyleaf braced herself to spring, but Brightheart, Foxleap, and Rosepetal were already launching themselves from the bushes on the far side of the clearing.

The three warriors raced at the fox with their teeth bared. "Get out of here!" screeched Rosepetal.

The fox jerked its head up, its eyes widening in alarm. It snapped at Foxleap, who was nearest, but the reddish-furred warrior ducked away and came at the fox from behind, raking his claws down its flank. Brightheart flung herself onto the fox's ear and hung there with her teeth clenched fast. Rosepetal flailed her paws at its nose, sending scarlet beads of blood flying onto the grass. The fox struggled briefly, then whipped around, flicking Brightheart into the bracken, and raced into the trees. The warriors pelted after it, still yowling.

Hollyleaf stayed where she was, hardly daring to breathe. The bracken had been crushed in the fight, and there was barely enough left standing to keep her hidden. During the scuffle, Cherrypaw and Molepaw had fled to the shelter of a bramble thicket on the far side of the clearing. Hollyleaf could just see them in the shadows, crouching in a three-colored huddle. At least they were safe. She had to get out of here before the warriors came back and picked up her scent on top of the fox's.

Just as she turned to leave, the bracken rattled and the fox leaped back into the clearing. Drool spilled from its jaws and its yellow eyes gleamed with fury and determination. Hollyleaf stared at it in dismay. It must have doubled back and lost its pursuers! The fox lowered its head and sniffed at the patch of grass where the apprentices had been training. Then it looked toward the bramble thicket, its ears flattening. There was a tiny squeak from the thorns, cut off abruptly as if Cherrypaw had whimpered and Molepaw had stuffed his paw in her mouth.

Hollyleaf gathered her haunches beneath her and sprang out of her hiding place. "Get away from those kits!" she hissed. "Or you'll have me to deal with!" She reared up on her hind paws and raked her claws down the fox's blood-spattered muzzle.

The fox glared at her, curling its lip to reveal sharp, stained teeth. Hollyleaf held her ground. "Get out of here!" she spat, feeling the fury of a whole Clan of queens ready to defend their kits.

In the distance, she could hear the warriors returning, pounding through the trees with calls of alarm. The fox ducked to one side, then turned and fled. Hollyleaf followed, relief making her ears ring. She dived into the undergrowth and kept on running, flattening one ear back for signs of pursuit. But the warriors had stayed with Cherrypaw and Molepaw and didn't come after the fox again. For a moment Hollyleaf wondered how much Cherrypaw and Molepaw had seen from underneath the thicket; would they tell their

Clanmates about the strange cat that had chased off the fox? Hollyleaf knew she had taken a big risk, but she had had no choice. She had saved the lives of those kits, and that was all that mattered.

CHAPTER 10

❧

Hollyleaf gave up trying to sleep and hauled herself out of the crumpled feathers. She couldn't remember the last time her eyes had stayed closed all night. When she had drifted off earlier, she dreamed she was back in the hollow, defending her Clanmates from foxes, helping them gather herbs, watching kits play in the sunshine. It only took moments before she jerked awake in the lonely dark, with a sharp pain inside her that memories would never ease.

She padded along the tunnel to the river-cave with a strange feeling of calm. Fallen Leaves was sitting in his usual place beside the water. Hollyleaf settled down next to him and waited until he met her gaze. "I'm sorry," she began. "I will never forget how you saved my life and gave me somewhere to stay when I thought I had lost everything. You have been a true friend, and I will always be grateful for that. But I don't belong here."

"I know," Fallen Leaves meowed. "I always hoped you would stay. I . . . I never had someone to share my home before. But your Clan needs you more than I do. You must realize that by now."

Hollyleaf nodded, looking down at her paws. "And I need them. But I don't know how to go back! So much has happened!"

"When the time comes, you will know," whispered Fallen Leaves, and when Hollyleaf lifted her head, he had vanished and she was alone by the rippling water.

A moon passed. Hollyleaf was even more restless than usual, creeping into ThunderClan's territory every day before dawn but always shying away from presenting herself in the hollow. She couldn't imagine what she would say, or how the cats would react. On the night of the full moon she climbed the ridge and looked down at the island in the lake, picturing the four Clans gathered there. Did they even remember her? Suddenly filled with doubt, Hollyleaf went back to the tunnels and curled into her nest, only to dream that she was at a Gathering surrounded by scornful, jeering cats who wanted to know why a loner was asking to join the Clans. Hollyleaf woke with a start, shivering. She was still a warrior, wasn't she?

After that she stayed inside the tunnels for several days, eating fish and patrolling endless stone passages until her paws were as rough as tree bark. Fallen Leaves had told her she would know when it was time for her to go back. She hoped he was right, and that the chance hadn't already passed her by.

She was finishing a late meal of minnow when there were soft paw steps behind her and she turned to see Fallen Leaves entering the river-cave. Hollyleaf hadn't seen him for a while, and she jumped to her paws with excitement. "Hey! Where have you been?"

Fallen Leaves held up his tail to silence her. "There are cats in the tunnels. Something bad is happening." He whipped around and headed into the tunnel that led eventually to the moor. Hollyleaf followed him, running to keep up. They had hardly left the faint light of the river-cave when she heard voices echoing through the darkness. Not ThunderClan cats this time but WindClan—and another voice she recognized, a tom who spoke louder than the others in a deep rumble that sounded like thunder as it rang off the stone. *Sol!* In a flash Hollyleaf remembered the tortoiseshell-and-white cat who had caused such trouble before, predicting the vanishing of the sun and trying to persuade Blackstar to turn his back on his warrior ancestors. *What's he doing back here?*

In front of her, Fallen Leaves stopped. The conversation traveled clearly along the tunnel.

"This is your chance for true glory!" Sol was saying. "One-star may want peace, but that is a sign of weakness! Attack ThunderClan through the tunnels, and victory will be easy over those mouse-munching idiots!"

"Sol's right!" called another cat; Hollyleaf was sure it was Owlwhisker. "We've listened to Onestar for too long. He should let us fight now, do what we've trained for, and teach those ThunderClan cats that we're stronger than they think!"

There was a chorus of yowls in agreement. Hollyleaf's fur stood on end. Her Clanmates were going to be attacked! She couldn't let this happen! Beside her, Fallen Leaves stiffened.

"There are other cats down here," he breathed into Hollyleaf's ear.

Very carefully, she turned and sniffed the air. Two ThunderClan cats were standing in a side tunnel, just around the corner. Hollyleaf inhaled again until she could identify the scents: Ivypool and her sister, Dovewing. She started to pad toward them, then stopped as there was a hiss from the WindClan cats.

"Did anyone hear a noise?" growled a warrior.

Fallen Leaves put his mouth close to Hollyleaf's ear. "You have to get them out of here. Your whole Clan needs you now. If WindClan is going to attack through the tunnels, you are the only one who can help them."

Hollyleaf looked at her friend. "It's time, isn't it?" she meowed softly.

Fallen Leaves nodded. "Go well," he murmured. "I will never forget you, Hollyleaf."

At that moment, there was a cracking noise from the side tunnel, nothing more than a pebble slipping underneath a paw, but echoed and magnified by the stone walls until it sounded as loud as thunder.

"What was that?" Owlwhisker growled. "Is some cat eavesdropping on us?"

Hollyleaf began to creep toward the thicker shadows where her Clanmates were hiding.

"Get us out of here!" she heard Ivypool whisper.

"I followed the voices to get here," Dovewing replied. "I'm not sure of the way out."

Behind her, Hollyleaf heard the WindClan cats stirring. It sounded as if more than one was coming to investigate.

Ivypool had heard them too. "They're coming to look for us! We have to go."

There wasn't time to lead these cats out from the safety of the shadows. Hollyleaf would have to show herself to them, let them know that she was a cat who could be trusted. She took a deep breath. All the moons of hiding, trying to forget she had ever belonged to a Clan, seemed to vanish in a single heartbeat. The blood of a warrior flowed through her veins. Nothing was more important than loyalty to her Clan.

She walked into the side tunnel and felt the air tingle as Dovewing and Ivypool tensed, ready to defend themselves.

"Come with me," she ordered into the darkness. "Quick!"

"No way!" Ivypool hissed. "You could be with them."

"I'm not," Hollyleaf mewed, trying to keep her voice calm.

"Prove it," Dovewing challenged.

"I shouldn't have to," Hollyleaf snapped. *Didn't these cats recognize ThunderClan scent when it was in front of them?* "For StarClan's sake, let's go."

In the faintest gleam of starlight filtering from the river-cave, Hollyleaf saw Ivypool's eyes widen as she exchanged a glance with her sister. "StarClan?" Ivypool echoed. "Then you—"

"Do you want to get out of here or not?" Hollyleaf interrupted.

"Yes, we do," Ivypool snapped back. "But how do we know you won't lead us farther in?"

Hollyleaf let out a hiss of frustration. Couldn't these questions have waited? And yet perhaps it wasn't surprising that these young cats had no idea who she was. She was going to be a stranger to many of her Clanmates after being away for so long.

"Because I'm a ThunderClan cat like you," she meowed, raising her voice over the pounding of her heart. "My name is Hollyleaf."

WARRIORS

MISTYSTAR'S
OMEN

ALLEGIANCES

RIVERCLAN

LEADER   **LEOPARDSTAR**—unusually spotted golden tabby she-cat

DEPUTY   **MISTYFOOT**—gray she-cat with blue eyes

MEDICINE CAT   **MOTHWING**—dappled golden she-cat
APPRENTICE, WILLOWSHINE (gray tabby she-cat)

WARRIORS   **REEDWHISKER**—black tom
APPRENTICE, HOLLOWPAW (dark brown tabby tom)

GRAYMIST—pale gray tabby she-cat
APPRENTICE, TROUTPAW (pale gray tabby she-cat)

MINTFUR—light gray tabby tom

ICEWING—white she-cat with blue eyes

MINNOWTAIL—dark gray she-cat
APPRENTICE, MOSSYPAW (brown-and-white she-cat)

PEBBLEFOOT—mottled gray tom
APPRENTICE, RUSHPAW (light brown tabby tom)

MALLOWNOSE—light brown tabby tom

ROBINWING—tortoiseshell-and-white tom

BEETLEWHISKER—brown-and-white tabby tom

PETALFUR—gray-and-white she-cat

GRASSPELT—light brown tom

QUEENS	**DUSKFUR**—brown tabby she-cat
	MOSSPELT—tortoiseshell she-cat with blue eyes
ELDERS	**DAPPLENOSE**—mottled gray she-cat
	POUNCETAIL—ginger-and-white tom

THUNDERCLAN

LEADER	**FIRESTAR**—ginger tom with a flame-colored pelt
DEPUTY	**BRAMBLECLAW**—dark brown tabby tom with amber eyes
MEDICINE CAT	**JAYFEATHER**—gray tabby tom with blind blue eyes
WARRIORS	(toms and she-cats without kits)
	GRAYSTRIPE—long-haired gray tom
	MILLIE—striped gray tabby she-cat
	DUSTPELT—dark brown tabby tom
	SANDSTORM—pale ginger she-cat with green eyes
	BRACKENFUR—golden brown tabby tom
	SORRELTAIL—tortoiseshell-and-white she-cat with amber eyes
	CLOUDTAIL—long-haired white tom with blue eyes
	BRIGHTHEART—white she-cat with ginger patches
	THORNCLAW—golden brown tabby tom
	SQUIRRELFLIGHT—dark ginger she-cat with green eyes

LEAFPOOL—light brown tabby she-cat with amber eyes

SPIDERLEG—long-limbed black tom with brown underbelly and amber eyes

BIRCHFALL—light brown tabby tom

WHITEWING—white she-cat with green eyes

BERRYNOSE—cream-colored tom

HAZELTAIL—small gray-and-white she-cat

MOUSEWHISKER—gray-and-white tom

CINDERHEART—gray tabby she-cat
APPRENTICE, IVYPAW

LIONBLAZE—golden tabby tom with amber eyes
APPRENTICE, DOVEPAW

FOXLEAP—reddish tabby tom

ICECLOUD—white she-cat

TOADSTEP—black-and-white tom

ROSEPETAL—dark cream she-cat

BRIARLIGHT—dark brown she-cat

BLOSSOMFALL—tortoiseshell-and-white she-cat

BUMBLEFLIGHT—very pale gray tom with black stripes

APPRENTICES (more than six moons old, in training to become warriors)

DOVEPAW—pale gray she-cat with blue eyes

IVYPAW—silver-and-white tabby she-cat with dark blue eyes

QUEENS (she-cats expecting or nursing kits)

FERNCLOUD—pale gray (with darker flecks) she-cat with green eyes

DAISY—cream long-furred cat from the horseplace

POPPYFROST—tortoiseshell she-cat (mother to Cherrykit, a ginger she-cat, and Molekit, a brown-and-cream tom)

ELDERS (former warriors and queens, now retired)

MOUSEFUR—small dusky brown she-cat

PURDY—plump tabby former loner with a gray muzzle

LONGTAIL—pale tabby tom with black stripes, retired early due to failing sight

SHADOWCLAN

LEADER   **BLACKSTAR**—large white tom with huge jet-black paws

DEPUTY   **RUSSETFUR**—dark ginger she-cat

MEDICINE CAT   **LITTLECLOUD**—very small tabby tom
APPRENTICE, FLAMETAIL (ginger tom)

WARRIORS   **OAKFUR**—small brown tom
APPRENTICE, FERRETPAW (cream-and-gray tom)

ROWANCLAW—ginger tom

SMOKEFOOT—black tom

TOADFOOT—dark brown tom

APPLEFUR—mottled brown she-cat

CROWFROST—black-and-white tom

RATSCAR—brown tom with long scar across his back

APPRENTICE, **PINEPAW** (black she-cat)

SNOWBIRD—pure-white she-cat

TAWNYPELT—tortoiseshell she-cat with green eyes

APPRENTICE, **STARLINGPAW** (ginger tom)

OLIVENOSE—tortoiseshell she-cat

OWLCLAW—light brown tabby tom

SHREWFOOT—gray she-cat with black feet

SCORCHFUR—dark gray tom

REDWILLOW—mottled brown-and-ginger tom

TIGERHEART—dark brown tabby tom

DAWNPELT—cream-furred she-cat

QUEENS
KINKFUR—tabby she-cat, with long fur that sticks out at all angles

IVYTAIL—black, white, and tortoiseshell she-cat

ELDERS
CEDARHEART—dark gray tom

TALLPOPPY—long-legged light brown tabby she-cat

SNAKETAIL—dark brown tom with tabby-striped tail

WHITEWATER—white she-cat with long fur, blind in one eye

WINDCLAN

LEADER
ONESTAR—brown tabby tom

DEPUTY   **ASHFOOT**—gray she-cat

MEDICINE CAT   **KESTRELFLIGHT**—mottled gray tom

WARRIORS   **CROWFEATHER**—dark gray tom

OWLWHISKER—light brown tabby tom
APPRENTICE, WHISKERPAW (light brown tom)

WHITETAIL—small white she-cat

NIGHTCLOUD—black she-cat

GORSETAIL—very pale gray-and-white she-cat with blue eyes

WEASELFUR—ginger tom with white paws

HARESPRING—brown-and-white tom

LEAFTAIL—dark tabby tom with amber eyes

ANTPELT—brown tom with one black ear

EMBERFOOT—gray tom with two dark paws

HEATHERTAIL—light brown tabby she-cat with blue eyes
APPRENTICE, FURZEPAW (gray-and-white she-cat)

BREEZEPELT—black tom with amber eyes
APPRENTICE, BOULDERPAW (large pale gray tom)

SEDGEWHISKER—light brown tabby she-cat

SWALLOWTAIL—dark gray she-cat

SUNSTRIKE—tortoiseshell she-cat with large white mark on her forehead

ELDERS   **WEBFOOT**—dark gray tabby tom

TORNEAR—tabby tom

CATS OUTSIDE CLANS

SMOKY—muscular gray-and-white tom who lives in a barn at the horseplace

FLOSS—small gray-and-white she-cat who lives at the horseplace

OTHER ANIMALS

MIDNIGHT—a star-gazing badger who lives by the sea

MISTYSTAR'S
OMEN

Hareview Campsite

Sanctuary
Cottage

Sadler Woods

Littlepine Road

Littlepine
Sailing
Center

Littlepine
Island

River Alba

Whitchurch Road

CHAPTER 1

❧

Mistyfoot stood at the edge of the rock and watched the water swirl below her paws. It was brown and thick with debris—twigs, scraps of leaf, even a knot of roots that had once held up a tree—and however hard Mistyfoot stared, she was unable to glimpse the stones on the bottom of the lake, or the distinctive flash of silver that gave away the position of a fish. She stretched down to lap at the surface with her tongue. The water tasted bitter and muddy.

"It's not the same, is it?" Leopardstar commented beside her. Mistyfoot raised her head and looked at her leader. Leopardstar's golden fur looked dull and dusty in the gray dawn light, and the dark spots that had inspired her name seemed to have faded in the last moon. "I thought when the water returned that everything would be as it was before," Leopardstar went on. She dipped her paw in the lake, staggering a little as she straightened up again, and watched the drips fall from the tips of her claws onto the stone.

"The fish will come back soon," Mistyfoot meowed. "Now that the streams are flowing, there's no reason for them to stay away."

Leopardstar gazed at the ruffled water. "So many fish died in the drought," she sighed, as if Mistyfoot hadn't spoken. "What if the lake stays empty forever? What will we eat?"

Mistyfoot moved closer to her leader until her shoulder brushed Leopardstar's fur. She was shocked to feel the she-cat's bones sharp just beneath the skin. "Everything will be fine," she murmured. "The beavers' dam has been destroyed, the rain has come, and the long thirst is over. It's been a hard greenleaf, but we have survived."

"Blackclaw, Voletooth, and Dawnflower didn't," Leopardstar snapped. "Three elders lost in a single season? I had to watch my Clanmates starve to death because there were no fish to catch, nothing left in the lake but mud. And what about Rippletail? He was as brave as any of the other cats who went to find where the water had gone—why didn't he deserve to come back? Did he go too far beyond the sight of StarClan?"

Mistyfoot let her tail curl forward to rest on Leopardstar's back. "Rippletail died saving the lake, and all the Clans. He will be honored forever."

Leopardstar turned away and began to pad up the shore. "He paid too high a price," she growled. "If the fish haven't returned with the water, we're no better off than we were during the drought." She stumbled, and Mistyfoot jumped forward, ready to support her. But Leopardstar shrugged her off with a hiss and continued over the stones, limping.

Mistyfoot followed at a respectful distance, not wanting to fuss over the proud golden cat. She knew Leopardstar was in pain most of the time now, worn down by a sickness that had resisted all of Mothwing's medicine skills, although it wasn't unknown: the ravaging thirst, the dramatic weight loss in spite of constant hunger, the growing weakness that dulled a cat's eyes and hearing. Mistyfoot felt her gaze soften as she watched Leopardstar reach the end of the pebbles and push her way into the ferns that ringed the RiverClan camp.

Suddenly there was a muffled cry from the depths of the undergrowth.

"Leopardstar?" Mistyfoot bounded into the green stalks. A few strides in, she reached her leader's side. She was slumped on the ground, her eyes stretched wide with pain, her flanks heaving with the effort to draw another breath. "Don't move," Mistyfoot ordered. "I'll fetch help." She thrust her way through the rest of the ferns and burst into the clearing at the heart of the territory. "Mothwing! Come quick! Leopardstar has fallen!"

There was the sound of racing paws; then Mothwing's sandy pelt, so close to the shade of Leopardstar's, appeared at the entrance to her den. The medicine cat paused, looking around, and Mistyfoot called, "This way!"

Side by side, the cats pushed through the ferns to their leader. Leopardstar had closed her eyes, and her breath rattled in her chest as she gasped for air. Mothwing bent over her, sniffing and tasting her fur with her tongue. Mistyfoot leaned forward but recoiled from the musty stench coming from the sick cat. Close up, she could see dirt and scurf in Leopardstar's pelt, as if the leader hadn't groomed herself in days.

"Fetch Mintfur and Pebblefoot," Mothwing mewed quietly

over her shoulder. "They haven't gone out on patrol yet. They can help us carry Leopardstar to her den."

Relieved to have an excuse to leave, and guilty that she wanted to, Mistyfoot backed away and raced to the clearing. She returned with Mintfur and Pebblefoot and watched as Mothwing eased Leopardstar to her paws, propped heavily on either flank by the warriors. Mistyfoot held the ferns aside as the cats half guided, half dragged their leader into the camp.

"Is Leopardstar *dead*?" Mistyfoot heard one of Duskfur's kits whisper.

"Of course not, dear. She's just very tired," Duskfur mewed.

Mistyfoot stood at the entrance to the den and watched Pebblefoot pat moss into place beneath Leopardstar's head. This was more than mere exhaustion. Already the den seemed darker, the shadows thicker, as though warriors from StarClan were gathering to welcome the RiverClan leader. Mintfur brushed past Mistyfoot as he left, his pale gray pelt smelling sharply of ferns. "Let me know if I can do anything else for her," he murmured, and Mistyfoot nodded. Pebblefoot followed, his head lowered and the tip of his tail leaving a faint scar in the dust.

Mothwing tucked Leopardstar's front paw more comfortably under the she-cat's chest and straightened up. "I need to fetch some herbs from my den," she meowed. "Stay with her; let her know that you are here." She rested her muzzle briefly against Mistyfoot's ear. "Be strong, my friend," she whispered.

The den seemed deathly quiet after Mothwing had gone. Leopardstar's breathing had grown shallow, a barely audible wheeze that did little more than flex the moss by her muzzle. Mistyfoot crouched down by her leader's head and stroked her tail along Leopardstar's bony flank. "Sleep well," she mewed softly. "You're safe now. Mothwing is gathering herbs to make you feel better."

To her surprise, Leopardstar stirred. "It's too late for that," rasped the she-cat without opening her eyes. "StarClan draws near; I can feel them all around me. This is my time to leave."

"Don't say that!" hissed Mistyfoot. "Your ninth life has barely started! Mothwing will heal you."

Leopardstar let out a grunt. "Mothwing has served me so well, but some things are beyond even her skills. Let me go peacefully, Mistyfoot. I won't fight this last battle, and neither should you."

"But I don't want to lose you!" Mistyfoot protested.

One clouded blue eye opened and gazed at her. "Really?" Leopardstar wheezed. "After what I did to your brother? To all the half-Clan cats?"

For a heartbeat, Mistyfoot was plunged back into the dark and stinking rabbit hole in RiverClan's old camp in the forest. Tigerstar and Leopardstar had united to form TigerClan, and in their quest for the purest warrior blood, they had imprisoned all cats with mixed Clan heritage. Mistyfoot and Stonefur, who had been the RiverClan deputy, had recently learned that Bluestar of ThunderClan was their mother. This had been enough to condemn them in Leopardstar's eyes, and she had allowed Tigerstar to persecute them until Stonefur had been killed, murdered in cold blood by Tigerstar's deputy,

Blackfoot. Mistyfoot had been rescued by Firestar and taken to ThunderClan until the terrible battle with BloodClan had ended Tigerstar's death-soaked rule.

"I never deserved your forgiveness," Leopardstar whispered, jerking Mistyfoot back to the cold, quiet den.

"Tigerstar was responsible for the death of my brother," Mistyfoot growled. "Tigerstar and Blackfoot. The time of TigerClan had nothing to do with the warrior code that I believe in. I was always loyal to RiverClan—and to you, as our leader."

Leopardstar sighed. "Your life has been harder than I wanted, Mistyfoot. Losing your brother and three of your kits. You have borne your heartache well."

Mistyfoot stiffened. No cat would ever know the pain she had felt when she buried her children. "Every queen knows that the life of a kit is a precious and fragile thing. I will see them again in StarClan, and I walk with them in my heart every day," she mewed.

There was a pause as Leopardstar strained to take a breath, and Mistyfoot half rose, ready to call for help. Then Leopardstar relaxed again. "I am sorry not to have known the joy of having kits. There was a time when I thought it might happen, but it was not to be." Her words faded away as though she was picturing something she had dreamed of long ago. "Perhaps it was for the best. But I would have been proud to call you my daughter, Mistyfoot."

Mistyfoot couldn't reply. Her heart ached with the familiar sorrow that she had never had a chance to know her real mother, Bluestar. The ThunderClan leader had revealed her darkest secret to Mistyfoot and Stonefur just before she died on the banks of the river. For a moment, Mistyfoot had been scorched by the love of a mother, but then it had vanished, leaving a cold emptiness that could never be filled.

She curled herself around Leopardstar, just as she had tried to warm Bluestar's sodden body all those moons ago.

"Sleep now," she murmured into Leopardstar's ear. "I'll be here when you wake."

CHAPTER 2

The wind had risen, stirring the bushes and making the waves splash against the shore, when Mistyfoot woke. The den was pale with dawn light that flickered as the branches of the rowan tree swayed in the breeze. Beside Mistyfoot, Leopardstar was cold and still. Mistyfoot rested her muzzle on the old cat's head, then slipped out of the den and padded through the sleeping camp down to the shore. She stared over the choppy gray water, wondering if Leopardstar had joined their ancestors yet.

Paw steps behind her made Mistyfoot turn. Mothwing was stepping carefully over the stones. "Leopardstar is dead," the medicine cat announced.

"I know," Mistyfoot meowed. She closed her eyes against the rush of pain. She felt Mothwing come to stand beside her, spilling warmth and softness from her fur. "I don't feel ready to lead this Clan," Mistyfoot confessed in a whisper without opening her eyes. "How can I follow in Leopardstar's footsteps?"

Mothwing rested her tail on Mistyfoot's back. "You are more than ready," she promised. "Think of the path you have traveled so far. You have seen more than most cats ever will in their lifetime."

"That's because I am old," Mistyfoot pointed out. "Black-claw was only a few seasons older than me! Sometimes I feel as if I have outstayed my welcome here, as if I should be walking in StarClan with Stonefur by now."

"That's mouse-brained, and you know it," Mothwing retorted. "You have a long life yet to live. Nine long lives, in fact."

Nine lives! For a heartbeat, Mistyfoot felt overwhelmed with tiredness. How would she find enough energy to lead her Clan when she could barely move her paws? Would she have a chance to feel sad about Leopardstar's death, with so much to do? Mothwing seemed to sense her hesitation.

"There will be plenty of time to grieve for Leopardstar. I will be here whenever you need me. You are not alone, Misty-foot. You must summon our Clanmates; tell them about Leopardstar. You are their leader now, and they need you as much as they needed Leopardstar."

Keeping her tail on Mistyfoot's spine, Mothwing led her back to the camp. Mistyfoot breathed in the delicate scent of herbs from her friend's pelt and began to feel better. "I couldn't do this without you," she murmured.

"Nor should you have to," Mothwing replied briskly. "I am your medicine cat, and I will do everything I can to help you."

The clearing was already filling up with cats, who circled anxiously, whispering. Mistyfoot jumped onto the broad willow stump outside Leopardstar's den and called to her

Clanmates. "Let all cats old enough to swim gather to hear my words!" In spite of her grief, she couldn't help feeling a rush of excitement as the cats stopped circling and settled on their haunches around the tree stump, gazing expectantly up at her. *Mothwing was right! They see me as their leader even before I have been given my nine lives and my new name!*

"Leopardstar has gone to walk with StarClan," she announced. A murmur of sadness spread through the cats like a gust of cold wind.

"We were lucky to have her as our leader for so many moons," Graymist mewed. "She was brave and strong-willed on behalf of all of us."

"She told me I was doing really well in my battle training," the apprentice Mossypaw commented mournfully.

Duskfur drew her kits closer with a sweep of her tail. "I had hoped she would live long enough to see these little ones become apprentices," she sighed.

Beetlewhisker stood up, his brown-and-white pelt gleaming in the early rays of the sun. "When will you be getting your nine lives?" he asked Mistyfoot.

Mistyfoot winced. This was what she had been afraid of, that she would scarcely have time to draw breath—let alone mourn the former leader—before she was plunged into her new life. But she had been Leopardstar's deputy for a long time, and she had always known what her duties would be when this moment came. And she couldn't help looking forward to the chance to walk with Mothwing among her warrior ancestors, to learn the secrets of the future that would help her to lead her Clan. "I'll go to the Moonpool as soon as I can," she declared.

Mothwing stirred, and Mistyfoot looked questioningly at her. "We can wait until tomorrow," meowed the medicine cat. "We must sit vigil for Leopardstar tonight."

A black tom stood up and nodded to Mistyfoot. "I speak for all the warriors when I say that I will be honored to serve you as my leader," he announced.

"Thank you, Reedwhisker," Mistyfoot purred. Her mind flashed back to the time she had nursed this cat at her belly with his littermates; he was the only one of her kits who had survived, and every day she took pride in the warrior he had become.

Petalfur twitched her tail. "Some of us can speak for ourselves," she mewed irritably. "But I will be as loyal to you as I was to Leopardstar, may she walk in peace among the stars."

"Mistystar!" called Troutpaw.

Mistyfoot narrowed her eyes at the pale gray apprentice. "Not yet, Troutpaw. Not until I have received my nine lives." *Tomorrow I will walk with our ancestors, and say good-bye to my warrior name forever.*

Mistyfoot jumped down from the tree stump and called to Grasspelt: "Could you lead a hunting patrol before sunhigh? Take Minnowtail and Mossypaw, and Icewing if she feels up to it."

The white she-cat sniffed. "Of course I'm up to it! I've spent the last three sunrises stuck in this camp, so I'm more than ready to stretch my legs."

Mistyfoot hid a purr of amusement. "You're allowed to rest as much as you want after journeying to the beavers' dam," she reminded Icewing. "But if you feel like hunting, then we'd all be grateful for your sharp eyes."

Reedwhisker padded up to Mistyfoot. "Would you like me to visit the other Clans and let them know about Leopardstar's death?"

Mistyfoot shook her head. "No. They'll find out soon enough. We must honor Leopardstar by carrying out our duties as usual."

"In that case, should I lead a boundary patrol?" Reedwhisker offered. "I want to be sure that the fox we scented yesterday hasn't come any closer to the camp."

Mistyfoot nodded. "Yes, please. And keep an eye out for squirrels or mice while you're on that side of the territory. In case there aren't many fish to be found in the lake yet." She wondered if any of her Clanmates knew just how empty the water seemed to be. *If they haven't noticed on their own, I'm not going to point it out to them. But we might need to stock the fresh-kill pile with other prey for a while.*

"You won't have to do this for much longer," mewed Graymist close to her ear.

Mistyfoot jumped. "Do what?" She wondered if she had said something about the lack of fish out loud.

Graymist nodded toward the cats who were gathering into groups. "Organize patrols. You'll have to appoint a deputy before moonhigh, won't you?"

"A deputy?" Mistyfoot echoed. "Yes, of course."

The she-cat looked at her closely. "Do you know who you'll choose? You must have thought about it before now."

Mistyfoot didn't think she could admit that no, she hadn't. Of course she had known that Leopardstar was sick, but she hadn't really imagined that the leader's ninth life would end. There was so much to do! And all of it seemed to rest on her shoulders. To her relief, Reedwhisker called Graymist to join his border patrol and Mistyfoot didn't have to answer.

For a moment the bushes were alive with movement as cats headed out on their patrols; then suddenly the clearing was empty and silent. Mistyfoot drew a deep breath and looked around. Everything was reassuringly familiar, from the well-trodden bare earth where the cats sat to eat and share tongues to the carefully draped brambles that hid the different dens. Only Mistyfoot felt changed beyond recognition, daunted and breathless at the thought of what lay ahead.

"Mistyfoot?" Willowshine was standing at the entrance to the medicine cats' den, which was shielded between two mossy rocks. She trotted across the flattened grass with her tail kinked over her back. "Do you want me to come with you to the Moonpool? When you go to receive your nine lives, I mean."

Mistyfoot blinked. "Isn't that Mothwing's duty?"

"Well, yes," mewed Willowshine, sounding a little uncertain. "But as it's your first time sharing tongues with our ancestors, I thought you might like more company."

Mistyfoot purred. "I'm not afraid of walking in StarClan, little one. But you are kind to offer, and one day I'm sure you will accompany your leader as they receive their nine lives. But it's Mothwing's responsibility this time."

Again there was a puzzling flash of hesitation in the gray tabby's eyes; then she nodded. "Of course," she meowed. "Whatever happens tomorrow, I wish you well." She ducked away, back to her den, leaving Mistyfoot frowning after her. *Whatever happens tomorrow?* Was there something she should be afraid of? She shrugged, deciding that Willowshine was just a little too eager to prove her merit as a medicine cat, and perhaps not quite experienced enough for all of the responsibilities.

She crossed the clearing to the Clan's favorite basking place, a sandy slope that was a poor substitute for Sunningrocks, according to the cats who remembered the forest. Dapplenose and Pouncetail lay in the soft golden light, their tails twitching and their eyes half-closed. *But I bet they haven't missed a single moment of what's happened this morning,* Mistyfoot thought.

"We need to find somewhere to bury Leopardstar," she mewed, feeling grief weigh in her belly like a stone.

The elders nodded, and Dapplenose stood up, shaking sand from her mottled gray pelt. "I know just the place. Follow me." Pouncetail got to his paws more stiffly, stretching out each ginger-and-white leg in turn. Dapplenose led them over the crest of a slope and into the spindly trees on the other side. She swerved along a half-hidden path through a dense patch of comfrey until they emerged in a little clearing, shaded by a young rowan tree with a clear view of the lake and the island where the Clans gathered at each full moon. Behind the island, the hills where WindClan lived rose up to meet the clouds—and beyond that ridge lay the forest, Leopardstar's first home.

"I've always thought this would be a good spot for Leopardstar to rest," Dapplenose explained.

Mistyfoot nodded. "It's perfect. Are you able to dig the hole, or should I fetch some help?"

Pouncetail snorted. "For StarClan's sake, trust us to do this one last duty for our leader! Do you think we've lost the use of our legs?"

Dapplenose lay her tail across her denmate's shoulders. "Ignore this bad-tempered old trout," she told Mistyfoot. "But he's right that we can manage. You should go back to the clearing and have something to eat. You look exhausted, and you'll need your strength for the journey to the Moonpool."

Feeling a little overwhelmed by the old she-cat's motherly sympathy, Mistyfoot thanked them and pushed her way back through the comfrey. In the clearing, Grasspelt's patrol had returned with a catch of two tiny minnows, and set out again. Duskfur was prodding the minnows thoughtfully, but when Mistyfoot appeared, she pushed them toward her. "You take these," she urged. "My kits and I can eat later."

Mistyfoot blinked. Was she so old that her Clanmates were worried about her ability to cope with becoming leader?

Duskfur seemed to guess her thoughts. "Let us help you however we can," she prompted gently. "We know the sacrifices you will be making for us from now on."

Mistyfoot didn't argue. She couldn't tell Duskfur how isolated she suddenly felt from the cats who had been her friends and denmates all her life. Leopardstar's death had changed everything. *Thank StarClan I have Mothwing,* she thought. *She's the only cat who understands how it feels to be responsible for the entire Clan.*

As she chewed on the minnow, she watched the two medicine cats carefully pull Leopardstar's body out of her den and cover her pelt with rosemary and watermint. The scent of the fresh herbs hung in the air, smothering the taint of death. Mistyfoot heard Willowshine warn Mothwing that they were using the last of their supplies of watermint, but Mothwing just shook her head and told her to keep going. "Leopardstar needs it more than we do now," she insisted.

Mistyfoot's heart swelled with warmth toward her old friend. She knew how lucky she was to have Mothwing as her medicine cat. There was no way she could even contemplate the path ahead without her.

As the light began to fade, the cats of RiverClan gathered around the body of their former leader for the start of the long night vigil. The air was filled with the scent of herbs, and the wind had dropped so that the waves were little more than a gentle whisper beyond the bushes. Mistyfoot sat at Leopardstar's head, watching her Clanmates file sadly past.

Mothwing appeared beside her. "Are you ready to name your deputy? The moon is rising."

The cats closest to them pricked their ears, and Mistyfoot felt their gazes prick her pelt. She nodded and stood up. "Let all cats old enough to swim gather to hear my words!"

At once the line of cats stopped moving and turned to face

her. They all knew what was coming. Would they approve of her choice? Mistyfoot wondered. Once more she felt her legs tremble beneath the weight of new duties, and she took a step toward Mothwing so she could draw strength from the warmth of the medicine cat's fur.

"It is time for me to name my deputy," Mistyfoot announced, her voice sounding sharp and high-pitched in the cool night air. "Reedwhisker, I invite you to walk beside me and help me to lead this Clan. May StarClan hear and approve my choice."

There was a moment of silence; then the cats broke into cheers. "Reedwhisker! Congratulations!"

Mistyfoot's son stepped forward, his dark gray eyes shining. "I am honored to be chosen," he purred. "And I will lay down my life to protect you and my Clanmates."

"Hopefully it won't come to that," Mistyfoot told him. She stretched out her neck to rest her muzzle on top of his head. Reedwhisker's fur still smelled as it had when he was her kit.

There was a cross-sounding mutter from the shadows at the edge of the clearing: "I bet she only chose him because he's her son!"

"Hush, Mossypaw!" snapped Minnowtail. "Reedwhisker is a loyal and brave warrior, and will make a great deputy."

I hope so, thought Mistyfoot. She had expected some criticism for naming her son as her deputy, but she wanted to believe that wasn't the reason behind her decision.

"A brave choice," murmured Mothwing in her ear. "But the right one, I think."

Mistyfoot felt a bit better, but she would have been more

comforted if Mothwing had mentioned some sign of approval from StarClan, or even an omen that foresaw her announcement.

"Excuse me, Mistyfoot?" Duskfur was standing in front of her. "Is it okay if I take my little ones off now? They're getting tired."

Mistyfoot looked at the two kits, who were yawning and blinking their huge, round eyes. "Of course," she purred.

As Duskfur herded her family across the clearing, the line of cats started moving again.

"Farewell, Leopardstar. May you have good hunting in StarClan."

"We'll meet again, old friend. Save me a place to enjoy the sun."

"Wow! I've never seen a dead body before! What's all that green stuff on her fur?"

"Rushpaw, go to your den if you can't behave properly. And put that watermint down!"

Finally Mistyfoot was alone in the clearing with Leopardstar and the elders, who would stay beside their former leader all night. Mistyfoot bent and touched her muzzle to Leopardstar's cool, leaf-thin ear. "May the sun warm your back and the fish leap into your paws," she murmured.

"I haven't heard that said for a long time," rasped Pouncetail. "Not since we lived in the forest."

"Graypool used to say it when Stonefur and I were going to sleep," Mistyfoot mewed. "It was her way of wishing us good dreams."

"Ah, Stonefur," sighed Pouncetail. "I still miss him." He looked at Mistyfoot, narrowing his eyes through the gloom. "You had much to forgive Leopardstar for, didn't you?"

Mistyfoot swallowed. "She was a good leader for most of her life," she replied. "That is what she should be remembered for." She lay down with her nose pressed against Leopardstar's fur. *I promise to be the strongest, wisest leader I can be. I will do my best to echo your loyalty to RiverClan and your courage to speak out on our behalf, and I will learn from your mistakes. I know that I don't need to prove to the other Clans that RiverClan is the strongest or most powerful. I just want my Clanmates to be happy and at peace.*

"And that is the best ambition of all," murmured a voice behind her.

Mistyfoot sprang up and spun around. A gray cat stood behind her, this thick fur glowing with starlight. "Stonefur!"

The cat nodded. "Did you think I would miss this night?" he meowed. "I have been watching you all this time, and I am so proud that you are going to lead our Clan."

Mistyfoot's tail drooped. "It should have been you."

Stonefur shook his head. "That was not my destiny. I wish you well, Mistyfoot. You will need great courage for what lies ahead, but remember that you are not alone. I will always walk beside you. We will meet again soon."

His fur began to fade, until Mistyfoot could see the dark leaves on the bushes behind him. "Wait!" she called. "What do you mean? Why will I need great courage? Is there a battle coming?"

But there was no answer, just a muffled snore from

Pouncetail, who was sleeping beside her. Mistyfoot stared wildly around the clearing, but her brother had gone. Had he been trying to warn her that something dreadful was on the horizon? There was no chance that Mistyfoot would be able to sleep now. She padded carefully past the sleeping elders and went to the entrance of the medicine cats' den.

"Mothwing!" she called in a loud whisper.

There was a faint murmur from behind the boulders; then the medicine cat appeared. She looked wide-eyed and ruffled, as if she hadn't been able to sleep either. "What it is?" she asked. "Is something wrong?"

"I need to go to the Moonpool now!" Mistyfoot told her. "Stonefur visited me in a dream, and there are things I need to ask him."

Mothwing looked alarmed. "Why? What did he say?"

"Nothing that made sense!" Mistyfoot hissed. "Come on, we have to go!"

"It would be safer to wait until dawn," Mothwing hedged. "Since we have to cross WindClan territory."

"No, we have to leave now," Mistyfoot insisted. "If trouble is coming, RiverClan cannot be without a leader any longer! There is so much I have to learn!"

Mothwing padded out from her den and shook a few clinging scraps of herb from her fur. "Yes," she murmured. "There is more to learn than you know."

CHAPTER 3

❧

The first light of dawn was beginning to appear on the horizon when Mistyfoot and Mothwing reached the top of Wind-Clan's ridge. It had been too early for any patrols, so they had crossed the moor unchallenged, traveling in silence apart from the soft brush of their paws on the grass. Mistyfoot paused to catch her breath at the crest of the hill and looked back down at the lake. The water looked thick and almost black from here, pushing against the curls and points of the shoreline. The RiverClan camp was a dark smudge on the far side; Mistyfoot pictured the cats in the clearing, and she wondered if any of them were looking up at the ridge at this moment, spotting her silhouetted against the milky sunrise.

Beside her, Mothwing shifted her paws. "We should keep going," she meowed. Mistyfoot was surprised that she didn't seem more excited about the nine lives ceremony. Was visiting the Moonpool and sharing tongues with StarClan just a matter of routine for medicine cats?

Their pace slowed as they began the long, steep scramble over the rocks. Mistyfoot had only traveled this way once before, and she had forgotten how hard it was—or perhaps her legs had just grown older.

"Is it much farther?" she panted after losing her grip on one boulder and almost falling off backward.

"No," Mothwing replied over her shoulder. "See those bushes up there? The path that leads down to the Moonpool is just behind them."

Mistyfoot's head was spinning by the time they pushed their way through the thorny branches and started to follow the spiraling path downward. Her paws slotted into the imprints left by generations of cats before, and for a moment she felt their pelts brush past her, bathing her in musky scent. *Welcome, welcome.* Did she hear their voices, too, or was it just her imagination?

Mothwing led her to the edge of the pool. It gleamed under the pale sunlight, reflecting the clouds and the swift flight of a bird across its surface. Mistyfoot's heart started to beat faster. This was it! She was actually going to be the leader of RiverClan! She glanced at Mothwing and was surprised to see that the medicine cat looked nervous too. The tip of her fluffy tail was twitching, and she seemed reluctant to meet Mistyfoot's gaze. Perhaps she was feeling anxious about the unfamiliar ceremony after all.

"You'll be fine," Mistyfoot reassured her old friend. "It's the first time for both of us, but we'll get through it together."

Mothwing just blinked. "Lie down at the edge of the pool," she instructed, "and let your muzzle touch the water."

Mistyfoot settled down with her paws tucked under her. The stone was cold beneath her belly, but the water was colder still, sparkling like ice against her nose. She took a deep breath and closed her eyes. "Good luck," she heard Mothwing say softly, as though she were very far away.

There was a rush of stars around her, and then a dizzying blackness swallowed her up. Mistyfoot fought the urge to cry out. *Am I falling?* There were whispers and cries in her ears, but none of them clear enough to hear, and the scents of many cats, some half-recognized, some strange and sharp. Just as Mistyfoot was about to shriek in terror, she felt firm sand underneath her paws. She opened her eyes and looked around. She was standing on a gently sloping shore beside a broad, shallow river that splashed over pebbles and carried the scent of fish. Above, the sky was bright and the sun blazed down, warming her fur. Mistyfoot felt an urge to wade into the water and let fish swim onto her claws; somehow she knew there would be no difficulty in catching a haul of prey.

The bushes behind her rustled, and a pale gray cat appeared. For a moment Mistyfoot thought it was her brother, Stonefur, but then she recognized the scent and knew it was Graypool, the RiverClan she-cat she had called mother for so long. Mistyfoot purred loudly, and in two strides Graypool was beside her, licking her fur and nuzzling her head with her chin. Mistyfoot buried her nose in Graypool's feather-soft chest, suddenly feeling like a kit again.

"I'm so worried I'll make a mistake in the ceremony," she confessed.

"Hush, little one," Graypool soothed her. "You'll be fine. There's nothing to get wrong; I promise. Are you ready?"

Mistyfoot straightened up and nodded. She was startled to realize that the shore was crowded with cats now, their fur lit by stars and their eyes shining with warmth. She wondered for a fleeting moment where Mothwing was, but then Graypool stepped forward and lifted her voice above the splashing of the river.

"My precious Mistyfoot, beloved nearly-daughter, I give you a life for loving your Clanmates as if each cat were your kit, borne of your body and your pain." She rested her muzzle against Mistyfoot's, and a bolt like lightning shot through Mistyfoot's pelt. She squeaked and leaped back in pain, but Graypool's eyes glowed at her, giving her strength, and Mistyfoot dug her claws into the sand to hold her ground. The fire beneath her skin passed and she gasped for breath.

"Thank you, Graypool," she whispered. The she-cat nodded and stepped back.

Then a familiar shape loomed over Mistyfoot, and she basked in her brother's scent. "I told you we would meet again," Stonefur purred. "I give you a life for treating all cats equally, for fighting against injustice and unfairness wherever it comes."

Mistyfoot braced herself, but the shock from this life was less severe, feeling instead like a wave of strength building inside her, swelling from nose to tail-tip until she felt as if she could leap over mountains.

The next cat was a slender, soft-furred gray tabby with eyes that reflected the blue of the sky. "Feathertail!" Mistyfoot cried. "I have missed you!"

Feathertail's gaze softened. "I have missed you too, Mistyfoot. I haven't forgotten the lessons I learned as your apprentice. The life I give you is for accepting your destiny, however hard that may seem. Some things are beyond our control; that doesn't mean they should be fought against."

This life was uncomfortable, prickling like thorns and choking her like a fishbone caught in her throat. Mistyfoot struggled to keep still and not spit out the invisible bone. Perhaps this was a warning of how difficult her destiny was going to be? Mistyfoot felt a tremor of unease.

"Welcome, Mistyfoot," purred a deep voice. She opened her eyes to see Crookedstar, leader of RiverClan before Leopardstar, looking down at her. Mistyfoot bowed her head. "You don't have to do that now," Crookedstar reminded her. "We are equals here. I give you a life with the wisdom and strength to carry the burden of leadership. It will weigh heavy, but remember that every problem is nothing more than a challenge to be overcome."

Mistyfoot's legs buckled as she felt a huge, invisible pressure crushing her. She forced herself to stand straight, and felt the pressure transform into a soft, powerful warmth. *I am strong enough to carry this burden,* she told herself.

The next life came from the broad-shouldered brown tabby Oakheart, who had been Crookedstar's brother and deputy. But Mistyfoot knew him now as something else: her father. "My beautiful daughter," he murmured, resting his muzzle against her ears. "I am so sorry I could not be a true father to you. Live well, believe in yourself, and we will walk in StarClan together one day. I give you a life with the courage to follow your heart," he purred, and Mistyfoot braced herself against the jolt of feeling that seared through her. She felt a flash of sorrow as her father stepped away from her, but almost at once another cat was close beside her, breathing warmly into her ear.

"Oh, my daughter," Bluestar whispered. "If only you knew how much I missed you."

Mistyfoot lifted her head and studied the dark gray she-cat. Bluestar looked young and lithe and strong, very different from the soaked and battered cat she and her brother had dragged from the river.

Bluestar let her tail-tip rest on Mistyfoot's flank. "The life I give you is for doing what is right, however hard that might be." The regret in her voice almost broke Mistyfoot's heart. She forced out a purr, in spite of the fire that was scorching through her blood.

"I know you only ever tried to do the right thing," she rasped.

Bluestar leaned forward until her muzzle was touching the tip of Mistyfoot's ear. "Thank you," she breathed.

A beautiful she-cat with delicate silver markings came forward. Mistyfoot tipped her head on one side. "Silverstream? Is that you?"

The she-cat purred. "Well met, Mistyfoot. I am so proud of what you have become. I give you a life for finding happiness, even in the most unlooked-for places. Whatever happens, never forget how to be joyful." When she touched Mistyfoot's nose, a bright silver light flashed, making Mistyfoot blink. Her fur tingled and she felt the hair stand up along her spine.

"Thank you," she murmured.

A dark gray tabby took Silverstream's place. Mistyfoot's heart ached as she gazed at him. "Oh, Rippletail. I'm so sorry you didn't return. You saved the lake, you know? The water came back!" *If not the fish,* she added silently, though she wasn't going to tell her former Clanmate that.

Rippletail dipped his head. "I only ever wanted to help my Clan," he meowed. "My life was worth that. The life I give you is for curiosity, for the courage to find out what lies beyond the horizon. Never turn down a chance to learn something more."

"I won't; I promise," Mistyfoot whispered as the heat burned through her once more. She was beginning to feel dizzy and weak, and her vision was blurred.

At first she thought no cat had come up after Rippletail. There was an empty space in front of her. She had one more life to come, didn't she? Then there was a tiny squeak below her, and Mistyfoot looked down at a small black kit with piercing green eyes.

"Perchkit! My baby!"

The tiny cat bounced on his paws. "I knew I'd see you again," he chirped. "They said I could give you a life, too. So mine is for bravery, even when you are walking into shadows. There will always be light, even in the darkest night."

He stretched up to press his nose against Mistyfoot's chin. She inhaled his precious kit scent and drank in the energy that flowed from him. *I never forgot you, not for a single moment.*

"Mistystar! Mistystar!"

The cats on the shore raised their voices, sending her new name echoing up to the sky. Two more cats pushed through the throng and wound around Mistystar's legs. "Pikepaw! Primrosepaw!" She felt a rush of love for her kits who hadn't lived long enough to become the warriors they should have been.

"We will be waiting for you," Pikepaw promised earnestly.

"We are so proud of you!" Primrosepaw added, pressing her cheek against Mistystar's shoulder.

Mistystar opened her mouth to tell her kits how much she missed them, but the light was turning gray and misty, and the shore vanished to be replaced by curved cliffs of stone. Mistystar was lying beside the Moonpool once more, her ears ringing and her fur still ruffled from the agony of the nine lives.

Mothwing padded up to her. "Are you all right?"

Mistystar blinked. She pictured the cats by the shore again, and knew there had been one missing. "You weren't there!"

Mothwing winced, then relaxed as if a weight had been lifted off her. "No." She held Mistystar's gaze without flinching. "You will always visit StarClan alone. They don't exist for me in the way that they do for you."

Mistystar stared at her friend in dismay. What was

Mothwing saying? She was a medicine cat! How could this be true? She fought to speak, even though the ground was lurching under her feet.

"You . . . you don't believe in StarClan?"

CHAPTER 4

♣

"But you've been our medicine cat for so long! Have you never walked with StarClan in your dreams?"

Mothwing shook her head. "You have your beliefs," she meowed calmly. "I have mine. The cats you see in your dreams guide and protect you in ways that I have lived without. I am skilled at healing and caring for my Clanmates, and that has been enough to serve my Clan."

Mistystar's mind was whirling. Surely this couldn't be happening! How could a medicine cat not believe in StarClan? Why had none of the cats said anything to her during the nine lives ceremony? They must know that Mothwing never walked with them. What about omens? Did StarClan bother to send any if Mothwing would never be watching for them? She took a step forward, suddenly desperate to get back to the lake, to find a footing for her paws on ground that seemed to have shifted.

"Come on, let's go home."

As Mothwing followed her up the paw-printed path, Mistystar thought she heard the medicine cat murmur, "I'm sorry." But there was nothing she could think of to say in reply.

They traveled quickly and in silence, leaping and scrambling down the tumbled rocks until they were standing on the short, springy grass of WindClan's territory once more. Scents from ThunderClan drifted to them across the narrow stream that marked the boundary between the two Clans. "Let's stop and tell Firestar what has happened," Mistystar suggested. The other leaders would have to learn about Leopardstar's death sometime.

Mothwing nodded. They jumped over the stream and trotted down the other side until they reached a clear path that led into the trees. Fresh ThunderClan scent hung in the air; they had clearly just missed a patrol. Mistystar took the lead along the trail, reminding herself that she was a Clan leader now, and had every right to visit her neighbors with this important news without being accused of trespassing. But it still felt strange to be walking in another Clan's territory without constantly looking over her shoulder, wary of ambush.

They reached the gap in the walls of the hollow and forced their way in through the thorns. Mistystar shook her head to dislodge the prickles that had caught in her nose. She didn't know how the ThunderClan cats put up with such an uncomfortable entrance to their home. Firestar was crossing the clearing to meet them.

"Is everything all right?"

Mistystar stood still and waited for him to reach her. "Leopardstar's dead," she announced.

Firestar lowered his head. "I'm so sorry," he whispered.

"We've just come from the Moonpool," Mothwing

explained. "Mistystar has received her nine lives."

Firestar dipped his muzzle even lower. "Mistystar," he mewed respectfully.

"Mistystar," echoed Graystripe, a sturdy tom who Mistystar had known since he was an apprentice back in the forest.

"Mistystar, Mistystar," called the other ThunderClan cats.

Mistystar felt a bit uncomfortable. She had never liked being the center of attention, and it seemed all the more strange because she was still getting used to her new name. "Thank you," she mewed when the cats were silent. "I have chosen Reedwhisker as my deputy. We look forward to a long and fair relationship with ThunderClan."

Firestar raised his head and lightly touched her muzzle. "How's RiverClan?" His tone was lighter, more relaxed; now that the formal greeting was over, he sounded more like the cat Mistystar had known—and confided in—for so long.

She told him about the loss of three elders, and that the drought had hit the whole Clan hard. Firestar was sympathetic, and Jayfeather offered Mothwing some herbs to replenish her stocks, including watermint. Laden with green-scented leaves, the RiverClan cats retraced their steps through the trees. When they broke out into the open and reached the stream again, Mistystar put down her mouthful of herbs.

"Does Jayfeather know that you don't believe in StarClan?" she mewed.

Mothwing nodded.

"What does he think?"

Mothwing carefully placed her herbs on a tussock of grass.

"He knows that I am a good medicine cat and will do anything to help my Clan."

Mistystar stared at her Clanmate in frustration. How could she be so calm and accepting? She longed to ask Mothwing about omens and dreams and ceremonies—all the responsibilities of a medicine cat that involved trusting in the unseen presence of their warrior ancestors. But standing in ThunderClan territory, still a long way from home, wasn't the right place for that conversation. The questions would have to wait. Mistystar picked up her herbs and leaped over the stream.

Mothwing followed, and they picked their way down to the edge of the lake to walk along the shore, which lay outside WindClan territory. As they neared the border with RiverClan, a WindClan patrol spotted them and raced up, bristling, but their fur flattened when Mistystar told them about Leopardstar's death, and the warriors offered sympathy and congratulations to Mistystar on receiving her nine lives. They promised to tell Onestar as soon as they returned to their camp.

Mistystar realized that she should let Blackstar of ShadowClan know as well, but by the time she reached the RiverClan camp her paws were too weary to walk another step. She wanted to be at full strength when she first met Blackstar as his equal, another Clan leader with the power to challenge him if one of his warriors so much as placed a whisker over their shared border. There was too much history between Mistystar and the ShadowClan leader—the memory of him killing Stonefur was too sharp—for her ever to contemplate an alliance with his Clan.

Reedwhisker met her as she limped toward her den. "Did you meet with our ancestors? Do you have your nine lives?"

Mistystar nodded. "Yes, I do." She forced herself to lift her head higher. "With StarClan's blessing, I will lead this Clan until the last breath of my last life."

"Hurrah! Mistystar!" Her Clanmates cheered, but Mistystar noticed Mothwing standing at the edge of the clearing, her gaze troubled.

"Mothwing said you'd seen Firestar and a WindClan patrol," Reedwhisker meowed. "Would you like me to take the news to Blackstar?"

Mistystar blinked gratefully at her deputy. "Thank you," she mewed. "Make sure you return before it gets dark."

Reedwhisker dipped his head and raced off. Mistystar watched him dive into the bushes on the far side of the clearing. She wondered if his littermates were watching from StarClan. She would have to tell Reedwhisker that one of her lives came from his brother Perchkit.

"Mistystar?" Dapplenose was standing a little way off. "We're going to bury Leopardstar now. Would you like to join us?"

"Of course," Mistystar meowed. She stretched her legs to ease some of the stiffness. Sleep could come later.

Almost the whole Clan gathered in the clearing by the lake to watch the elders gently scoop earth over Leopardstar's body. Mothwing stood by the former leader's head and spoke the words of the ceremony, letting them drift in the air like scent.

"May StarClan light your path, Leopardstar. May you find good hunting, swift running, and shelter when you sleep."

Mistystar stared at Mothwing's golden pelt, wondering what the other cats would do if they knew the truth. Mistystar was surrounded by Clanmates, their cheers of her new name still echoed in her ears, yet she had never felt more alone. How could she lead her Clan without a medicine cat who believed in their warrior ancestors? Why had none of the StarClan cats told her the truth? Were they angry with RiverClan for having a medicine cat who could never fulfill all her duties? And yet they had still given Mistystar her nine lives. . . .

After the ceremony, Mistystar headed to Leopardstar's den beneath the rowan tree and started to pull out the dusty bedding. A matted chunk of moss got stuck at the entrance to the den, and Mistystar dug in her hind paws as she struggled to yank it free. Graymist joined her, and together they tugged the moss into the open air. It smelled damp and musty, making Mistystar sneeze.

"You must be exhausted," Graymist commented.

Why does everyone keep telling me how tired I must be? "I'm fine," Mistystar snapped, a little more sharply than she intended.

Graymist tipped her head on one side and studied Mistystar. "Is everything okay? You seem upset."

Mistystar shrugged as she clawed at the chunk of moss, breaking it into small pieces that would be easier to carry out of the camp. "There's a lot to do," she mewed. "And I miss Leopardstar."

"We all do," Graymist reminded her. "But there's no rush

for you to fill her paw steps. With all the Clans still recovering from the drought, things should be peaceful for a while. Don't be too hard on yourself."

Mistystar felt a sudden urge to confide in Graymist about Mothwing, to tell her how lost she felt without a medicine cat who would be able to share tongues with StarClan. But this was too huge a secret to share with her Clanmates. She would have to find a way of dealing with this alone. She touched Graymist lightly on the flank with her tail.

"I'm fine," she meowed. "I'll clear this away later. I just want to get some sleep now."

Graymist looked doubtful. "What about clean bedding? Shall I have the apprentices fetch some for you?"

Mistystar shook her head. "I can sleep on what's left. I'll add it to their duties tomorrow." Graymist trotted away, and Mistystar crawled into the narrow den beneath the rowan tree. Even though the moss had been cleared out, Leopardstar's scent still clung to the walls and the branches overhead. Mistystar curled up with her nose tucked under her tail and shut her eyes. As she drifted into sleep, she wondered if she would dream herself back into StarClan, where she could question her ancestors about Mothwing, but instead she found herself searching through a dark, empty landscape, with the sound of running water just out of reach and no cats to answer her cries.

She was woken the following day by the sound of the rowan branches clashing in the wind. A few leaves tumbled into the den, blown by a gust that pierced Mistystar's fur. For a moment, Mistystar stared at the curved earthen walls around her, wondering where the other warriors were; then she remembered that Leopardstar was dead, she was now the leader of RiverClan, and this would be her den for the rest of her life. *My nine lives.*

Outside she heard Mothwing giving Willowshine instructions: "Thanks to Jayfeather, we have plenty of watermint and tansy, but our stocks of comfrey are running low and we should gather more while the plants are still growing. I used most of our cobwebs on Rushpaw's cut when he fell off that tree trunk, so we need to stock up on those, too."

Mistystar recalled Willowshine's offer to come to the Moonpool with her, and she felt her stomach churn as she realized Mothwing's apprentice must know the truth about her mentor's lack of faith. There was such a large part of her training that could never come from Mothwing. Had Willowshine spoken to the other medicine cats about it? Mistystar pushed herself to her paws, feeling every one of her seasons as she stretched her spine. She padded out of her den just as Willowshine was making for the entrance to the camp.

"Wait, Willowshine! I'll come with you!"

The medicine cat turned, looking surprised. "Er, okay, Mistystar."

Mistystar saw Mothwing watching them from the far side of the clearing. The golden cat's expression was impossible to read. Was she afraid of what Willowshine might say, or was she relieved that the truth was out? Mistystar ducked through the gap in the bushes and fell in beside Willowshine as they pushed their way through the dripping ferns.

"Yuck!" squeaked Willowshine as a leaf spilled sparkling raindrops onto her neck fur.

"We need the rain," Mistystar reminded her, swerving to avoid a particularly wet-looking clump of stalks.

"Couldn't it fall at night, and let us stay dry during the day?" Willowshine complained, half joking, as she shook her pelt.

"Perhaps you should put in a request to StarClan," Mistystar teased back.

Willowshine was negotiating a prickly tendril that lay across the path. "I'll try," she replied, sounding amused.

"So, how's the training going?" Mistystar asked, hoping that her question didn't sound forced.

Willowshine swerved to avoid a puddle. "It's great," she mewed. "Mothwing's teaching me how to combine herbs to make them more effective. She knows so much about plants! I don't know if I'll ever be able to learn it all."

"I'm sure you will," Mistystar meowed. "What about the . . . the StarClan side of your duties? Has she taught you about that, too?"

Mistystar had drawn level with Willowshine now, so she could see the little cat blink and look away. "Mothwing is the best mentor I would wish for," she replied.

Her evasive answer spoke volumes to Mistystar. *She knows that Mothwing doesn't believe in StarClan!* For a moment, Mistystar was torn. She didn't want to challenge Willowshine's loyalty and respect for her mentor, but how could they ignore the fact that Mothwing could not fulfill all her medicine cat duties? Mistystar stopped and turned to face Willowshine.

"I know the truth," she mewed. "Mothwing didn't come with me to StarClan when I received my nine lives. That's why you offered to come, isn't it?"

Willowshine nodded, her blue eyes full of pain. "It's not Mothwing's fault! She's the best medicine cat RiverClan could have!"

"But what about visiting the Moonpool, sharing tongues with StarClan, recognizing signs from our ancestors? Those are all part of a medicine cat's responsibilities," Mistystar pointed out.

"I can take care of those!" Willowshine insisted. She rolled a piece of fern under her front paw. "When I started training, Leafpool visited me in my dreams. She helped me learn the things that Mothwing couldn't teach me. I know enough to help; I promise!"

Mistystar shook her head. "I'm sure you do, little one. But you are too young to carry all that responsibility alone. Mothwing should have said something long before we got this far."

Willowshine's fur fluffed up and she opened her mouth to speak, but Mistystar raised one paw to stop her. "Don't say something you might come to regret, Willowshine," she warned. "This isn't up to you now. Go collect the herbs for Mothwing, and I'll see you back in the camp."

Willowshine shut her mouth with a snap and thrust her way into the long grass. Mistystar watched her go for a moment, then turned and headed back to the clearing. Mothwing was standing in the center of the empty camp as if she was waiting for her.

"Did you speak with Willowshine?" Mothwing asked.

Mistystar nodded. "You have a loyal and brave apprentice," she remarked.

"I couldn't be more proud of her," Mothwing agreed. "But my . . . my relationship with StarClan has nothing to do with her. You shouldn't have questioned her about it."

"It has everything to do with her!" Mistystar flashed back. "You are supposed to be training her to be a medicine cat! That means being able to walk in StarClan and speak with our warrior ancestors!"

Mothwing's hackles rose. "I have never stopped Willowshine from doing that. I would never tell her what she should believe."

"But you should believe in StarClan, too! You are our medicine cat! Can't you see that you are betraying your Clan by living your entire life as a lie?"

"I am *not* lying!" hissed Mothwing. "I have never pretended to do anything I cannot."

Mistystar glared at her old friend. "Actually, I think you have. You have risked the safety of your Clan by not being able to read signs from StarClan or walk with our ancestors at the Moonpool. I'm sorry, Mothwing, but you can no longer consider yourself a medicine cat."

CHAPTER 5

❧

Mothwing flinched as if Mistystar had struck her. "I have served my Clan for many seasons," she argued. "I have guarded the health of every cat as if they were a kit of my own. Leopardstar trusted me."

"Leopardstar didn't know the truth!" Mistystar snapped. "Did she?"

Mothwing shook her head. "No," she admitted. Her eyes clouded with sadness. "What do you want me to do now?"

Mistystar twitched the tip of her tail. "I don't know. Restock your supplies with Willowshine, and let me figure something out. We don't want every cat in the Clan learning about this." She walked away, feeling her stomach churn. Had she really just dismissed her medicine cat? *Oh, StarClan, why didn't you tell me the truth when you had the chance?*

Rapid paw steps sounded, and Mallownose appeared at the head of his hunting patrol. He was carrying a tiny minnow in his mouth, which he dropped in the space where the fresh-kill pile should be. Robinwing, Petalfur, and Minnowtail placed similar-sized prey beside the miniscule fish. Minnowtail's apprentice, Mossypaw, was covered in stinking green weed but had nothing to contribute that could be eaten.

Mistystar stared at the pile in dismay. "Is that it?" she gasped. "That won't feed Duskfur's kits, let alone the rest of us!"

"I'm sorry," meowed Mallownose. "The water may have come back, but the fish haven't. The lake is empty."

"Apart from weeds," Mossypaw put in crossly, trying to pull the slimy fronds off her ears.

"I warned you that rock was slippery," sighed Minnowtail.

Mistystar felt a wave of panic rise in her chest. "We'll have to look elsewhere for prey, then. Start hunting away from the lake for different kinds of prey."

Mossypaw made a face. "Yuck! Who wants to eat fur and whiskers?"

Mallownose flicked her with his tail. "Any cat who doesn't want to starve," he growled.

"StarClan must really hate us if they won't bring the fish back," Mossypaw muttered.

Mistystar bristled. *There is no way StarClan would punish us for letting Mothwing be our medicine cat, is there? No, of course not. She has been our medicine cat since before we came to the lake; why would StarClan turn against us now? And yet if they sent us a sign guiding us to a better source of prey, who would see it?*

The bushes at the entrance quivered, and Reedwhisker pushed his way through. "Blackstar says he is sorry to hear that Leopardstar has lost her last life, and looks forward to greeting you at the next Gathering," he announced to Mistystar. His gaze fell on the puny pile of minnows. "Great StarClan! Did everyone eat already?"

"No," meowed Mistystar. "We were just discussing finding other places to hunt until the fish return to the lake."

Reedwhisker nodded. "I can take a patrol into the marshes now if you like. And Mintfur?" He called to the pale gray tom who was washing himself on the far side of the clearing. "Why don't you take the apprentices upstream to see what you can find in the reeds beyond the border?"

For a moment Mistystar was taken aback by Reedwhisker's brisk string of commands; then she remembered that he was the deputy now, and it was his duty to organize patrols. "Right, thanks, Reedwhisker," she mewed. "I'll come with you, if that's okay?"

Reedwhisker looked surprised. "Of course it is. Icewing, Pebblefoot, will you join us?" The two warriors had just returned from a border patrol, but they nodded and trotted over. Mistystar fell in behind them as they filed out of the camp. She felt Mothwing watching her from the entrance to the medicine cats' den, but she didn't turn around. It was too painful to look into her old friend's eyes and know that she had been keeping a secret that threatened the whole Clan.

There was a strong wind blowing across the marshes, scented with rain. Mistystar's fur stood on end as she trekked across the sodden ground, leaping from tussock to tussock of spiny grass. The lake beckoned invitingly, sending waves fluttering over the stony shore. But Mistystar reminded herself that the water was empty, that the end of the drought had not brought an end to RiverClan's hunger. *Oh, StarClan, did Rippletail die in vain?*

Suddenly Icewing let out a hiss and stiffened as a vole crept out of a clump of grass. The white cat pounced a fraction too late, and the vole shot away. Icewing stumbled over a muddy rut, and for a moment it looked as if the vole was safe. Then Mistystar realized it was heading toward her, so she leaped forward, blocking the vole's path with her front paws, and thrust her head down so that it practically ran into her jaws. One sharp, frantic bite and the creature lay dead at her feet.

"Good catch!" called Reedwhisker.

Mistystar looked at Icewing, who had stumbled to a halt beside her, panting. "We did it together," she meowed. Icewing nodded, too breathless to speak.

Up ahead, Pebblefoot was crouching at the foot of a wind-warped pine tree. "I can see a squirrel," he yowled over his shoulder.

"Don't climb up after it!" Mistystar warned. RiverClan cats most definitely did not belong in trees. "Wait until it comes down!"

Pebblefoot scraped his claws impatiently down the trunk. There was a brief gray blur, and the squirrel dropped down from one of the lower branches and set off across the marsh, its fluffy tail bobbing behind it. Pebblefoot tore after it, sending scraps of grass and mud flying up from his hind paws. With a start, Mistystar realized he was running too fast to see where he was.

"Stop, Pebblefoot!" she screeched. "You're too close to the border!"

Reedwhisker bounded after his Clanmate, but the

squirrel leaped the final tussock of marsh grass onto the smooth, cropped surface of WindClan's territory and took off up the slope. Pebblefoot raced after it, straight into a patrol of shocked-looking WindClan cats who had just appeared around the side of the hill. A brown warrior named Antpelt sprang forward to block his path.

"Trespasser! Prey thief!" he screeched.

CHAPTER 6
♣

"He's not stealing prey!" Mistystar yowled, pounding past the scent markers and skidding to a halt beside her startled Clanmate.

"I'm sorry," Pebblefoot puffed. "I wasn't looking where I was going."

Antpelt's hackles rose. "Oh, I think you knew exactly where you were going," he sneered. "Onto territory with better prey than yours!" His eyes raked over the RiverClan warriors, and Mistystar winced as she saw their scrawny frames through an outsider's eyes. It was painfully obvious that the RiverClan cats hadn't had a proper meal in moons.

Ashfoot, the WindClan deputy, stepped forward. "Mistystar, I heard about Leopardstar's death, and I am truly sorry. But what are you doing, letting your warriors stray onto our territory? Did you forget to replace your border markers?"

Her tone was gentle, but Mistystar heard reproach beneath it. What kind of leader allowed her own patrol to cross a boundary? "I'm sorry, Ashfoot," she meowed, struggling to keep her fur flat. "It was a genuine mistake. Pebblefoot just got carried away chasing that squirrel."

"Well, it's ours now," Antpelt put in. "So you can remove

your mangy pelts from our territory before we make you." He raised one front paw and let his claws slide out. Pebblefoot glared at him, with the fur rising along his spine.

"Antpelt, enough!" ordered Ashfoot. "Mistystar, take your cats home. I suggest you renew the border markers to remind your warriors to hunt inside their own territory in future."

Feeling her pelt burn with shame, Mistystar dipped her head. "Yes, Ashfoot. May StarClan light your path."

"And yours," Ashfoot mewed briefly before summoning her warriors with a sweep of her tail. "Antpelt, put your claws away. Come on, back to camp."

The WindClan cats raced away over the turf, their bellies low enough to brush the grass. Mistystar led her Clanmates back to the border and didn't stop until they were well past the markers—which were plenty strong enough. Pebblefoot was still bristling.

"Antpelt treated us like mangy rats," he fumed. "And how dare Ashfoot tell you to renew the border markers? You're a leader! She's only a deputy!"

Mistystar sighed. "She was just making a point, Pebblefoot. You did cross the boundary, after all. Let's see if we can catch something that doesn't run into a different Clan, okay?"

She watched her warriors spread out across the marsh, lifting their paws high to avoid tripping over the tussocks, and flattening their ears as they tried to pick up the scent of prey. *We train to catch fish, not mice and voles,* she thought. *We're as hopeless as kits on dry land. Oh, StarClan, why are you letting us starve?*

* * *

Three sunrises later, with the fresh-kill pile still pitifully small, Mistystar spotted the faint outline of a half-moon floating between the clouds. That night the medicine cats from all four Clans would gather at the Moonpool to share tongues with StarClan. Mistystar cast her mind back to previous half-moons, realizing that she could hardly remember one when Mothwing hadn't sent Willowshine in her place on the excuse that a sick or kit-heavy cat needed her to stay in the Clan. How had Leopardstar not realized that Mothwing was neglecting so many of her responsibilities?

After a day of fruitless hunting in the bushes around the camp, Mistystar settled outside her den and waited for one of the medicine cats to leave. She saw Mothwing emerge from between the rocks, and for a moment Mistystar thought the golden cat might be making one last attempt to prove her right to be RiverClan's medicine cat. But then Willowshine padded out behind her.

"Thank Jayfeather for the herbs," Mothwing instructed. "And ask Kestrelflight if Tornear's cough cleared up with the poultice of bright-eye and lovage."

Willowshine nodded. "See you later," she meowed, stretching up to brush her muzzle against Mothwing's. With an anxious glance at Mistystar, she trotted out of the camp.

Mistystar stood up. Mothwing had vanished back into the shadows behind the rocks, and the clearing was silent apart from the murmurs of sleepy warriors in their nest. Mistystar pushed her way through the ferns and went down to the edge of the lake. She paced along the shore, feeling the stones smooth beneath her paws. Sparkling reflections of stars swirled and danced on the surface of the water—the empty, fishless water that mocked the RiverClan cats and their hungry bellies. Mistystar stared at the silvery patterns, desperately trying to read a message in their shapes. Should they be fishing in a different way? Were the fish about to return? Perhaps the hunger was nearly at an end.

But how would she know if there were any messages to be seen? She wasn't a medicine cat! Mistystar hissed and sank her claws into the grit between the pebbles. Mothwing had made it impossible for her to lead her Clan with any sort of confidence.

"Oh, Stonefur!" Mistystar whispered. "I can't do this alone!"

Mistystar tossed and wriggled all night, unable to get comfortable in her nest. The fresh moss seemed full of thorns, and she was convinced there was a lump of gorse caught up in it. As the first rays of the sun slanted through the rowan branches, she jumped up and trotted into the clearing. She just caught sight of Willowshine's gray striped tail whisking into the medicine cats' den. Mistystar followed and stood in the entrance. The two medicine cats blinked at her from the shadows.

"Willowshine, from now on you will be RiverClan's sole medicine cat," she announced. Her heart pounded, and she dug her claws into the earth to stop her legs from shaking. "Mothwing will no longer live with you in this den."

"That's not fair!" cried Willowshine. "I still have so much to learn!"

"StarClan will help you," Mistystar mewed. She looked at Mothwing, who was staring at her in dismay. "I've had enough time to think about this. Mothwing, you have served River-Clan for many seasons, and we are grateful. As an elder, you will be well cared for. No cat needs to know about . . . anything."

Mothwing stepped forward. "Mistystar, I know you want to punish me—"

"This is not about punishment!" Mistystar interrupted. "This is about doing what is right for the Clan!"

Mothwing twitched one ear. "Don't you think the Clan has suffered enough change recently, with the loss of Leopard-star? Let them come to terms with that before you make them accept something else. You are not the only cat who has their best interests at heart, Mistystar. I'll announce my retirement at the next Gathering, but not before." Her blue eyes flashed briefly with anger.

Mistystar gritted her teeth. *She must see that I have no choice in this! She cannot be a medicine cat if she doesn't believe in StarClan!* "Very well," she hissed. "You may stay here for the rest of this moon."

She started to back away, but stopped as Mothwing moved toward her. Placing her muzzle close to Mistystar's ear, she murmured, "I am so sorry."

So am I, thought Mistystar. *You were my closest friend.* But there was nothing to say, so she just shook her head and walked quickly away from the rocks, feeling her heart break with every step.

"Mistystar! Watch this!" It was Podkit, Duskfur's sturdy son. He had sunk his claws into a twig and was dragging it toward the nursery. "I caught this giant fish and I'm going to feed the whole Clan!" he squeaked proudly.

Mistystar purred. "Great catch, Podkit. Make sure it doesn't eat you first!"

"It won't. I killed it with one paw!"

Duskfur appeared at the entrance to the nursery. "Podkit! I hope you aren't bothering Mistystar!"

"He's not," Mistystar assured her. "If he can catch a fish that size, we might have to make him a warrior already!"

"Really?" gasped Podkit, his eyes huge.

"Of course not," snapped his sister, Curlkit, who was wriggling out past their mother. "You're such a minnow-brain!"

"Don't be rude to your brother," Duskfur chided. "If you can't play nicely, one of you will have to go back to the nest."

"She started it," Podkit muttered, slicing the bark of the twig with his tiny claws.

Duskfur rolled her eyes. "Tell me it gets better," she begged Mistystar. "Some days I feel I do nothing but scold them from dawn until dusk!"

"It does get easier," Mistystar promised, though inside she felt a stab of agony that her time with four playful kits had passed so quickly.

Duskfur shuffled her paws as if she realized she had said

something clumsy. "We're all so pleased that you're our leader," she mewed earnestly. "Not that I didn't like Leopardstar, of course, but every cat thinks you're the best choice for RiverClan."

Even though we're still hungry? Mistystar wondered. *What will they say when we lose one of our medicine cats at the next full-moon?*

"There was one thing I wanted to talk to you about," Duskfur went on. "I found Curlkit up to her belly in mud yesterday by the stream, and I wondered if we could put up some sort of barrier to keep kits away from the edge of the water. I know it's inside the boundary of the camp, but I'd hate for there to be an accident with a very small kit."

Mistystar nodded. "That's a good point. The recent rain has made that bank very slippery, and I've nearly lost my footing there myself. I'll ask Grasspelt if he can sort something out. He can get the apprentices to help."

"He'll be lucky," grumbled Pouncetail, getting up from outside the elders' den. "Our bedding was supposed to be changed today, but there's been no sign of any apprentices."

Pebblefoot looked up from the shrew that he was chewing unenthusiastically. "Really? I definitely told Rushpaw and Hollowpaw that they had to do it before we did battle practice after sunhigh."

"Well, you'd better check their hearing," grunted Pouncetail.

Pebblefoot pushed the remains of the shrew away from him and stood up. "If you haven't seen them, where are they?" he pondered, looking troubled.

"They could be collecting fresh bedding first," Mistystar suggested, not wanting the apprentices to get into trouble unnecessarily.

Robinwing crossed the clearing and dropped a bundle of moss on the ground outside the warriors' den. "I didn't see them when I was gathering this," he remarked.

Troutpaw and Mossypaw padded into the camp, dragging a wet, dark-furred creature between them.

"Is that a rat?" squeaked Curlkit. "Gross! There's no way I'm eating that!"

Duskfur flicked her daughter's ear with her tail. "Then you'll have to go hungry," she snapped. "This isn't the time to start being fussy."

Mistystar went to greet the apprentices and their mentors, Graymist and Minnowtail. "Have you seen Hollowpaw and Rushpaw? They were supposed to be clearing out the elders' den, but no cat has seen them."

Graymist frowned. "They weren't on the marshes. Did you see what Troutpaw and Mossypaw caught? That should feed us for a while!"

Troutpaw looked proudly over the spine of the bedraggled corpse. "It took ages to drag it back!" she declared. "My teeth ache now!"

Privately Mistystar shared Curlkit's feelings about tucking into a rat—that was ShadowClan food, not RiverClan. But she nodded and mewed. "Well done! Now, where else might Hollowpaw and Rushpaw be?"

Mossypaw shrugged. "I don't know. They were muttering

about something last night when I was trying to go to sleep, but I didn't hear what they were saying."

Mistystar felt the ground dip beneath her paws. Was she losing control of her entire Clan? No fish, prey scarce on land, a medicine cat who didn't believe in StarClan, and now half the apprentices gone missing?

Just then, the brambles behind the medicine cats' den rustled, and Rushpaw and Hollowpaw emerged, looking triumphant and somewhat ruffled. They were each carrying a tuft of moss.

"Where have you been?" demanded Pebblefoot. "The elders' den should have been cleared out ages ago!"

Hollowpaw dropped his mouthful of moss. "We were collecting fresh bedding!" he protested.

Pouncetail prodded the dusty moss with his paw. "From where? Some other cat's manky nest?"

"You can use what I've collected," Robinwing meowed. He narrowed his eyes at the apprentices. "I don't know where you found that, but stick to our usual supplies in future, okay? There's no point in refilling a den with moss that is going to be uncomfortable, especially for the elders."

"Whatever," Rushpaw muttered. "We were just trying to help."

Mistystar studied the apprentices closely. From the state of their rumpled fur, they looked as if they had traveled a long way in search of bedding for the elders. Exceptional commitment, or had they been looking for something else as well? She felt a flash of fear that they might have been trying to fish on their own. With the lake this full, that was strictly forbidden for younger cats. She'd have to warn Pebblefoot and Reedwhisker to keep an eye on them during future patrols.

The apprentices clawed out Pouncetail's and Dapplenose's old bedding and replaced it with Robinwing's fresh supply. Then they joined their Clanmates at the fresh-kill pile, as the cats divided up the prey. Mistystar noticed that Hollowpaw and Rushpaw only shared a tiny minnow between them. Were they feeling guilty for not pulling their weight properly that morning? She sighed. Whatever they had been up to, she didn't want any of her Clanmates punishing themselves with further hunger.

She looked at the rocks that guarded the medicine cats' den. Willowshine and Mothwing seemed to be avoiding Mistystar as much as they could. Was Willowshine even watching out for omens? Or was StarClan ignoring them after all?

CHAPTER 7

♣

A run of stormy days kept the RiverClan cats confined to their camp; none of them minded getting their fur wet by choice when it came to swimming, but they hated torrential rain as much as any Clan. At last the wind eased and the rain lightened to a fur-flattening drizzle. Mistystar and Reedwhisker stood on the rocks at the edge of the lake and stared into the water. It was slightly clearer than before, and one or two tiny silver shapes darted about in the shadows, but there were still no large fish such as trout or carp.

"Is it worth fishing today?" Pebblefoot called, crunching over the stones toward them.

Reedwhisker shook his head. "Not unless you want to chase minnows again. Oh, I meant to tell you that Hollowpaw and Rushpaw asked if they could do some battle training on their own today. They know their assessments are coming up and they wanted to practice the crouch-and-leap technique we taught them."

Pebblefoot looked surprised. "I didn't realize they were taking the assessments so seriously. I sometimes wonder if Rushpaw wants to go straight to the elders' den when he reaches twelve moons. I've never met an apprentice who is so good at finding shortcuts to getting things done!"

Mistystar snorted. "Perhaps he'll just be a very efficient warrior." She headed back up the shore, and the two warriors fell in beside her. "We can't keep waiting for the big fish to return," she mewed quietly before they reached the camp. "And our territory isn't big enough to provide enough land prey to support us all. We'll have to think about expanding upstream."

"It does seem like the only option," Pebblefoot agreed. "Hunting patrols have already caught a few birds in the reeds just beyond the border. Do you think we should go even farther?"

Mistystar nodded. "I'll take a patrol that way myself today. I don't want to announce the expansion to the whole Clan yet, but every cat knows we are running out of food."

"Would you like me to come too?" Reedwhisker offered.

"No, thank you. I want you to lead a patrol along the border with WindClan and renew those scent markers, just in case they're still waiting for us to cross over again. And Pebblefoot, will you take a hunting patrol onto the marshes?" The senior warriors nodded.

Back in the clearing, Reedwhisker started selecting cats for his and Pebblefoot's patrol while Mistystar looked around for warriors to accompany her upstream. She was just about to call out to Grasspelt when Mothwing approached. Mistystar felt her fur bristle. *Why am I so hostile? Mothwing used to be my friend!*

Mothwing's blue eyes looked troubled. "Do you know

where Hollowpaw and Rushpaw are?" she asked.

"They're practicing for their assessment," Mistystar told her.

"Are you sure? I heard them telling Mossypaw and Trout-paw that they had found something none of the warriors knew about, but they couldn't say what it was because it was a big secret. Do you think they're up to something?"

For a moment Mistystar longed to be able to talk openly to Mothwing, like they had done so many times before. *I always thought we would lead our Clan together!* But Mothwing had kept a bigger secret than anything the apprentices might be hiding, and Mistystar couldn't see how they could find a way back to how things used to be. "They were probably just showing off," she told Mothwing. "Don't worry about them." She sounded more dismissive than she had intended, and Mothwing shrank back as if she had been hit.

"I just thought I should let you know," she mewed. She turned and walked away before Mistystar could say anything else.

Mistystar forced herself to concentrate on the upstream patrol. "Grasspelt! Could you come over here? Bring Icewing and Mintfur!"

The three warriors trotted over. They bristled with excite-ment when Mistystar told them that they would be exploring beyond the border.

"It makes sense, if we don't have enough prey around the camp," Grasspelt meowed.

"Do you want us to set border marks?" asked Icewing.

"Not yet," mewed Mistystar. "I don't know how far we'll get today. We're just looking for hunting possibilities at the moment."

They left the clearing and picked their way down to the edge of the narrow stream. As Duskfur had said, the shore was muddy and slippery from the recent rain, and Mistystar felt her paws sink deeper with every step. The cats clung to the bank and scrambled through the long grass until they emerged from the trees that enclosed RiverClan's territory. Just beneath their feet, the stream was swollen and fast-flowing, impossible to fish in even if the cats wanted to. Mistystar clawed her way along the steep slope, keeping her head below the top of the bank. Her fur was soon slicked with reddish-brown mud, and her paws kept slipping. Behind her, Icewing fared better because she was more lightly built and seemed able to leap between patches of less sodden grass. Her denmate Grasspelt plodded grimly along at the rear, cursing under his breath every time he lost his footing.

At last Mistystar's pads were so clogged with wet soil that she couldn't keep a grip on the bank any longer. She scrambled up to the top and peered over the edge. Huge expanses of flat land, rippling with dark green grass, stretched away on both sides of the stream. Feeling very exposed under the vast gray sky, Mistystar reared up on her hind legs and peered over the stems. The stretch of grass ended at a row of cloud-colored Twoleg dens, three of them side by side with dark-leaved plants growing up the walls. As Mistystar stared, she spotted a flash of movement beside one of the dens, a blur of gray-brown fur.

"Kittypets!" growled Grasspelt beside her. "Two of them, by the looks of it."

A second shape had joined the other; then both vanished around the side of the den.

"If there are other cats around, there might be less prey for us out here," Icewing warned. Her fur stood on end, and she was clearly uncomfortable about being so far outside their territory in such an open, unprotected place.

Mistystar lifted her muzzle and sniffed the air. "I can't smell any trace of them," she commented. "Wouldn't kittypets be too lazy to come all the way over here if they have enough slop to eat from their Twolegs?"

"Probably," grunted Grasspelt. He started nosing through the grass, his ears pricking. "This way!" he whispered over his shoulder.

Mistystar and Icewing tracked him along the edge of the grass to a bramble thicket that hung over the bank of the stream. Grasspelt slowed down as they approached the brambles, lowering his belly until it almost hung on the ground, before he plunged forward with both front paws outstretched. The air was split with squeals; Mistystar and Icewing raced up to see him looming over a nest of young, hairless mice. They dove in, killing the baby mice with swift, careful blows so as not to spoil the delicate bodies.

When everything was quiet, they stood back and looked down at the instant fresh-kill pile. "That was a good find," Mistystar praised Grasspelt.

Her Clanmate shrugged. "It's hardly enough to replace a lake full of fish."

"But it's a start," mewed Icewing. She scooped up the mice, gathering the tails in her teeth. The others helped her, and they began to make their way back down the stream, holding their prey out of the mud as they struggled to keep their footing.

Back in the camp, their Clanmates fell hungrily on their catch. "Mice are almost as yummy as trout!" Podkit declared, munching a soft, pink ear.

There were enough mice for every cat to have half each. Mistystar watched her Clanmates eating and felt a surge of satisfaction. Perhaps hunting farther upstream would be the answer until the fish came back. She looked up at the sky, wondering if her warrior ancestors agreed. *If Mothwing can't hear you, could you send a sign to Willowshine instead?*

She became aware of raised voices at the edge of the fresh-kill pile. "You can't have another one, Mossypaw," Reedwhisker was saying. "Hollowpaw and Rushpaw haven't had theirs yet."

"They should be here, then!" Mossypaw argued.

"Here they come," mewed Graymist. The two apprentices were trotting through the entrance.

"Look!" called Mallownose. "Fresh mice!"

"Great," mewed Hollowpaw, sounding less than excited.

"How was your battle practice?" Mistystar asked. She watched the young cats closely, mindful of what Mothwing had said about their private boasting.

"Really good!" Rushpaw meowed.

"I was the best," Hollowpaw declared.

"Where did you go?" Mistystar put in.

Rushpaw looked surprised. "Oh, you know that elderflower bush by the holly tree? There's a clear space under there that is just right for battle training."

"Excellent," Mistystar murmured. She was beginning to feel guilty about quizzing them. "Reedwhisker saved a mouse for you."

The apprentices exchanged a glance. "We're not hungry right now," mewed Hollowpaw. "Is it okay if we have it later?"

"Yes, of course." Mistystar turned away but looked back over her shoulder. "And well done for working so hard. I know things aren't easy at the moment, but I'm proud of you for keeping up with your training."

Rushpaw twitched his tail. "We're just doing what any loyal cat would do," he insisted. "You can count on us, Mistystar."

CHAPTER 8

✤

Keeping her weight balanced over her haunches so that she didn't tip forward and fall in, Mistystar sliced her paw through the water. Her claws sank into the minnow's narrow body and she flicked it triumphantly onto the rock beside her. The tiny fish flapped for a moment before lying still.

"Nicely done!" called a voice, making Mistystar look up in surprise.

Beetlewhisker was watching her from the top of the shore. His brown-and-white fur stood out sharply against the gray stones.

"It's still not much more than a mouthful," Mistystar pointed out, glancing down at her catch in disappointment. Reedwhisker had taken a patrol upstream that morning in search of more prey outside the territory, but Mistystar had wanted to check for herself the state of the lake.

"At least the big fish are coming back!" Beetlewhisker purred.

Mistystar put her head on one side. "They are?"

Beetlewhisker nodded. "Oh, yes. I saw a huge trout yesterday, longer than my tail. Mothwing told me to leave it alone, though."

"She did?"

"Yes, to give the lake a chance to build up its stocks again. She said we should let the bigger fish build up their numbers and breed again before we start catching them."

Mistystar felt her mouth fall open. "She didn't mention this to me."

Beetlewhisker blinked. "Well, maybe she thought you'd feel the same?" He sounded uncomfortable, and Mistystar felt sorry for challenging him. He wasn't the cat she needed to speak to about this. She stood up and picked up her minnow.

"I'd better add this to the fresh-kill pile," she meowed. "See you later, Beetlewhisker."

She left the warrior standing rather unhappily on the shore, and threaded back through the ferns to the camp. She dropped her fish onto the pile and went to the medicine cats' den. Mothwing was inside alone, doing something complicated with a heap of leaves.

"Why did you tell Beetlewhisker not to catch the trout?" Mistystar demanded.

Mothwing looked up. "Because we want to let the lake recover first," she meowed. "What's the point of taking all of the big fish as soon as they appear?"

"That should have been my decision," Mistystar insisted. She knew she was being stubborn—Mothwing had a fair point—but she couldn't help feeling that she was being deliberately undermined.

"You weren't there!" Mothwing pointed out. "And I'm allowed to have an opinion, aren't I?" There was a hint of challenge in her gaze, which made Mistystar bristle even more.

"You know what? I'm not sure anymore! Not after lying to the Clan about StarClan!"

"I didn't lie!" Mothwing flashed back.

"By letting us believe you could be our medicine cat, you did."

Mothwing stared at her. "Are you saying you don't trust me to do anything?"

Mistystar felt her tail droop. "I don't think I do," she murmured. "Everything's going wrong, the Clan is still hungry, and I need StarClan to know that they can send us signs at any time."

"Willowshine will tell you if she sees a sign."

"Will she really? Or is her loyalty to you too strong?" Mistystar suddenly felt very tired. "Please accept that you can no longer be a medicine cat, Mothwing. Before StarClan gives up on us completely."

Mothwing curled her tail over her back and padded out of the den. "Just because I don't believe in StarClan, Mistystar, you don't have to give up your faith in them," she whispered on her way past.

As Mistystar followed Mothwing away from the rocks, she heard a small commotion beside the fresh-kill pile. Mossypaw was bickering with Troutpaw over who should have the last piece of squirrel. *At least they're getting a taste for land prey,* Mistystar thought. She didn't have the energy to sort out the apprentices' quarrel, so she headed for the entrance and pushed her way into the middle of the territory, where the bushes grew most densely. It was quiet and sheltered under here, and she found a patch of dry leaves to lie down on.

She listened to the leaves on the holly tree rattling in the breeze, and watched a few late elderflower petals drift down in front of her. Something stirred in her mind. Hadn't Rushpaw described a place under an elderflower bush next to a holly tree where he and Hollowpaw had practiced their battle techniques? Mistystar looked around. Holly trees weren't common in their territory, and she was pretty sure there wasn't another one so close to an elder bush. But the ground was smooth and the layer of fallen leaves undisturbed; there had been no fighting here for a long while. Had Rushpaw lied?

Mistystar shrugged. She'd question where the apprentices were again later. Whatever they were up to, it could wait. She closed her eyes and pictured her Clanmates roaming across the marsh and up the stream in search of food. Was Beetlewhisker right? Were the trout really coming back to the lake? And if so, would her warriors be able to resist catching them until the water was fully stocked?

Mistystar felt warm breath on her ear, and a familiar, heartbreaking scent wreathed around her. "There are more sources of prey than the lake," whispered a voice. Mistystar whirled around, peering into the shadows.

"Stonefur? Are you there?"

There was nothing but silence. But Stonefur had visited her! StarClan was still watching them. *We are going to survive!* Mistystar thought joyously.

Suddenly the branches crashed and Reedwhisker burst

through the bushes. "Mistystar! Come quickly! Hollowpaw and Rushpaw are in trouble!"

Mistystar leaped up. "Where are they?"

Reedwhisker skidded to a halt, his expression grim. "By the Twoleg dens."

Mistystar didn't ask for an explanation. She just followed her deputy at a sprint through the bushes, down to the stream, and along the muddy bank that led out of their territory. *What in the name of StarClan are Hollowpaw and Rushpaw doing there? They weren't part of Reedwhisker's patrol.*

Reedwhisker clawed his way to the top of the bank with Mistystar close behind him, and the two cats stood panting on the vast stretch of grass. Reedwhisker pointed with his tail. "Mallownose, Graymist, and Robinwing are by the boundary; can you see?"

Mistystar narrowed her eyes against the wind. She could just make out the pale-furred shapes of her Clanmates crouching by the long wall of stones that marked the edge of the field. "Where are the apprentices?"

"On the other side of the wall, by the Twoleg den. They're trapped in a corner by a pair of dogs." Reedwhisker glanced at Mistystar. "It looks pretty dangerous."

"We have to get them out!" Mistystar exclaimed.

"Of course," Reedwhisker meowed. "I just wanted to warn you, that's all."

But Mistystar was already tearing over the grass, leaping high with each stride to avoid being caught in the dense stalks. Reedwhisker caught up to her with a few bounds, and they raced side by side to the wall where the others were waiting.

"Are the dogs still there?" Reedwhisker demanded.

Graymist nodded, her eyes huge and her fur fluffed up. Mistystar jumped on top of the wall. She almost fell off again when she saw the two huge black-and-brown dogs snarling at the edge of the Twoleg den. Cowering under a tiny stone ledge were the RiverClan apprentices.

"Help, help!" shrieked Hollowpaw as one of the dogs thrust its muzzle under the ledge.

"Get back, you brute!" Rushpaw hissed, and Mistystar saw one of his paws flash out, catching the dog on its nose. The dog merely shook its head and curled its lip again. Twin strands of drool hung from its jaws.

"Great StarClan," Mistystar whispered.

Reedwhisker appeared beside her on the wall. "You and the others distract the dogs," he meowed. "I'll go along that fence"—he gestured with his tail to a narrow wooden barrier running from the wall to the Twoleg den—"and lead Hollow-paw and Rushpaw out."

"It's too far for you to go on your own!" Mistystar gasped, studying the distance between the wooden fence and the tiny ledge of stone.

"The apprentices won't come out on their own," Reed-whisker meowed. "You have to trust me, Mistystar."

Mistystar gazed at her son. "I do trust you," she mewed. "Just be careful, please."

"I will," Reedwhisker promised. "I value my pelt even more than you do," he teased over his shoulder as he turned to the warriors crouching below. "Come up here!" he called. Graymist, Mallownose, and Robinwing scrambled onto the wall and balanced beside Mistystar. Reedwhisker started to trot along the top of the stones. "When I'm almost at the Twoleg den, make some noise!" he ordered.

"Are you going to let him do this?" Graymist whispered to Mistystar.

"We don't have a choice," Mistystar replied grimly. *Oh, StarClan, please watch over him!*

The cats watched in silence as Reedwhisker picked his way along the narrow strip of wood. His black pelt looked like a shadow as he crept noiselessly closer to the Twoleg den. When he was less than a fox-length away, Mistystar lifted her head.

"Dog-breath!" she screeched. "Over here, you foulmouthed creatures!"

One of the dogs spun around, its hackles raised. It barked, and the other dog turned to join it.

"Scared of us, are you?" taunted Mallownose.

"Come on, flea-pelts! Pick on someone your own size!" yowled Robinwing.

The dogs took a pace toward the wall. Behind them, Mistystar saw Hollowpaw and Rushpaw peep out from under the ledge. They looked as tiny as kits, and even more vulnerable.

"Too scared to come any closer?" jeered Graymist, standing on her toes. "We'll give you a proper fight!"

The dogs sprang forward, crossing the short, muddy grass in a few strides. Mistystar gripped the stone tightly to keep herself from fleeing. At the far end of the wooden fence,

Reedwhisker jumped down and raced along the side of the Twoleg den to where the apprentices were hiding.

"Come on!" Mistystar heard him call. "This way, quick!"

Hollowpaw and Rushpaw started to creep out from underneath the ledge. *Faster, faster,* Mistystar willed them.

In the brief silence, the dogs' attention had turned away from the cats on the wall. One of them swung its massive head back toward the Twoleg den. When it saw the three cats outlined sharply against the pale gray stone, it let out a growl. With a mad scrabble of gigantic paws, the dogs whirled around and started to hurtle back toward Reedwhisker and the apprentices.

"No!" screeched Mistystar. Without thinking, she leaped down behind the dogs. "Come back here! Take me instead!"

"Get back to the wall!" yowled Reedwhisker, who had reached the apprentices and was standing in front of them, shielding them with his tail.

"Run!" Mistystar hollered. She was almost at the dogs' heels now; mud was splashing into her face from their racing paws, and she was almost knocked off her feet by one of their thick-furred tails. She sprang up and grabbed the end of the tail in her teeth. At once the dog skidded to a halt, jerking Mistystar forward. She braced herself and sank her teeth deeper into the fleshy tail. The dog circled, and Mistystar found herself being dragged sideways.

"Let go, Mistystar!" she heard Mallownose shout from the wall. Mistystar gritted her teeth and clung on. She could feel the dog's breath hot on her neck and the stench was enough to make her gag, but she knew she couldn't let go.

There was a rapid pounding of paws, and suddenly Graymist and Robinwing were beside her, rearing up on their hind legs to slash at the dog. With a yelp, it jumped backward. Mistystar lost her grip and stumbled onto her knees. Graymist shoved her up to her feet, and the three cats raced back to the wall.

"Where's Mallownose?" Mistystar yowled, realizing that the top of the stones was empty.

"Helping Reedwhisker," Graymist panted.

Mistystar whirled around and saw the light brown warrior clinging to the back of the other dog, distracting it while Reedwhisker pushed Hollowpaw and Rushpaw up to the top of the fence. As soon as the apprentices were clear, Mallownose sprang from the dog's shoulders onto the fence beside them. The narrow strip of wood shuddered and buckled as the three cats clung on.

"Reedwhisker! Watch out!" Mistystar shrieked. The deputy was crouching down, waiting for the fence to stop shaking before he jumped up. Both of the dogs leaped at him, jaws bared, drool flying from their cheeks. They landed with a thud and a dreadful tearing sound. Reedwhisker let out a shriek of pain that tore Mistystar's heart in two.

"Reedwhisker! No!"

CHAPTER 9

✿

Mistystar bunched her hindquarters beneath her, ready to spring down, but Robinwing held her back.

"Wait! Mallownose has him!"

The brown warrior had dug his claws into the top of the fence and lowered himself down until he could sink his teeth into Reedwhisker's scruff. He hauled the barely moving cat out of the dogs' reach and carried him along the wood, with Hollowpaw and Rushpaw stumbling in front of him. The dogs sprang and snapped at them from below, but Mallownose kept going, his eyes bulging from the effort of holding his Clanmate.

Mistystar pushed the apprentices out of the way as they stood trembling on the wall, and stretched out to take her son from Mallownose. The black tom was moaning softly, and a huge gash stretched across his flank. The wound was so deep that Mistystar could see the white gleam of bone at the top of his hind leg.

"Oh, StarClan," she whispered.

"We're so sorry," Hollowpaw whimpered. "We were just looking for food."

"Kittypet food," Rushpaw added. He hung his head. "We found some here before, and it didn't taste too bad. We thought if we got enough to eat here, we wouldn't have to take anything from the fresh-kill pile."

Mistystar stared at the apprentices, resisting the urge to claw their ears off until they screamed as loudly as Reedwhisker had. *They never meant for any cat to get hurt. They thought they were helping.*

Robinwing stepped alongside Mistystar. "Let's get Reedwhisker back to the camp," he meowed. He and Mallownose stood at the foot of the wall while Graymist and Mistystar lowered Reedwhisker onto their shoulders. The warriors stumbled a little under the deputy's weight, then braced themselves and began the slow trek back through the grass. Mistystar walked at Reedwhisker's head, trying to stop it from bouncing against Mallownose's elbow. Graymist followed, with the apprentices on each side of her. The young cats were too dazed and miserable to speak.

They kept to the top of the bank, not wanting to risk Reedwhisker falling into the still-swollen stream. Once they reached the bushes inside RiverClan territory, Graymist and Mistystar went ahead to hold branches out of the way. Reedwhisker's body was still whipped by stray twigs, though, and Mistystar whimpered every time he was lashed by another loose branch.

As they entered the camp, Graymist yowled, "Mothwing! Quick!"

Mothwing's golden head poked out from the elders' den.

"What is it?" Scraps of moss clung to her fur, and Mistystar guessed she had been building herself a nest.

"Reedwhisker is hurt!" Mallownose told her, but Mothwing was already pushing her way out of the branches and running across the clearing. The warriors let Reedwhisker slip gently to the ground.

Mothwing stared at the gaping wound. "We need cobweb, comfrey, marigold, watermint," she began. "Robinwing, fetch some soaked moss. Do I smell *dog*?"

"Yes," mewed Mallownose. "He was bitten by at least one, if not two."

"In that case, we need to get this wound as clean as possible." Mothwing ran her paw lightly along Reedwhisker's spine. "I don't think anything's broken, but let's keep him still anyway."

Mistystar stepped forward. Her heart was pounding so hard she could hardly speak. But she reached out with one paw and moved Mothwing away from Reedwhisker. "Let Willowshine do this," she mewed.

Her Clanmates stared at her. "Mistystar, what are you doing?" Graymist exclaimed. "Mothwing is our medicine cat!"

"Not anymore," Mistystar replied softly.

Mothwing blinked. "Are you sure you mean this? Reedwhisker is very, very sick."

"Willowshine knows what to do," Mistystar whispered. "StarClan will help her."

Mothwing flinched, then turned away. "I'll get her," she mewed.

"I don't understand!" growled Robinwing. "What's going on?"

"I know what I'm doing," Mistystar insisted.

Willowshine raced up. "Mothwing said Reedwhisker was hurt!" She stopped and stared down at the deputy, whose wound was staining the earth beneath him as scarlet as a sunset. "Great StarClan!"

Mistystar lifted her head high. "I know you can heal him, Willowshine. Please, help him."

Willowshine opened her mouth to protest, then shut it with a snap and began examining the injury. Mistystar gazed down at her son. *I won't lose you too,* she vowed. *I know you need StarClan's help to survive this, and Mothwing can't give you that. I'm doing the right thing; I must be.*

A crowd of cats gathered around Reedwhisker. Mothwing brought herbs to Willowshine, then left. Mistystar heard murmurs ripple around the Clan, ranging from puzzled to angry.

"Where's Mothwing going?"

"How can she turn her back on an injured Clanmate? Surely that's breaking the medicine code!"

"Mistystar said she wasn't the medicine cat anymore."

"What? In the name of StarClan, why not?"

Because to Mothwing, StarClan doesn't exist! Mistystar thought desperately. She watched as Willowshine carefully rinsed Reedwhisker's wound, then packed it with cobwebs and freshly pulped herbs. Reedwhisker's eyes remained closed, and his breathing was so shallow his flank barely moved.

Mistystar couldn't bear to see him suffer any longer. She padded out of the camp and headed into the densest part of the territory. She crawled into a patch of brambles and curled up, wrapping her tail over her nose.

StarClan, we need you now! Guide Willowshine's paws; help her to heal Reedwhisker's injuries and make him strong again. Please don't take my last kit from me!

The air stirred beside her, and a faint scent drifted through the thorns. Mistystar lifted her head. "Stonefur?" She could just make out a shape against the brambles, gray-furred and broad-shouldered. "Stonefur! Have you come for Reedwhisker? Please don't take him to StarClan yet!"

Her brother leaned toward her until she felt his breath on her cheek. "Reedwhisker's life hangs by the thinnest fish scale," he whispered. "He needs all the help he can get."

"Then speak to Willowshine!" Mistystar begged. "Tell her what she should do!"

Stonefur shook his head, almost in sorrow. "The lake is not the only source of prey," he mewed, echoing what he had said before. "RiverClan has another medicine cat."

"But Mothwing doesn't believe in you! How can she be a true medicine cat? She has lied to the whole Clan, and she will be forever blind to what you tell her."

"Did StarClan tell you how to give birth to your kits?" Stonefur queried.

Mistystar gazed at her brother in astonishment. "No, of course not."

"So you trusted your instincts, and acted alone?"

"Well, I had Mudfur to help me, but yes, I guess my instincts told me what to do," Mistystar admitted. She had no idea where this was leading. Beside her, Stonefur was starting to fade. Mistystar reached out with her front paw, trying to hold the vision where it was.

"Perhaps you should trust Mothwing to act alone," came the last whisper.

Dazed, Mistystar shoved her way out of the brambles. On the last tendril, a pale green pod balanced, so delicate that Mistystar could almost see through it. Something made her pause, and as she watched, the pod began to split open. A damp, folded brown creature emerged, not much thicker than a twig. The sides of the pod fell away, leaving the creature clinging to the bramble. Mistystar watched, entranced, as the tiny shape stretched out first one wing, then the other. They gleamed in the pale light, thinner than gossamer and lifted by the softest breeze. As the wings dried, bolder colors appeared: rich fox-colored brown, bright circles of blue edged in white, and specks of black that looked like the opposite of stars. It was a moth!

Does it know what it is? Mistystar wondered. *Fly, little one! That's what your wings are for!*

The moth clung to the tendril, its wings trembling. Then, with a twitch of its hair's-breadth legs, it flexed its wings and let the breeze lift it into the air. It hung for a moment above the bramble; then its wings folded and unfolded in a single heartbeat and the moth soared up through the brambles, flitting past the thorns and out into the cold, crisp sky.

Mistystar realized she had been holding her breath. Did the moth have its own StarClan? Or had it really emerged all on its own, known how to spread its wings and take flight purely by instinct? Stonefur's words came back to her, and Mistystar's fur started to tingle. *You sent this moth, didn't you, Stonefur? You meant this to be an omen—an omen for me that I should trust Mothwing's instincts, and not judge her for what she does not do.*

CHAPTER 10

❧

Mistystar raced back to the camp and burst through the entrance. The clearing was empty and quiet. There was no sign of Reedwhisker or Willowshine or the cats who had clustered around them. Surely Reedwhisker hadn't died! Was she too late? She spotted Graymist emerging from the dirtplace and called over to her.

"Where is he? Where is Willowshine?"

Graymist looked at her, and Mistystar flinched from the judgment in her gaze. "They are in the medicine cats' den," she meowed.

Mistystar couldn't bear to ask how Reedwhisker was. She fled to the rocks and peered in. Willowshine was bent over the deputy's still, black shape. "Is . . . is he alive?"

"Just," mewed Willowshine without looking up. "I'm doing everything I can."

Mistystar stepped forward. "Where is Mothwing?"

Anger prickled from Willowshine's fur. "In the elders' den. Where you sent her."

Mistystar swallowed. "I made a mistake," she whispered. Then she turned and ran out of the den. She went over to the bush that sheltered the elders in their twilight moons and ducked her head into the den. "Mothwing?"

There was a faint stirring in the shadows. "Yes?"

"Mothwing, Reedwhisker needs you." Mistystar paused. "*I* need you. Please don't let me lose my son."

Mothwing padded across the den and pushed her way out as Mistystar stepped back. Her blue eyes were wary and watchful.

"I was wrong," Mistystar confessed. "You are still the RiverClan medicine cat. It is not up to me to take that away from you." She pictured the moth, proud and strong and utterly confident that it could fly without any help. "Please forgive me, Mothwing."

Mothwing stretched until her muzzle rested on top of Mistystar's head. "I will do everything I can for Reedwhisker," she promised. Then she brushed lightly past Mistystar and vanished into her old den.

Mistystar forced herself not to follow. Reedwhisker was in the best place to recover; she would only get in the way. Suddenly she knew where she had to go. She turned and trotted toward the entrance. She met Beetlewhisker just outside. "Is Reedwhisker okay?" the warrior asked.

"Mothwing and Willowshine are with him," Mistystar replied. When she saw his look of surprise, she added, "RiverClan is blessed by StarClan to have two medicine cats. You can tell the rest of the Clan that, if you wish."

Beetlewhisker held her gaze for a moment, then nodded. "As you say, we are very lucky," he meowed.

Mistystar began to move off. Beetlewhisker called after her, "Do you want some company?"

Mistystar shook her head. "No, thank you. I'll be back later; I promise."

She jumped over the stream and ran across the marsh, bouncing from tussock to tussock to keep her paws out of the mud. As she trotted along the shore, she looked across the ruffled water to the RiverClan camp, hidden among its sheltering bushes. "StarClan, help Mothwing and Willowshine," she prayed.

At the stream that divided WindClan from ThunderClan, she started to climb. She didn't meet any patrols, though she saw a group of WindClan cats racing over the moor in the distance. She still couldn't figure out how they managed to move so fast. Up and up she climbed, until her paws ached. At last the circle of bushes appeared above her, and she found herself at the top of the paw-dented path that led down to the Moonpool.

She settled down with her nose just touching the ice-cold water, and closed her eyes. She wanted to dream herself into StarClan, find Stonefur, and let him know that she had seen his sign. A soft breeze ruffled her fur and she opened her eyes expectantly. To her disappointment she was still beside the Moonpool. Bare walls of stone encircled her, and the gray sky above was empty of stars. Mistystar felt a faint tremor of alarm. Was it a bad omen if StarClan wouldn't let her in?

Then she noticed a cat walking down the path toward her. For a moment she didn't recognize the sturdy shape and long brown pelt; then she realized it was Mudfur, the medicine cat who had stayed behind in the forest because his bones were too old for the Great Journey. Mistystar scrambled to her feet.

Mudfur padded closer until he was facing her, barely a fox-length away. He dipped his head in greeting, then gestured with his tail. "Let's sit," he suggested. Still stunned by his appearance, Mistystar folded her haunches underneath her. Mudfur took a long breath. "I realized that Mothwing didn't believe in StarClan quite quickly," he began, staring out over the pool. "But I never saw any reason to challenge her. I could tell she was going to be a good medicine cat. She was smart and calm, and kinder than I was to cats in pain! Being a medicine cat is first and foremost about serving your Clan, and I knew that Mothwing would do that with every beat of her heart."

"But what about the rest of her responsibilities?" Mistystar argued. "Seeing signs from StarClan, performing ceremonies?"

"StarClan can speak to any cat they want," Mudfur replied. "We all have dreams, not just medicine cats. As for ceremonies, if Mothwing said the right words, how would any cat know what she thought in her own mind?"

"But there was a sign! You chose her because you found the wing of a moth!"

Mudfur looked down at his paws. "Ah, yes, so I did. At least, that's what made my mind up. Maybe it was a real sign; maybe it wasn't. If it was, then it meant StarClan saw her skills before any of us did. And if it wasn't, well, I figured they'd find a way to tell me something different before too long."

"But they never did, did they?" Mistystar whispered. "StarClan allowed Mothwing to become our medicine cat even though they knew she would never listen to them."

"I've had a long time to think about this," Mudfur meowed. "Faith is not just about believing in warrior ancestors. It means being loyal to whatever is most important to you. For Mothwing, this is her Clan and her Clanmates. What else does a medicine cat need?"

Mistystar looked at the Moonpool, gray and lightless beneath the sky. What else, indeed? Mothwing had not stopped caring for her Clan since the moment she became Mudfur's apprentice. Like the moth, she had taught herself to fly alone.

"Mistystar?"

Mistystar jerked around. Mudfur had vanished, and Mothwing was standing behind her. Why was she here, and not with Reedwhisker? The breath suddenly caught in Mistystar's throat. "Reedwhisker. . . ?" she rasped.

"Is sleeping peacefully," Mothwing finished for her. "There are no signs of infection, and as long as he stays still for a while, the wound will heal."

Mistystar sagged with relief. "Oh, thank StarClan," she breathed. Then she straightened up. "And thank *you*, Mothwing. For . . . for everything. How did you know I was here?"

"I didn't," Mothwing replied. "But I often come here when I need some time to think. All the wisdom of the medicine cats that have come before me must have rubbed off on these stones somehow!"

"And yet you don't believe in anything that they do," Mistystar murmured.

Mothwing looked sharply at her. "I believe in the importance of learning from what has been discovered before. And in how precious health is, and how hard I must work to preserve it in all my Clanmates. The fact that the world of signs, omens, and dreams that have hidden meanings is closed to me doesn't feel like something is missing, Mistystar. I respect what you believe. You must respect what matters to me."

Mistystar nodded. "Who would have thought that a moth would have so much to teach me?" she whispered, half under her breath.

"What did you say?"

Mistystar let her tail rest on her friend's shoulder. "Just something for me to remember," she purred. "Now, shall we let our old bones rest for a while before we go back to our Clan?"

CLOUDSTAR'S
JOURNEY

ALLEGIANCES

SKYCLAN

LEADER

CLOUDSTAR—small pale gray tom with white patches and very pale blue eyes

DEPUTY

BUZZARDTAIL—ginger tom with green eyes

MEDICINE CAT

FAWNSTEP—light brown tabby she-cat

WARRIORS

(toms and she-cats without kits)

NIGHTFUR—black tom
APPRENTICE, OAKPAW

QUAILHEART—dappled gray tom

STOATFUR—orange-and-white tom
APPRENTICE, TANSYPAW

WEASELWHISKER—brown-and-ginger tom
APPRENTICE, ACORNPAW

FERNPELT—dark brown tabby she-cat

MOUSEFANG—sandy-colored she-cat
APPRENTICE, SNAILPAW

RAINLEAP—silver tabby she-cat with blue eyes
APPRENTICE, MINTPAW

APPRENTICES

(more than six moons old, in training to become warriors)

OAKPAW—gray tabby tom

ACORNPAW—light brown tom

SNAILPAW—dark brown tabby tom

TANSYPAW—cream-colored she-cat

MINTPAW—pale gray she-cat

QUEENS

(she-cats expecting or nursing kits)

BIRDFLIGHT—light brown tabby she-cat with long fur and amber eyes

HAZELWING—orange tabby she-cat with green eyes (mother to Webkit, a pale gray tom; Hatchkit, a dark gray tom; Emberkit, an orange she-cat; and Mistlekit, a silver tabby she-cat)

ELDERS   **PETALFALL**—rose-cream she-cat with green eyes

STARLINGFEATHER—dark brown tom with amber eyes

HAWKSNOW—brown tabby tom speckled with white

THUNDERCLAN

LEADER   **REDSTAR**—dark ginger tom

DEPUTY   **SEEDPELT**—gray she-cat with darker flecks

MEDICINE CAT   **KESTRELWING**—dark brown tabby tom

SHADOWCLAN

LEADER   **DAWNSTAR**—creamy brown she-cat

DEPUTY   **SNAKETAIL**—brown tabby tom

MEDICINE CAT   **MOLEPELT**—small black tom

WINDCLAN

LEADER   **SWIFTSTAR**—dark gray tom

DEPUTY   **MILKFUR**—creamy white tom

MEDICINE CAT   **LARKWING**—silver-and-black tabby she-cat

RIVERCLAN

LEADER   **BIRCHSTAR**—light brown tabby she-cat

DEPUTY   **SLOEFUR**—black she-cat

MEDICINE CAT   **ICEWHISKER**—silver-gray tom

HIGHSTONES

BARLEY'S
FARM

WINDCLAN
CAMP

FOURTREES

FALLS

OWL-
TREE

RIVER

SUNNING-
ROCKS

RIVERCLAN
CAMP

CHAPTER 1

♣

Stripes of sunlight dappled the forest floor and the air was thick with the scent of damp new leaves. Cloudstar jerked his head up as he caught sight of a flash of dark gray movement above him: a squirrel, darting between the branches with its tail streaming behind like a feather.

"Are you just going to watch it?" meowed Buzzardtail, twitching his nose. The sturdy ginger deputy went to the trunk of the tree and peered up. "Or are you hoping it will find its own way to the fresh-kill pile?"

Cloudstar snorted. "I'll leave that one for the apprentices to catch." He lifted one paw and rubbed it behind his ear. "My old bones are enjoying this sun too much to go chasing about in the trees."

"What's that nonsense about old bones?" Buzzardtail demanded. "You're barely older than I am, and I've certainly got a few more chases and battles in me."

Cloudstar stepped around his deputy and headed for a patch of pale green ferns. "Ah, but I've been worn down by the burdens of leadership," he teased.

There was a rapid thud of paw steps as Buzzardtail hurtled

after Cloudstar and swiped him over his haunches, claws sheathed. "The only burden you'll have is those kits of yours keeping you awake once they arrive. I heard Birdflight tell Hazelwing that she's going to let them sleep in your den to give her some peace."

Cloudstar purred. "They'll be welcome," he mewed. "I can't wait to meet them."

Buzzardtail rolled his eyes. "You might not feel that way when they start pulling your tail and chewing your whiskers."

"I don't recall you putting up much of a fight with your three when they wanted to play!" Cloudstar reminded him. Snailpaw, Tansypaw, and Mintpaw were apprentices now, strong and good at climbing trees like all SkyClan warriors, but Buzzardtail had been as soft as honey with them when they were born.

Buzzardtail grunted. "Just you wait. Chasing that squirrel will seem easy compared to looking after kits!"

The sound of a twig snapping distracted them, and both cats stared into the bracken. A blurry shape was just visible through the green stems. Cloudstar opened his mouth to taste the air. "Is that a ThunderClan patrol?" he called.

The ferns parted and a speckled gray face appeared. "Cloudstar? You wouldn't be chasing squirrels into our territory, would you?"

Cloudstar snorted. "Of course not, Seedpelt. SkyClan cats know how to respect borders." He spoke lightly, but he wasn't about to let the ThunderClan deputy challenge him for no reason.

Seedpelt nodded and stepped through the bracken until she was less than a fox-length from the SkyClan cats. She stretched out her neck and sniffed.

"Our border marks are in the right place," Buzzardtail growled.

Seedpelt opened her blue eyes wide. "Of course they are," she purred. "I wasn't accusing you of anything, Buzzardtail."

"For once," muttered the SkyClan deputy.

"Is everything all right, Seedpelt?" called a voice from beyond the bracken.

"Fine, thanks, Nettleclaw," Seedpelt replied without taking her eyes from Cloudstar. More quietly, she asked, "I trust all is well in SkyClan?"

"Yes. Is there a reason why it wouldn't be?" Cloudstar felt his hackles rise.

Seedpelt's eyes glinted. "It's not often I find the leader and deputy forming their own patrol. Rich pickings for rival Clans wanting a fight, I'd have thought."

"We're not frightened of you," Buzzardtail snarled. He took a step forward, but Cloudstar held him back with a twitch of his tail.

"Don't let her get to you," he warned his old friend. "Seedpelt, I'll grant you the respect of not watching where you set your border marks, but we will not tolerate a single Thunder-Clan paw on our territory."

Seedpelt bowed her head. "We wouldn't dream of it, Cloudstar."

Cloudstar twitched his ears, indicating to Buzzardtail that

he should follow, and the two cats headed into the trees. As soon as they were out of earshot of the ThunderClan patrol, Buzzardtail spat, "What was that furball going on about, telling us we're an easy target for rival patrols?"

Cloudstar shrugged. "Seedpelt was just trying to distract us from the fact that her patrol was closer to our border than they should have been. That clump of ferns has always been a barrier between the territories, and ThunderClan patrols are supposed to leave their marks on the far side."

Buzzardtail stopped in his tracks, his fur bristling. "They were lucky we didn't claw their ears!"

Cloudstar kept walking. "I'm sure Seedpelt was shocked to find us there, and she knows we'll be checking for Thunder-Clan scent marks from now on."

Buzzardtail stomped behind him, still muttering. "Those ThunderClan cats think they can hunt where they like. If Duskstar hadn't given them that strip of SkyClan territory to start with, they wouldn't walk all over us as if our scent marks meant nothing. I know he was our leader, but really, it was a mouse-brained decision."

Cloudstar gazed into the trees on the far side of the border. They grew more densely there than in the rest of the SkyClan, mostly oaks with thick trunks and gnarled, heavy branches that bent low to the ground. He hadn't been born when Duskstar made the startling announcement at a Gathering that he would surrender part of his territory to ThunderClan, but the decision still sat uneasily with his Clan. "Duskstar had his reasons," he meowed to Buzzardtail.

"What, that he had bees in his brain?"

Cloudstar shook his head and tried to imagine himself in Duskstar's place, worn down by constant battles over a line of trees with old, fragile branches, while the sheer volume of leaves made it too easy for squirrels and birds to hide. "This part of the forest offered better hunting for ThunderClan warriors than for us. And he knew that ThunderClan queens had recently had several litters of kits, and their need for food was greater than their territory could provide. We may be rivals, but there have always been five Clans in the forest. If one is in danger of starving to death, it is our duty to help them survive."

"That's not part of the warrior code," growled Buzzardtail.

"No, but obeying your leader is," Cloudstar pointed out, keeping his tone light. "Thanks to Duskstar, in fact. You remember he was responsible for this part of the warrior code? And right now, your leader is ordering you to return to the camp to see what the hunting patrols have caught for us!"

"He's back!"

As soon as Cloudstar and Buzzardtail wriggled under the brambles that surrounded the SkyClan camp, four tiny shapes hurtled across the hard-packed earth. "Cloudstar! Hazelwing said you'd teach us a battle move! Please?"

Cloudstar gently disentangled himself from the flurry of gray and orange pelts. "You seem to be quite good at pouncing already," he mewed.

An orange tabby she-cat hurried over. "Kits! Kits! Leave

poor Cloudstar alone!" She turned to Cloudstar, her green eyes apologetic. "I'm so sorry. I don't know where they get their energy from. The only way I could get them to give Birdflight any peace in the nursery was by promising you'd show them a battle move."

Cloudstar looked down at the four eager faces by his front paws. "It's no problem, Hazelwing. I'm sure I can keep them amused for a while."

The biggest kit, a pale gray tom, bounced on his toes. "Does this mean we're going to start our warrior training?" he squeaked.

"Not quite, Webkit," Cloudstar meowed. "You'll have to wait another five moons for that. Now, wait for me by the hazel bush and do some stretches to warm up." The kits scrambled away, Webkit racing ahead with his brother Hatch-kit, while their sisters, Emberkit and Mistlekit, followed a few paces behind.

"Do you think our kits will be so lively?" murmured a soft voice beside Cloudstar.

He turned to look into Birdflight's amber eyes. She looked tired, her belly swollen under her long brown fur. "You should be resting," he reminded her. "Come on, let me take you back to the nursery."

Birdflight flicked her tail at him. "I've had enough of being stuck inside. Let me get some fresh air!"

Cloudstar pressed his face to her belly. Something rippled against his cheek. "I think that one's going to match Webkit for liveliness," he predicted.

Birdflight purred. "I can't wait to meet him," she purred.

"Or her," Cloudstar put in. "Two of each would be nice, like Hazelwing's litter. Or maybe three toms to look after their sisters."

"My daughters will be able to take care of themselves!" Birdflight retorted, her eyes warm. "Perhaps they'll look after their brothers?"

Cloudstar rested his muzzle on top of Birdflight's head. He felt the tips of her ears brush against his chin like the wings of a moth. "I'll teach them everything I know so that no harm comes to them," he promised. "Even when they are warriors, I'll still watch over them. They will be the most precious parts of my life—alongside you, of course." He closed his eyes and breathed in Birdflight's sweet scent. *Thank you, StarClan, for giving me everything I could have dreamed of. My Clan is strong and happy, our borders are safe, and soon Birdflight and I will have kits of our own. You have been kind to me.*

"Cloudstar! Cloudstar!" Mistlekit was calling to him from beside the hazel bush. With a sigh, Cloudstar stepped away from Birdflight and started toward the far side of the clearing. But a frantic crackle of twigs stopped him in his tracks, and he spun around to see Fernpelt leading her hunting patrol back into the camp. Her eyes were wide and worried, and she headed straight for Cloudstar once she was clear of the brambles.

He looked past her to see what the patrol was carrying. To

his shock, only Snailpaw held any prey: a rather damp-looking squirrel, its gray tail dragging along the ground. "Is that all?" Cloudstar exclaimed.

Fernpelt stood in front of him, her pelt bristling. "There was nothing to find!" she told him. "We went to the border beside the pine trees, but the woods were empty. Snailpaw did well to catch that squirrel."

"And that was only because it was half-drowned in a puddle," muttered Acornpaw. Like the other cats on the patrol, his fur was ruffled and smeared with mud.

"But it's almost greenleaf," Cloudstar meowed. "The prey should be jumping into our claws!"

Fernpelt shook her head. "Not in that part of the forest. The Twolegs are making so much noise just beyond the border that they've scared everything away. If there is any prey left, we can't smell it over the stench from the monsters."

Cloudstar narrowed his eyes. Gigantic yellow monsters had been shifting huge piles of earth just beyond their boundary for a while now. They hadn't crossed into SkyClan territory, so Cloudstar had paid little attention. Twolegs were always doing strange things, but they rarely strayed over the borders.

Stoatfur stepped quietly up to Cloudstar. He had been part of Fernpelt's patrol. "I don't think we should hunt along that border from now on," he meowed. "The yellow monsters seemed much closer today, and it could be dangerous."

Cloudstar shook his head. "I don't agree. We know that Twolegs take trees from treecutplace, but they've never troubled us anywhere else. They don't even bring their dogs into that part of the territory. Once the prey gets used to the noise from the yellow monsters, it will come back. You had bad luck hunting today, that's all."

CHAPTER 2

♣

Cloudstar lay in his nest beneath a densely leaved elderberry bush and dreamed. He was in a forest of wide-spaced trees—oak, birch, beech, and ash—all growing so tall that their tops were lost in the wispy clouds. Their branches were perfectly placed for swift, unhindered climbing, and the ground was clear of brambles or tangled ferns so a cat could leap safely down in pursuit of prey or enemies. But Cloudstar knew there would be no enemies here, not even from rival Clans, because this was StarClan, where his ancestors lived peacefully alongside one another as they watched over the cats below.

A few blades of sunlight sliced through the trees, sending flashes of warmth across Cloudstar's gray-and-white pelt as he padded between the trunks. The air rippled with the scent of prey and new growth, and his claws tingled with the urge to spring up the nearest tree and soar skyward, seeing the forest from a completely different view as it unfurled beneath him. Soft paw steps behind him made him turn.

A dark ginger she-cat who Cloudstar recognized from his nine-lives ceremony was padding toward him. "Maplestar!" He bowed his head.

"Greetings, Cloudstar," Maplestar purred. "Welcome to StarClan."

Cloudstar looked up. "Is everything okay?" he asked, suddenly feeling a chill beneath his pelt. "Did you bring me here for a reason?"

The orange cat twitched her ears. "Everything's fine. We just wanted to see you, to tell you how proud we are of you."

Cloudstar arched his back and purred. "Thank you. It is an honor to lead my Clan."

Maplestar brushed her tail along his flank. "Walk with me," she invited. Side by side, the cats padded between the tree trunks, moving from sunlight to shadow and back to sunlight again. "SkyClan has been at the heart of the forest, the heart of the warrior code, since cats first made this place their home. Did you know we were the first Clan to mark boundaries? Clear Sky, who led us then, saw how our territory could feed and shelter us, and he knew that he had to protect it from outsiders who were jealous of our prey and security."

Cloudstar meowed, "We still mark the borders in his memory. No SkyClan cat will forget the debt we owe to him."

There was a rustle in a clump of ferns at the side of the path. A black-and-brown tom stepped out and nodded to them. "Greetings, Maplestar, Cloudstar."

Cloudstar tipped his head on one side. Beside him, Maplestar twitched her tail. "Cloudstar, this is Rowanstar."

Cloudstar bowed. "I am honored to meet you," he mewed.

Rowanstar flared his nostrils, as if he was annoyed that Cloudstar failed to recognize him. "I was one of the leaders who decided that boundaries should be patrolled and marked daily, as part of the warrior code. Clear Sky may have traced the first outline of our territory, but I was the leader who made the borders as strong as stone."

There was a cough from Maplestar. "As I recall, Rowanstar, the issue was raised at a Gathering only after your patrols were caught once too many times in ThunderClan's territory."

The dark-colored tom bristled. "If ThunderClan had marked their boundary clearly, my cats would never have accidentally strayed."

"You both brought honor and strength to SkyClan. But the greatest contribution to the warrior code came from me," rumbled a voice behind them.

The three cats whirled around to see a dark brown tom with yellow eyes standing on the path. His thick coat was underlaid with soft black fur, so that he looked as though he were outlined in shadow. Cloudstar pricked his ears. "Duskstar!" he meowed.

Duskstar dipped his head. "Greetings, Cloudstar. I trust you haven't forgotten the life that I gave to you? To have faith in your instincts, and know that your word is law?"

"I haven't forgotten," Cloudstar promised.

The brown tom looked at the other two cats. "Maplestar, Rowanstar, it is rare that we three meet in this woods. We are all part of the noble history of SkyClan, but it is thanks to me that the leaders of all five Clans know that their judgment is final, that their word goes unchallenged. Cloudstar, you must use this power wisely, for the good of your Clan rather than personal gain. Learn to lead from our examples, and your path will be clear and straight."

Cloudstar bowed. "I am honored to follow in your paw steps." He looked down at his paws. *I have to ask!* "Duskstar, did you ever regret giving ThunderClan that strip of forest?"

There was a heartbeat of silence, and Rowanstar looked aghast. Then Duskstar said quietly, "Wherever our heart lies, we have a duty to preserve the survival of all five Clans in the forest. I could not watch our neighbors starve when we had prey to spare." The brown tom went on. "Hold your head high, Cloudstar. SkyClan is the noblest of all the Clans, with the strongest borders, the bravest warriors, and the most skillful hunters. You have nothing to fear from Twolegs, or their monsters, or the animals they have bent to their will. SkyClan will endure forever!"

The clouds above the trees seemed to sink through the branches until Cloudstar was surrounded by mist. The cats around him blurred and faded, their pelts vanishing against the background of leaves and trunks. Then Cloudstar felt soft feathers tickling his nose in time with his breathing, and heard the rustle of dry moss as he stirred.

"Cloudstar? Are you awake?" A small tabby she-cat, her striped fur the color of bracken in leaf-fall, was peering down at him. The scent of herbs hung on to her pelt, and there was a scrap of tansy clinging to her whiskers.

"Fawnstep?" Cloudstar scrambled to sit up. "Is Birdflight okay? Is there something wrong?"

The medicine cat took a step back, giving Cloudstar room

to climb out of his nest. "Birdflight is fine," she purred. "I wanted to speak with you about something else."

Cloudstar shook his pelt to dislodge a piece of moss, then led the way into the clearing. The dawn was clear and still, promising a warm day full of prey-scent and stable branches for climbing. "What is it?" Cloudstar asked, turning back to Fawnstep.

She ducked her head. "I'd rather speak outside the camp, if you don't mind."

"Oh, okay." Cloudstar twitched his tail, inviting her to go first. They squeezed under the brambles and emerged into a glade of silver birches, whose cobweb-colored leaves whispered in the softest breath of wind. Fawnstep pushed her way through the long grass that grew between the slender gray trunks and headed deeper into the woods. Cloudstar trotted after her.

"Don't go too far, or we'll run into the dawn patrol," he warned.

Fawnstep stopped beside a tree stump and sat down, curling her tail over her paws. "There have been omens," she began.

Instantly Cloudstar tensed. "What kind of omens?"

Fawnstep looked serious. "I think these signs involve what the Twolegs are doing on the edge of our border. I think Sky-Clan is more threatened by them than we realize."

Cloudstar thought of his dream, and knew he would be able to reassure Fawnstep, whatever she was worrying about, but he wanted to hear her speak first. "Tell me what you have seen."

"Yesterday, in the fresh-kill pile, there was a blackbird with no head. The day before, I found a sparrow with no wings, and later a squirrel without a tail." The medicine cat's voice was high-pitched with alarm, and her blue eyes were huge.

Cloudstar shrugged. "The apprentices must be hunting clumsily. I'll have a word with them later."

Fawnstep shook her head. "I've already spoken to them. They told me the prey was in one piece when they caught it."

"So what do you think it means?" Cloudstar prompted. He still felt untroubled, boosted by the memory of his dream with three noble leaders assuring him that SkyClan would survive forever.

"Our prey is being diminished, made smaller," Fawnstep meowed. She traced a circle in the leaf mulch with her front paw, then sliced across it, cutting it in half. "Our hunting is getting smaller—literally, from what we find in the fresh-kill pile to the places we can hunt."

"You mean, because of what the Twolegs are doing?"

Fawnstep nodded. "The noise and stench have scared off the prey already. And we don't know what the Twolegs are doing there. What if they cross our boundary and start to take over our territory? We know they don't respect scent marks."

Cloudstar rested the tip of his tail on Fawnstep's shoulder. "There's no reason to believe that will happen. Trust me. I walked with other SkyClan leaders in StarClan last night, and they promised that no harm will come to us. I appreciate you telling me this, but I'm sure it's just a sign that we need to take more care with our hunting."

He turned to go, and Fawnstep stood up behind him. As he walked away, she called out, "I'll keep looking, Cloudstar. Something is coming, I fear."

As Cloudstar entered the circle of birch trees, the long grass rippled and Birdflight sat up. Crushed grass showed where she had been sprawling on her side, basking in a beam of sunlight. Cloudstar trotted over and rubbed his muzzle against her shoulder. "How are those wriggly little ones today?" he murmured.

"Alive and kicking!" Birdflight replied, sounding breathless. "It helps to walk, sometimes. Will you come with me?"

"Of course," mewed Cloudstar. "But we're not going far. I don't want to have to carry you back!"

"Cheeky fox!" Birdflight scolded, flicking him with her tail.

They padded out of the birches and walked through the trees toward the river. The undergrowth thinned as the ground sloped down to the water. Birdflight settled herself on a patch of soft grass and Cloudstar sat beside her. The water flowed swiftly past, too deep for wading—not that any Sky-Clan cat would willingly get their paws wet.

"Our kits will love playing here when they're old enough to leave camp," Birdflight commented, gazing around the flat, sandy shore.

Cloudstar nodded to a rock that stood at the edge of the beach. "I remember jumping off that for the first time when I was a new apprentice. I thought I was flying!"

"Until you bumped your head and went wailing back to the camp," Birdflight put in. She was several moons older than him, and had been a warrior already when he was made an apprentice.

"It didn't put me off for long, though," Cloudstar retorted. "I came back the next day and landed on the far side of that tree stump!" He rested his front paw on Birdflight's bulging flank. "I'll teach our kits to keep trying, even if things go wrong at first. They're going to be so brave."

"Just like you," purred Birdflight.

"And kind and smart like you," Cloudstar murmured, burying his nose in her soft fur.

"Well, we can only hope so," Birdflight teased. She rolled over and sat up, looking straight into Cloudstar's eyes. "I am very proud to be having your kits," she whispered. "No cat could wish for a better father than you."

"Or a better mother than you," Cloudstar replied. He closed his eyes to drink in her scent, and as he did he felt the stirrings of warrior ancestors around him, wishing him well and watching over him, his mate, and his kits forever.

CHAPTER 3

❧

Cloudstar crouched down, balancing his weight on his haunches as his hind claws sank into the soft bark. Then he pushed hard and thrust upward, reaching out with his forepaws for the branch above. His claws slid for a heartbeat, then gripped the tree limb and held his weight just long enough for him to swing his hindquarters up and climb onto the branch.

"Whoa! Way to go, Cloudstar!" chirped a voice far below.

"Seriously? 'Way to go, Cloudstar!' He's our *leader*, don't you know?" snapped a different voice.

"Sorry, Cloudstar!" called the first cat. "I was just really impressed!"

Cloudstar suppressed an amused purr as he steadied himself in the tree and looked down at the apprentices below. He loved these sessions with his young Clanmates, when he got to indulge his love of climbing—sometimes so fast that it felt like *flying*—while teaching them a few of his favorite tricks. Cloudstar always sent the mentors off on a hunting patrol, leaving him alone with the apprentices so he could see for himself their excitement, the moment their nerves about being so high up gave way to delight in the power it gave them over their prey and their enemies.

"Okay, Tansypaw," he meowed down to the cream she-cat, who was standing on her hind legs with her front paws resting on the trunk of the tree. "Since you were watching so closely, why don't you join me?"

"Yeah, and give us all some peace down here," muttered her brother Snailpaw.

"Snailpaw and Mintpaw can follow whichever route you choose," Cloudstar added, making Tansypaw shoot a triumphant glance over her shoulder at her littermates. *There's plenty of time for you to learn to control your high spirits,* Cloudstar thought. *Let's make use of them now to give you courage that might be lacking in the others.*

Sure enough, Snailpaw and Mintpaw moved more slowly toward the tree, their neck fur ruffled and their eyes huge and serious. Snailpaw's dark brown pelt merged with the bark as he found his first paw holds just above his head; Mintpaw's fur glowed pale gray in the shadows. The leaves just below Cloudstar shook frantically, and Tansypaw emerged, clinging to the trunk, her ears flat with the effort.

"Move onto that branch there," Cloudstar instructed, pointing with his tail. "Then you'll be able to jump up to me."

Tansypaw blinked, then reached out with one front paw and rested it on the branch.

"Unsheathe your claws again," meowed Cloudstar. "You'll need them for gripping." He ran his own smooth pad over the branch. He often climbed claws-sheathed now, for extra speed and to prove to himself that he could. *After all, squirrels don't have claws like ours!*

Tansypaw was just gathering herself to jump when Snail-paw and Mintpaw scrabbled up the trunk. "Be careful," Tansypaw yelped. "You're shaking my branch!"

"Pretend it's the wind," Cloudstar suggested. "You have to learn to climb in all kinds of weather, otherwise we'd go hungry every time there was a breeze!"

Tansypaw gritted her teeth and leaped toward Cloudstar, legs flailing. He stepped backward and grabbed the young cat's scruff as she scrabbled madly for the branch. He hauled her next to him, waiting until she had found her balance.

"Wow! That was easy!" Tansypaw puffed. Cloudstar disentangled his jaws from her neck fur and nodded.

By now, Snailpaw and Mintpaw had made it onto the lower branch. Cloudstar instructed them to jump one by one, then braced himself to catch them when they leaped close enough. Snailpaw jumped too high, and Tansypaw had to grab his tail to stop him from slithering straight over the branch and down into empty air. Mintpaw made a much neater leap and landed without Cloudstar's help. The pale gray she-cat purred in delight.

"Right," Cloudstar meowed. "Let's head for the next tree."

"But we've only just climbed this one," Snailpaw protested. "I don't want to go down again straight away."

Cloudstar twitched his ears. "Who said anything about going down again? Our enemies would pounce on us! We're going to practice branch-skipping!"

Snailpaw's eyes bulged, but Tansypaw danced excitedly.

"Yes! I've always wanted to learn how to do that!"

Snailpaw let out a yelp as the branch bounced. "Stop jiggling, Tansypaw!" he shrieked.

Cloudstar stepped forward and steadied the young cat against his shoulder. "You're okay, Snailpaw. Tansypaw, remember that the branch is more sensitive to your weight the farther you go from the trunk. You can bounce your enemies off, but not your Clanmates!"

Once Snailpaw had found his balance again, Cloudstar jumped onto the next branch up. "I'll show you how to cross to the nearest tree, and you follow from where you are." He felt three pairs of eyes scorching his gray-and-white pelt as he stepped carefully to the end of the branch. It was thinner than the one below, and for a moment Cloudstar felt his belly lurch as the limb dipped toward the ground. Then it steadied, and he took a deep breath, fixing his eyes on the next tree.

"Look for a branch that is at least as thick as the one you're on," he told the apprentices. "And without too many twigs or leaves, because they could get in your way. Most of all, be realistic. You're not going to be able to jump farther up here than you can on the ground. When you get it right, it will feel like flying, but as far as I know, cats have never had wings!"

He gently let out his breath, then sprang forward, stretching out his front legs toward the closest twigs. It was an easy jump—he didn't want to scare the apprentices in their first lesson—and he landed lightly with all four paws on the new perch. He spun around and nodded to the young cats staring anxiously from the other tree. "Come on!"

Tansypaw went first. She screwed up her face in concentration until her pink nose almost disappeared in cream-colored fur. Then she launched herself out of the tree, hung briefly in midair, and slammed into the neighboring branch. Cloudstar braced himself to leap down and help her, but Tansypaw managed to dig her claws into the bark and haul herself onto the tree.

"I did it!" she yowled triumphantly.

"Excellent!" meowed Cloudstar. "Snailpaw, now it's your turn. Look at the place where you're going to land, that's right. Keep your eyes fixed there . . . and *jump!*"

The dark brown tabby flew out of the tree as if all the cats in ThunderClan were chasing him and made a desperate grab for the end of Tansypaw's branch. For a moment he dangled from his front paws, his hind legs swinging into space, but with a grunt of determination he swung his back feet underneath him and scrambled onto the branch.

"Great!" called Cloudstar. Even Tansypaw looked impressed.

Finally it was Mintpaw's turn. Cloudstar watched her closely; she was smaller than her littermates, so this was going to feel like a bigger jump. Staring at the end of the branch until her eyes almost crossed, Mintpaw sprang into the air with a tiny squeak. Tansypaw and Snailpaw shuffled out of her way as she landed next to them, balanced almost perfectly on all four paws.

"Wow! That was awesome!" Tansypaw mewed. Mintpaw looked thrilled.

Cloudstar jumped down to join them. "Ready for some fun?" he challenged. "Watch where I go, give each other time to land, and if you don't feel like you can do any of the jumps, there's no shame in letting me know, and we can all go down to the ground again. It's not a competition or an assessment."

Three small heads nodded at him. Cloudstar wriggled around to the far side of the trunk and gazed into the trees, judging where to head next. There was a pine tree close by, but the apprentices weren't ready to do battle with those spiky needles just yet, so Cloudstar aimed for a young oak tree with thick, well-spaced branches. He checked once to make sure the others were following, then thrust himself into the air. *I feel sorry for the other Clans. Who'd want to be trapped on the ground all the time, never knowing the rush of air through your fur or the sight of the forest spreading out around you?*

The three cats followed, one by one, this time looking more confident as they landed beside him. "Oak bark is particularly good for paw holds," Cloudstar explained as he trotted along the branch. "It has deeper grooves than birch, for example, which can feel like ice, especially if it's wet."

In a series of joyous, soaring leaps, he led the apprentices around the edge of the pine forest, close to the boundary where the Twolegs were moving earth. The air was thick with noise and tremors from the yellow monsters, and Mintpaw squealed in alarm when one of them loomed out of the trees below them, churning along the ground with strange, elongated paws.

"Get back against the trunk!" Cloudstar ordered. There

was nothing to suggest that the yellow monster was hunting cats, but he didn't want to take any chances. The cats were in a sycamore tree now, with broad green leaves that offered good cover. Cloudstar waited until the apprentices were pressed against the trunk, then curled his body around them, facing out. He'd wait until the yellow monster had passed before taking them to the next tree.

Suddenly the roaring of the monster got even louder, and the tree began to tremble. "What's happening?" yelped Snail-paw.

"The monster must be stuck," Cloudstar meowed, trying to peer down through the leaves. He could see the yellow shape directly below, its paws flinging up mud and leaves as they churned on the spot. As Cloudstar leaned over, the tree shuddered so violently that he lost his grip and started to plunge headfirst off the branch. There was a searing pain in his haunches as all three apprentices sank their teeth into his fur and dragged him back up.

"Cloudstar!" gasped Mintpaw. "You nearly fell!"

The tree was swaying now, and shaking so hard that leaves were starting to fall around them. "We need to get out of here!" Cloudstar panted. "Follow me!"

He began to pull himself along the branch, keeping three sets of claws dug into the bark while he moved one foot at a time. The closest tree to them was a fir; the apprentices would have to learn about the dangers of prickly needles sooner than Cloudstar had hoped. Halfway to the end of the branch, the tree lurched sideways. Behind him, the apprentices shrieked in terror. Cloudstar looked down and saw the ground looming toward him. The tree was *falling*!

"Hold on to the trunk!" he yowled, slithering around and hurtling back to the others in a single stride. Whimpering, the young cats clung to the trunk with their front paws. Cloudstar hung on to the branch and tried to keep the apprentices in place with his body. The tree hovered in the air for a moment as if it was trying to resist, then plunged downward with a dreadful crashing of branches. Cloudstar's branch hit the ground and folded in on itself, swallowing him in leaves and twigs with a deafening roar. Cloudstar felt his claws being yanked out of the bark, and the world went black around him.

"Cloudstar? Are you there?" A trembling mew roused him, coming from somewhere in a tangle of leaves near his haunches. Cloudstar struggled to sit up, spitting out scraps of dirt. His spine stung and one of his paws felt strange and numb, but he could move all his legs, and his vision cleared when he shook his head.

He scrambled out and clambered over the debris to the heap of leaves. "Tansypaw? Snailpaw? Mintpaw?"

He started to dig down, carefully at first then increasingly frantic. He could hear the yellow monster bellowing close by, as if it wanted to crush the fallen tree into shards. *We have to get out of here!* Then his paw struck against something furry and solid, and Tansypaw's head popped up.

"Cloudstar! The tree fell!" she squeaked.

"I know," he said grimly. He sank his teeth into Tansypaw's scruff and hauled her out. Snailpaw was underneath her, the breath knocked out of him, but at least he was awake and squirming. Cloudstar helped him out and told him to lie still while he got his breath back.

Tansypaw was peering down into the tangle of broken branches. "Where's Mintpaw?" she yowled.

Cloudstar pushed Tansypaw out of the way and stared into the shadows. A tuft of pale fur was just visible under some shattered twigs. Cloudstar jumped down and carefully moved the twigs aside. Mintpaw was lying very still, her eyes closed, but her flank rose and fell steadily, and she murmured when Cloudstar touched her. *She's alive!*

He hoisted her onto his shoulders and clambered back up to the others. "Is she dead?" Snailpaw wailed, staring at his sister in horror.

"No, but we need to get her to Fawnstep as quickly as we can," Cloudstar meowed. "Are you two okay to run?" The apprentices nodded bravely. Cloudstar straightened Mintpaw on his shoulders, then started to pick his way out of the crushed branches. He could hear Snailpaw and Tansypaw helping each other behind him.

They had almost reached the edge of the destroyed tree when there was a terrible creaking noise, and the earth beneath Cloudstar's paws shook so much that Mintpaw slithered to the ground.

"Watch out!" screeched Tansypaw.

Cloudstar looked up just as the fir tree plunged toward him. For a moment he was frozen, imagining what it would feel like to be crushed beneath branches laden with pine needles; then he sprang backward, dragging Mintpaw's limp body with him, and the tip of the fir tree crashed to the ground less than a tail-length from his muzzle. Beyond the fallen tree, a yellow monster roared in triumph. A Twoleg sat astride it, raising his naked pink paw in the air as he gestured to his companions standing among the trees.

"StarClan, help us!" whispered Snailpaw. "The Twolegs are destroying the forest!"

CHAPTER 4

Cloudstar's spine was throbbing as he stumbled into the clearing and let Mintpaw slide to the ground. Tansypaw and Snailpaw collapsed beside her, their fur full of debris and their eyes round with horror.

"What in the name of StarClan has happened?" gasped Mousefang, running over to Snailpaw and sniffing at her apprentice's fur in disbelief.

"The forest is being crushed!" Snailpaw whimpered. "A monster knocked down the tree we were in!"

"Oh my whiskers, you could have been killed!" Mousefang yowled. "Fawnstep! Come quickly!"

The medicine cat trotted out of her den, her nostrils flaring as she smelled the fear and scent of broken branches. She raced over to Mintpaw and gently rolled the apprentice onto her side. "Mintpaw, can you hear me?"

By now the clearing was filling with cats, wide-eyed and murmuring in hushed tones. Fernpelt hurtled out of the warriors' den and stared in horror at the cats lying on the ground. "My kits! What have you done to them?" She glared accusingly at Cloudstar.

He shook a piece of twig from his fur and faced his Clanmate. "The Twolegs and their monsters have invaded our territory," he reported, feeling his heart wrench with each word. *I have to be strong. My Clan needs me more than it ever has before. I can't let them see how scared I am.* "The apprentices and I were in a tree when it was pushed over by one of the yellow monsters."

Fernpelt let out a faint shriek. The brambles crackled and Buzzardtail emerged, followed by the rest of his hunting patrol. They were dragging a small squirrel, but nothing more. Buzzardtail took one look at the cats lying on the ground and ran to the side of his mate. "Fernpelt, what's going on?"

"They were in a tree!" she whimpered. "They almost got killed!"

Buzzardtail looked at Cloudstar. Cloudstar nodded. "I was with them," he mewed. "StarClan saved us, for sure."

The deputy turned to follow Fernpelt to the injured cats, but paused for a moment. "We've lost that border, haven't we?" he mewed quietly to Cloudstar.

"Yes. I'll take a patrol at nightfall to assess the damage. Will you come with me?"

Buzzardtail twitched his ears. "Of course." As he padded over to join Fernpelt, Quailheart brushed past him with a mouthful of herbs from Fawnstep's den.

"I've brought comfrey, marigold, and poppy seeds," she reported, placing the bundle at Fawnstep's paws.

The medicine cat looked up from Mintpaw's unmoving body. "I can't find any broken bones or wounds. I think she's just stunned. Get someone to help you take her into my den, and sit with her until I've treated the others."

"I'll carry her," meowed Buzzardtail. He crouched down and Quailheart heaved the small gray cat onto his shoulders. The deputy straightened up and walked slowly to the medicine cat's den with Quailheart on his heels.

"Tansypaw is bleeding!" wailed Fernpelt, who was examining her daughter's cream pelt.

"Okay, I have cobweb and marigold for that," Fawnstep mewed calmly. "Snailpaw, what are your injuries?"

The apprentice sniffed at his pelt. "I feel like the tree fell right on top of me," he complained. "But I don't see any blood."

Fawnstep began applying a mixture of marigold and comfrey to the cut on Tansypaw's hind leg. "Can you move all your legs? Any numbness?" Fawnstep called across to Snailpaw.

The apprentice stretched each leg in turn with a slight wince, then shook his head. "Good," mewed Fernpelt. "Eat half a poppy seed and get some rest. The poppy will help you sleep, but be prepared for the bruises to feel even worse tomorrow."

"And what about you?" mewed a soft voice in Cloudstar's ear. "Are you hurt?"

He turned and looked into Birdflight's troubled blue eyes. "I ache all over," he admitted. "But I don't need any herbs."

Birdflight blinked. "Fernpelt's right. You could have died."

"There are always dangers in the forest," Cloudstar pointed out.

"Not like this! Not inside our territory!" Birdflight gazed at him. "It's bad, isn't it?"

"Yes," Cloudstar admitted. "It's bad."

"Should we prepare to leave?" asked Nightfur, padding over with his apprentice, Oakpaw, beside him.

"And go where?" Mousefang demanded. "Twolegplace? Across the river? RiverClan might have something to say about that."

"We're not going anywhere," Cloudstar declared, drawing in a painful breath as he raised his voice. Around him, his Clanmates fell silent and stared at him. "We are safe here. Tomorrow we will assess how far the Twolegs have invaded, and set new border marks. This is our home."

"But we don't know how far the Twolegs will come!" blurted Hazelwing. "My kits are far too small to survive falling trees!"

"No, we're not," Hatchkit insisted. "I'll chase those Twolegs off if they come anywhere near us! Grrrr!"

"We don't stand a chance against the yellow monsters," Rainleap put in. "SkyClan is going to be *destroyed*!"

"Never say that!" Cloudstar snarled. "As your leader, I will give my last breath to keep you safe. I promise the Twolegs will not harm a hair on our pelts or touch one branch of our homes. StarClan is watching over us—how else would we have escaped the falling tree today? They know that this is our home, and they will protect it."

"Are you sure?" meowed Stoatfur. He was standing beside Tansypaw, keeping his apprentice still while the poultice on her wounds dried. "Did you see them fighting the Twolegs and their yellow monsters? Did they catch you as the tree fell?"

"That's not the way StarClan works, and you know it,"

Cloudstar replied, forcing his fur to stay flat. "We must have faith."

"And we must have faith in Cloudstar, too," rasped a frail voice from the edge of the clearing. A rose-cream she-cat with dark green eyes stood trembling at the entrance to the elders' den. "He has led us well until now, and we should listen to him."

"Thank you, Petalfall," Cloudstar meowed, dipping his head. "You need to get some rest. One of the apprentices will bring you something to eat."

The elderly cat turned to go back into her den. "Ah, don't trouble the young ones with chasing after me," she grunted. "Let them feed the rest of the Clan first. Toothless old badgers like me don't deserve the pick of the fresh-kill pile."

In three strides, Cloudstar had crossed the clearing and was standing close to Petalfall. "Never let me hear you talk like that!" he hissed quietly. "You served your Clan as well as any cat here—in fact, better than most." *If you hadn't started suffering with the falling sickness, you would be leader in my place. You know that as well as I do.* Before the previous leader, Flystar, had lost his ninth life, his deputy Petalfall had been forced to retire to the elders' den after suffering a number of alarming fits, when she lost consciousness for a while and trembled on the ground like a wind-tossed leaf. Fawnstep seemed to keep the fits at bay with tiny doses of poppy seed, but the she-cat was far frailer than she should have been, and rarely ventured out of the camp now.

"Petalfall, are you refusing to eat again?" called a voice

from inside the elders' den. It was Starlingfeather. There was a rustling sound and the dark brown tom stuck his head out of the branches. "I heard what happened by the border," he meowed to Cloudstar. He turned to Petalfall. "Sounds like Cloudstar has enough to sort out without you making a fuss about food," he snorted. "Now get in here and stop distracting him." The old tom's tone was curt, but Cloudstar noticed the way he gently laid his tail across Petalfall's shoulders to steer her back to her nest.

Slowly the clearing emptied, with Birdflight helping Hazelwing round up the thoroughly overexcited kits and herd them back to the nursery. Cloudstar and Buzzardtail were left alone. Shadows gathered beneath the trees, and above them the purple sky was starting to show claw-pricks of starlight.

"When do you want to go to the border?" Buzzardtail asked.

Cloudstar tilted his head and listened for a moment. The forest was quiet now, and the earth beneath his feet was still. The Twolegs and the yellow monsters had stopped whatever they were doing. "Let's round up a patrol right away," Cloudstar suggested. "The sooner we're back, the longer we'll all have to rest before dawn."

Accompanied by the gentle rustle of leaves and the occasional hoot of a lonely owl, Cloudstar led his warriors along one of their familiar hunting paths. His paws rang softly on the packed earth, and his breath clouded around his muzzle. *Oh my precious home. I grieve for the wounds that have been done to you. I promise I will never leave you, not until it is time for me to walk in StarClan.*

Cloudstar's thoughts were jerked back to the present by a stifled curse from behind him.

"Great StarClan, what is *that*?" Weaselwhisker had stopped dead and was staring at the heap of splintered branches and fast-wilting leaves that blocked the path in front of them.

"Is that the tree you were in?" gasped Mousefang.

Cloudstar looked at the leaves. This was an oak, not a sycamore. "No," he mewed. "Our tree is closer to the border."

"Then they've come even farther than you thought," Buzzardtail meowed. "How can we possibly tell our Clanmates that the camp is safe?" His voice rose with thinly veiled panic.

Cloudstar sank his claws into the damp earth. "There is no reason for the Twolegs to destroy our forest! We have lived here unchallenged for countless moons. StarClan has given me no warning that anything will change, so we have no option but to set new border marks and carry on as we always have done." To make his point, he walked up to the crumpled branches and left his scent mark defiantly on the withered leaves.

"And you think the Twolegs will take notice of that, do you?" muttered Weaselwhisker. His brown-and-ginger pelt looked gray in the half-light.

"What else can we do?" Cloudstar retorted, trying to sound strong rather than bleak with despair. "The warrior code tells us to mark our borders daily. From now on, this is our border."

"And if the Twolegs leave the fallen trees alone, we can still hunt as far as the old border," Mousefang put in.

"Hunting what? Tasty morsels like this?" Stoatfur asked, flicking a squashed and shriveled worm toward his Clanmate. There were several littered on the path around them. "Even they've had the good sense to try to escape."

"*This is our home*," Cloudstar insisted through gritted teeth. "SkyClan will survive as it always has, by the skill of its hunting and the courage to adapt to a changed territory." He lifted his head and stared at each of his warriors in turn. "Anything else will be considered a direct challenge to my leadership, and to the warrior code."

One by one, the cats nodded.

"Stay strong," Cloudstar urged them. "Have faith in our ancestors, and in the home they chose for us. We have a right to be here, more than the Twolegs and their monsters."

Buzzardtail looked away, and Cloudstar heard him murmur, "I don't think the Twolegs live by our code."

"Go back to the camp and get some rest," Cloudstar ordered. "I'll stay here tonight to keep watch. From now on, one of us will be on guard at this border every night. We will not leave our territory unprotected for a moment." As he watched his warriors file away into the trees, Cloudstar felt a pain deep in his chest that had nothing to do with his fall in the tree. *May StarClan go with you, my precious Clanmates*, he prayed silently. *And may our ancestors keep you safe where I cannot.*

CHAPTER 5
&

Cloudstar was jolted awake by a terrible clattering noise. He was curled on the trunk of one of the fallen trees, enclosed by leaves that dangled limply as they died with the broken branches. He sprang up and peered over the top of his makeshift den. In the harsh dawn light, the remains of SkyClan's former border looked ravaged and horrifying. Shattered trees lay everywhere, with the brown earth churned up around them like an open wound. Cloudstar looked wildly at the line of trees still standing behind him. Were the Twolegs destroying even more of the territory?

But those trees were standing as tall as ever, though their branches trembled with the noise. Cloudstar looked back at the devastation and saw one of the fallen trees quivering as if it was trying to make its way back into the forest. With a jerk, it started to slide along the ground, in a din of scraping bark and snapping branches. Cloudstar realized it was being dragged on a long, silver tendril attached to a yellow monster, whose paws scrabbled at the mud as it tried to get a grip on the slippery leaf mulch. Slowly, slowly, the tree was hauled away from its stricken companions until it disappeared behind one of the huge mounds of earth. There was a volley of Twoleg shouts, and another yellow monster crawled forward, trailing a silver tendril that was bound tightly around the trunk of the next tree.

But somehow this didn't seem as troubling as the devastation of the trees in the first place. *And the Twolegs are leaving the standing trees alone today. Perhaps they have destroyed as many as they want.* Cloudstar jumped down, set fresh border marks on the trunks of the trees still standing, and ran back into the woods.

When he entered the camp, Fawnstep met him. She looked as if she hadn't slept for a moon; her fur stood on end and was littered with scraps of dirt, and her eyes were huge and bulging. "Have they destroyed more trees?" she demanded as soon as Cloudstar wriggled free from the brambles.

"Not today," he reported. "The Twolegs seem to be moving the trees they pushed down yesterday."

Fawnstep's eyes narrowed. "Moving them? Where? Why?"

Cloudstar headed for his den, longing to wash the dust from his fur. "How am I supposed to know?" he snapped. "It's bad enough having Twolegs troubling our borders. I'm not going to start knowing how their brains work!" He pushed his way into his den and flopped into his nest.

Fawnstep followed him and hovered at the edge of the quiet, shadowy space. "I'm sorry," she mewed. "I know we'll never understand the ways of Twolegs. But if we could just figure out what they're doing, we might know how much danger we're in."

Cloudstar looked at her. "Have you received any more

omens?" He was reluctantly starting to acknowledge the headless and wingless prey as a warning of what was happening now.

Fawnstep blinked. "No more omens, but my dreams are full of darkness and falling trees and the screams of kits." She shuddered as she spoke, and Cloudstar felt a stab of pity for his gentle, intuitive medicine cat.

"I think all our dreams will be like that for a while," he murmured. "Let me rest for a bit, and tell Buzzardtail to get on with organizing the patrols. We'll hunt as normal, tell him." He tucked his nose beneath his tail and closed his eyes as he listened to Fawnstep pad softly out of the den.

Cloudstar had barely dozed off when Stoatfur woke him up, prodding him with one paw. "Sorry to disturb you, Cloudstar," he mewed. "Buzzardtail asked me to lead a border patrol, but with three of the apprentices out of action, I need you to make up the numbers."

Cloudstar hauled himself stiffly out of his nest and stretched each leg in turn. "Okay," he meowed. "Let's go."

He let Stoatfur take the lead, and walked beside Quailheart and Rainleap as they headed into the dense trees that lay between the camp and the border with ThunderClan. The yellow monsters rumbled in the distance, and where the ground was bare of leaf mulch, Cloudstar could feel the earth trembling beneath his paws. *Where are they taking the trees? And why?* The cats were used to fir trees being harvested by Twolegs, but not the trees that shed their leaves in the coldest seasons.

Stoatfur directed Rainleap to refresh the first border mark they came to, on a tree stump covered with ivy. At the next, a twisted hazel tree, Stoatfur nodded to Cloudstar, offering him the task. Cloudstar stepped forward, enjoying the role of a warrior rather than leader. He was about to rejoin the patrol when a hiss through the bracken stopped him.

"Patrolling the borders again, Cloudstar?" The bracken rustled and a dark ginger tom stepped through. "Seedpelt told me she'd seen you here recently. Is SkyClan lacking in warriors?"

Cloudstar forced his fur to stay flat. "There is no reason why a Clan leader shouldn't patrol with his warriors," he growled. "After all, isn't that what you're doing here, Redstar?"

The ThunderClan leader flicked his tail as if he was bored of the subject and padded forward until he was almost muzzle to muzzle with Cloudstar. "What's all this noise we hear coming from your territory?" he asked, leaning close to peer into Cloudstar's eyes. "Is there trouble in SkyClan?" His yellow eyes gleamed hungrily.

Behind him, Cloudstar heard Quailheart snarl. "No, no trouble at all," Cloudstar replied. "Just some Twolegs playing with monsters beyond the far boundary. My Clanmates know better than to fret about every little thing a Twoleg does. Is the noise making your warriors nervous, Redstar?"

The ThunderClan leader curled his lip, and Cloudstar felt a small stab of satisfaction that he had gotten under Redstar's fur. "Nothing scares ThunderClan warriors!" Redstar growled.

Cloudstar turned to leave. "If they have any sense, they should be more wary of SkyClan warriors!" he called over his shoulder. His Clanmates fell in behind him as he stalked away from the hazel tree, leaving Redstar glaring after them.

Once out of sight of the ThunderClan cat, Cloudstar stepped off the path to let Stoatfur take the lead again. The orange-and-white tom looked anxious. "Don't you think you should have told Redstar the truth?" he meowed. "That our border has been destroyed, and we have lost territory?"

Cloudstar stared at him. "Have moths got into your brain? Why would I let ThunderClan know there is anything wrong?"

Stoatfur scraped one paw over the ground. "Because if the Twolegs destroy much more of the forest, we might need ThunderClan's help."

"ThunderClan warriors can't chase off Twolegs and monsters!" Rainleap snapped. "I'd rather die than ask them for help!"

Cloudstar twitched his ears. "That's a little extreme, Rainleap. But you're right: SkyClan will fight its own battles."

"What about the territory that used to belong to us?" Stoatfur persisted, nodding toward the dense strip of oak trees just beyond the SkyClan scent marks. "If we lose much more from the far side of our hunting grounds, we should ask Thunder-Clan to give it back."

Cloudstar bristled. "SkyClan can survive without it. I will never go groveling to Redstar to get us out of trouble, and we can't go back on Duskstar's decision to let them have that territory. It would be like challenging all our ancestors, as well as the warrior code." He gazed at each of his warriors in turn, wincing at their troubled eyes and ruffled pelts. *I have to stay strong for them.* "SkyClan will survive, without the help of ThunderClan. We are strong, skillful, and more honorable than any of the five Clans of the forest. Trust me, warriors. The Twolegs will not destroy our home."

By the time they returned to the camp, the sun was high, blazing down through the trees. Cloudstar headed straight for the stream at the edge of the camp, just beyond the elders' den, and took a long drink. His pelt felt itchy and dusty, and his legs ached, but he had insisted on double-checking all the border marks. He didn't trust Redstar. Cloudstar was beginning to fear he had been too relaxed about letting ThunderClan warriors cross the border by a few paw steps, in the interest of keeping things peaceful with their closest neighbor. Now he wanted to maintain a much stricter border, with more frequent patrols and marks refreshed three times a day, not just twice.

Padding back into the clearing, Cloudstar's belly rumbled. He trotted over to the fresh-kill pile and stopped short with a yelp of dismay. There was only a tough-looking starling and the remains of a vole under the elderflower tree. "Haven't the hunting patrols returned yet?" he called to Weaselwhisker, who was sunning himself on the tree stump in the center of the clearing.

Weaselwhisker lifted his head and peered over the edge of

the stump. "Yes, and gone out again," he reported.

"And this is all they caught?" Cloudstar exclaimed.

Weaselwhisker nodded. "They said the woods where the trees have fallen are empty, and the rest of the territory is so noisy that prey is being frightened away from there, as well."

Cloudstar cursed under his breath. "I'll go out myself," he told Weaselwhisker. Perhaps one cat alone would have a better chance of stalking nervous prey. Ignoring the pangs in his belly, he turned away from the fresh-kill pile and headed back into the woods. The trees hummed with the noise of the yellow monsters. It drowned out the rustling of the leaves, the creaking of branches, and any sound of birds or squirrels that might offer good hunting. Cloudstar felt a worm of alarm squirm in his belly. *There must be something we can eat!* Suddenly feeling impatient at being trapped on the ground, he leaped up the trunk of the closest tree and hauled himself into the branches.

He could still hear the monsters up here, but now the leaves whispered around his ears, and a soft breeze lifted his fur. Cloudstar pressed his ear to the bark and heard the tiniest scratching sound. *Squirrel!* Lifting his head, he waited for a moment, opening his jaws so that the scents of the forest flooded in. His prey was farther up the tree, on one of the thinnest branches. SkyClan warriors tended to avoid hunting at the tops of the trees because it was more dangerous, with the branches much less able to bear their weight, but hunger quelled Cloudstar's nerves. He clawed his way upward, stretching his tail behind him to keep his balance. There was a desperate scrabble above him as the squirrel spotted Cloudstar launching himself up, but Cloudstar put on an extra burst of speed and slammed one of his front paws into the tiny fluffy creature before it had a chance to run.

He studied his catch disappointedly. It was hardly old enough to be out of its nest, and wouldn't feed an elder let alone a warrior. But it was a start. Peering down through the leaves, Cloudstar carefully dropped the squirrel between the branches, then scampered down the trunk to bury it beneath a heap of earth and twigs until he collected it later.

He hunted until the sunbeams slanted low through the trees and the first star appeared in the hazy sky. He was exhausted, his pelt ruffled and filthy, and the stiffness along his spine had sharpened to a fierce burn. But all he had to add to his squirrel was a blackbird, plump enough but hardly a good meal for more than two cats. Unearthing the squirrel, Cloudstar dragged his fresh-kill back to the camp.

Birdflight was waiting for him on the far side of the brambles. "Where have you been? Weaselwhisker said you went out hunting on your own!"

Cloudstar nodded. "Let me put these on the fresh-kill pile, and let's eat together."

"I've already eaten," Birdflight meowed. "I'm sorry, I should have saved some for you." Cloudstar was about to protest when his gaze fell on the pile beneath the elderflower tree. There were a few scraps that might have been the vole he had seen earlier, but nothing else. He spun around to face Birdflight. "Has every cat eaten?"

She flinched at his fierce tone. "I think so," she mewed. "Petalfall shared hers with Hazelwing and the kits. She said she wasn't hungry."

Cloudstar curled his lip. "She's said that before."

Birdflight's eyes widened. "You think she's deliberately letting the other cats eat her share?"

Cloudstar nodded. "But if there isn't enough food to go around, we'll all have to go hungry for a while. Just until the prey comes back. Buzzardtail!" He called to his deputy, who was sharing tongues with Fernpelt outside the warriors' den. "From now on, we'll eat once a day, at dusk. There isn't enough prey for two meals a day."

Buzzardtail looked startled. "We'll starve!"

"No, we won't," Cloudstar snapped, fighting the panic rising inside his chest. "We survive on one meal during leaf-bare. Why should this be different?"

"Because we need to eat more in the warm seasons in order to survive leaf-bare!" Buzzardtail pointed out. "We won't have the strength to hunt if we're hungry all the time."

"Then figure out a different way to hunt!" Cloudstar hissed. He whirled around and stalked to his den. *They look to me for answers, but how am I supposed to conjure prey out of an empty forest?*

There were soft paw steps behind him, and Birdflight followed him into the den. "Cloudstar, I'm worried about you."

"Well, I'm worried about everyone," Cloudstar muttered, circling in his nest to flatten the moss.

"That's your duty, as our leader," Birdflight mewed. "But I just have to worry about you—and our kits, when they come.

Cloudstar, they need their father! If you work yourself to death before they arrive, I'll have to raise them alone! Please, take care of yourself for their sake, if nothing else."

Cloudstar reached out and rested his muzzle on Birdflight's shoulder. "I'm sorry. I will look after myself, I promise. And the rest of the Clan. Everything will be fine when the monsters leave and the prey comes back."

Birdflight squeezed in beside him. Cloudstar shuffled to the edge of the nest to make room for her swollen belly. "Do you really believe SkyClan will survive this?" Birdflight murmured as she settled against him.

"Of course," Cloudstar purred. "StarClan would not have made me leader if they did not know for certain that I would be able to save my Clan. Now sleep, my precious. Our kits need us both to be strong."

CHAPTER 6

Cloudstar stood at the edge of the Great Rock, washed in silver moonlight, and gazed down at the cats below. Countless pairs of eyes gleamed up at him, ears pricked, the only sound the whispering of the leaves from the four giant oaks. *How long have the five Clans gathered here?* Cloudstar wondered. *And how long will they continue? Until the Twolegs destroy these trees as well?*

There was a quiet cough from the foot of the rock, and Cloudstar saw Buzzardtail looking expectantly at him. Three sunrises had passed since Cloudstar and the apprentices were caught in the falling tree, and the Twolegs had encroached no farther onto SkyClan's territory. Instead they had cleared the ruined trees away and started to place rows of large gray stones, sharp and square, in the empty space. There was still too much noise, and the prey had not yet returned—leaving SkyClan thin and hungry on reduced fresh-kill—but Cloudstar felt a stirring of hope that the worst was over.

He had wanted to say nothing about the Twolegs at the Gathering, and let the other Clans believe that all was well in SkyClan. But Buzzardtail insisted that he had to acknowledge there was something going on. They knew that the noise of the yellow monsters had reached ThunderClan, and it was impossible that RiverClan hadn't heard something too. Better to acknowledge what the Twolegs are doing, Buzzardtail had argued, than let rumors spread among the other Clans.

Greenleaf held sway in the forest, weighting the trees with glossy green leaves and plumping the prey. The other Clans reported overflowing fresh-kill piles, healthy litters of kits, and new warriors who looked as strong and sharp as their seniors. Cloudstar pictured the scant pile of food beneath the elderflower bush, the scrawny elders, and the wails of Hazelwing's kits when their bellies ached with hunger.

Scraping his claws over the silver stone, he lifted his head. "Cats of all the Clans, I am proud to speak for the SkyClan cats. Hazelwing's kits continue to grow, and are wearing us all out with their games!" There was a purr of amusement from below, mostly from she-cats and elders. "I look forward to presenting them to you as apprentices in three more moons. My warriors are hunting with great skill for their Clanmates, and like you we are grateful for the fresh-kill that greenleaf brings to the forest." He paused and took a breath. *Stay calm! Don't let them see that you are worried one tiny whisker about what is happening.*

"I'm sure some of you have heard the rumblings of Twolegs and their monsters just beyond our border." There were nods and murmurs from below the rock, and Cloudstar felt Redstar stiffen beside him. "Well, you know Twolegs, always trying to ruin something!" Cloudstar's throat ached as he tried to keep his tone light. "They've taken a few trees at their edge of our territory, but we have plenty more. The Twolegs will get bored soon and take their monsters somewhere else." He narrowed his eyes and tried to meet the gaze of as many warriors as possible from the other Clans. "We in SkyClan would hate for you to waste time on rumors and lies about what may be going on in our territory." Cloudstar let an edge creep into his tone, but then he caught sight of Buzzardtail looking alarmed, and softened his voice a little. *I don't want to seem like I am trying to hide something.* "And by the next Gathering, I hope to have even better news. Kits of my own, thanks to Birdflight!"

There were mutters of approval; Cloudstar hoped he had distracted the cats from gossiping about Twoleg nonsense. He stepped back from the edge of the rock and sat down again. Redstar leaned over and murmured in his ear, "Glad to hear that SkyClan doesn't mind sharing their territory with Twolegs."

Cloudstar shot a fierce glance at the ginger tom, and reminded himself with an effort that this was the night of the full moon, so hostility between Clans was forbidden. "Of course we aren't sharing our territory with Twolegs," he meowed, opening his eyes wide as if surprised that Redstar would have such a mouse-brained idea. "Our borders are strong, and our scent marks refreshed as usual."

"More often than usual, I've noticed," Redstar commented, with the tiniest flick of his tail.

Cloudstar was saved from replying by Swiftstar, the Wind-Clan leader, standing up and stretching each leg in turn. "Ah, I'm getting too old to sit on this cold rock for long," he grunted. "Shall we join the others?"

Dawnstar of ShadowClan and Birchstar of RiverClan nodded, and jumped side by side down from the Great Rock. Birchstar looked plump and content beneath her glossy pelt, and even Dawnstar looked less lean than usual. Cloudstar made a deliberate effort to fluff up his fur to hide his jutting ribs. In spite of his promise to Birdflight, he had been eating less than any of his warriors. *The prey will come back before our kits arrive*, he told himself.

Fawnstep was waiting for him at the foot of the rock. "Cloudstar, can we talk?" Her blue eyes looked anxious.

Cloudstar followed her into the shadows behind the stone. "It's the other medicine cats," Fawnstep told him, her voice trembling. "They've all had dreams about us, about SkyClan being swallowed up by yellow monsters, trampled like dust beneath falling trees. Molepelt of ShadowClan is convinced we will all be dead before the next Gathering!"

"Molepelt of ShadowClan should worry more about his own warriors and less about sticking his muzzle into other Clans' business," growled Cloudstar. "He's no better than a gossiping elder! He can hardly take care of his own pelt, let alone an entire Clan."

"But the others listen to him," Fawnstep persisted. "And they are all worried about SkyClan."

Cloudstar raised his head. "Do they live in our camp? Have they seen our hunting patrols working tirelessly to find enough food for us? Do they know that the trees have stopped falling? Or have you told them we are starving to death, crippled by Twolegs and their pathetic monsters?" His voice was harsher than he intended, and Fawnstep winced.

"I have told them that we are fine and can take of ourselves," she mewed sharply. "I would never tell them anything else."

Cloudstar felt a stab of guilt for doubting his medicine cat. "I know you wouldn't. I'm sorry. Now, let's join the others before we fuel more gossip from our neighbors."

It was a strain to stay cheerful and seem interested in what was going on in the other Clans, and Cloudstar was relieved when the cats began slipping away from the hollow in search of a brief rest before dawn. He led his Clanmates back along the river at a run, wrinkling his nose at the stench of ThunderClan scent marks at the edge of the shore. SkyClan was allowed to follow the edge of the water to reach Fourtrees, but Redstar seemed determined to keep them trapped on the pebbles by a wall of reeking scent.

Quailheart met them just inside the brambles. His eyes were full of sorrow. "It's Petalfall," he meowed as soon as Cloudstar and Fawnstep emerged from the thorns. "She's had another falling fit, and she's so weak she can hardly open her eyes."

Fawnstep and Cloudstar ran to the medicine cat's den. The old she-cat lay in a faint moonbeam that filtered through the branches above her. Her rose-cream pelt was stretched tight over her jutting hip bones, and her eyes were sunken into her skull. The scent of death clung to her fur and her breath rattled in her chest. She raised her head when Cloudstar and

Fawnstep entered and opened her mouth to speak, but suddenly her whole body stiffened, her legs shot out, and her eyes rolled back. She started to tremble and foam bubbled at her lips.

Fawnstep crouched beside her. "It's all right, Petalfall," she soothed. "It will be over soon."

A high-pitched moan came from between Petalfall's clenched teeth. "Bring me two poppy seeds," Fawnstep meowed to Quailheart. The tom hurried to the store, and Cloudstar hunkered down beside the sick cat.

"Two poppy seeds?" he queried. "Is that safe?" He knew that one poppy seed was usually all Fawnstep would allow a cat to eat.

Fawnstep didn't take her eyes from Petalfall's wretched, shaking body. "Would you rather she kept having these terrible fits? If I can keep her in a deep sleep, she'll have a chance to rest and regain her strength."

Cloudstar looked down at the sharp bones that seemed about to pierce the old cat's pelt. It didn't seem to him that Petalfall had a whisker of strength left in her frail body. She needed food more than sleep, but the Clan couldn't give her that. Cloudstar swallowed the urge to yowl in despair.

Slowly, Petalfall stopped shaking. Cloudstar drew his tail softly over her flank. "Everything's fine, Petalfall. Rest now."

The old cat blinked, and one faded blue eye focused on Cloudstar. "Don't lie to me, Cloudstar," she rasped, so quietly that Cloudstar had to bend closer. He winced at the stench of her breath, and hoped she hadn't noticed.

"I may be old, but I'm not dumb," Petalfall croaked. "I know we are in great trouble. Oh my poor Clan. We have survived so much, yet now we will be destroyed by Twolegs."

"No, Petalfall!" Cloudstar mewed in her ear. "SkyClan can still survive this!"

The clouded eye swiveled to hold his gaze with a stony glare. "Promise me, Cloudstar," the old cat wheezed. "Promise me you will not let the Twolegs drive us from our home."

"I promise," Cloudstar whispered. "This is where SkyClan belongs. For as long as I have my nine lives, we will never leave the forest."

CHAPTER 7

❧

Faint, cream-colored beams of light filtered through the branches, heralding the sunrise. Cloudstar tried to straighten his hind leg without disturbing Petalfall. The old cat had eaten the poppy seeds and fallen into a deep slumber, broken only by rumbling snores. Cloudstar had stayed beside her, too troubled to close his eyes but unwilling to let Petalfall sleep alone. She was used to being warmed by the fur of the other elders close beside her.

"Cloudstar!" Fawnstep's soft mew pierced the hushed den. "Stop wriggling, or you'll wake Petalfall! Why don't you go for a walk?" The medicine cat loomed out of the shadows. "Go on, I'll lie beside Petalfall until she wakes."

Cloudstar heaved himself up, stumbling on numb paws, and crept out of the den. Outside, the air was already warm and tiny flies buzzed around his ears. The camp was silent; it was too early even for the dawn patrols. Cloudstar crawled under the bramble bush and trotted through the quiet trees. For once, the forest was silent. It was too early for the Twolegs and their yellow monsters to be awake. But the silence felt wrong. Cloudstar's ears buzzed as he strained to hear the sound of any other living creatures. There were no bird-calls greeting the dawn, no squirrels scampering along the branches, not even butterflies stirring with the first rays of the sun. The forest felt empty, lifeless, and for the first time in Cloudstar's life, unwelcoming.

He emerged from the woods where the trees had been felled and stood on a splintered stump to survey the devastation. This part of the forest had changed beyond anything Cloudstar could recognize. Where was the tiny path used by badgers and deer that had led to the open heathland beyond? Or the holly bush that had once sheltered Cloudstar and his fellow apprentices during a hailstorm? All the trees had gone, and now the squares of gray stones were being covered with smaller, bright red stones. Some rows were tall enough to have gaps in them, some spaces reaching all the way to the ground and others stopping at the height of a young Twoleg. Something stirred in Cloudstar's mind. These constructions looked familiar . . . half-built, but definitely something he had seen before.

Twoleg nests! The Twolegs are building new nests on SkyClan's territory!

Cloudstar looked around him. This was *his* home! Not the Twolegs'! Cloudstar felt a pain in his chest as if a Clanmate had died. There would be no chance to reclaim this part of the territory. It was lost forever, to Twolegs and their kits and monsters. Would they stop here? Or keep swallowing up the forest, tree by tree, until nothing remained? Cloudstar felt a yowl rise in his throat, and he tipped back his head and let his cry echo his despair across the half-built stone nests.

"My home! My precious home!"

His legs felt heavy as stone as he made his way back to the camp. What was he going to tell the Clan? They deserved to keep some whisker of hope. Perhaps Cloudstar didn't have to force them to face the truth yet—at least, not until he had figured out a way for them to survive this. When he crawled through the brambles, he knew this was not the time to tell them anything. A soft keening sound came from Fawnstep's den; it was Starlingfeather and Hawksnow, mourning their denmate.

Fawnstep squeezed through the entrance to her den and trotted over to meet Cloudstar. "Petalfall died a few moments ago," she mewed. Her eyes were clouded with sorrow. "She was peaceful at the end. She slept well after you promised her Sky-Clan would be okay."

Cloudstar closed his eyes. *Run swiftly to StarClan, Petalfall. Don't look back. Your Clanmates will miss you, always.*

Starlingfeather and Hawksnow emerged from Fawnstep's den, rumps first, as they carefully dragged Petalfall's body into the sunlight.

"We will sit vigil for her today," Fawnstep explained to Cloudstar. "It's so hot, we must bury her body at dusk."

Cloudstar nodded. "Do you have enough herbs?" he asked. Quailheart had followed the elders out with a mouthful of soft green leaves, and was strewing them over Petalfall's fur so that the clearing filled with their grassy scent.

"I think so," Fawnstep replied. She looked at the nursery, her eyes troubled. "I'll go tell Hazelwing so she can prepare the kits. Cloudstar, it's rare I would give any orders to my Clan leader, but please, don't go out on patrol today. You need to rest as much as any of us, and without you, the Clan will have no hope at all." She ran her tail lightly along her spine as she padded away.

Cloudstar walked over and lay down beside Petalfall's head. Her eyes were closed, and she looked as if she were sleeping. *Go well in StarClan, my old friend.* The air stirred beside him, and Birdflight sat down. She was already panting from the heat.

"Do you want to move to the shade?" Cloudstar suggested, but Birdflight shook her head.

"My place is here, beside Petalfall," she meowed.

"It's like another piece of our past has been ripped away, along with the trees," Cloudstar murmured as he rested his muzzle on Petalfall's herb-sweet cheek.

"I know," mewed Birdflight. "Fawnstep told me you promised Petalfall everything would be fine, and SkyClan would not lose its home, but how can you be so certain? We cannot fight the Twolegs!"

"StarClan is watching over us," Cloudstar reminded his mate. "If we give up, we are only showing that we don't trust them to keep us safe. Have faith in them, especially now that Petalfall walks among the stars, too."

"I wanted her to meet our kits," Birdflight whispered.

"She will see them from wherever she is," Cloudstar vowed.

Buzzardtail sent out the early patrols, leading one group himself before joining Cloudstar beside Petalfall. Hazelwing had ushered her kits past, the four of them wide-eyed with curiosity at the unmoving cat. Emberkit had tried to lick Petalfall's ear to see if she tasted different now, and received a clout over her own ear from her angry mother. The whole camp was quieter than usual, muffled by sadness, yet the sun had scarcely reached the treetops before the rumbling of the monsters started up, and now Petalfall's fur quivered gently from the tremors through the earth.

Buzzardtail settled beside Cloudstar for his vigil. They sat in silence, breathing in the scent of the herbs, each with his own memories of the former deputy. Birdflight had retreated to the shade, where she lay on her side, panting in spite of the soaked moss Fawnstep had placed beneath her head.

Suddenly the brambles crackled and Mousefang burst into the clearing. "Fetch Fawnstep!" she cried.

Behind her, Nightfur's black pelt emerged from the thorns, rump first as he guided his apprentice Oakpaw through the branches. The gray tabby tom was smeared with mud and held one front paw off the ground, wincing every time he lurched forward on his other three legs. Cloudstar leaped to his feet.

"What happened?" he demanded.

Nightfur was grim faced. "We were hunting at the edge of the trees." He nodded toward the border ravaged by Twolegs. "Oakpaw found a squirrel and chased it onto the empty ground, where the Twolegs are laying red stones. He fell into a ditch they must have dug."

Fawnstep had run from her den by now and was sniffing Oakpaw's shoulder. "You're lucky," she commented. "I don't think any bones are broken. Come to my den and I'll find something to help with the pain." She led Oakpaw away, letting him rest his weight on her shoulder.

Buzzardtail came to join Cloudstar and Nightfur. "Fawnstep's right," he growled. "Oakpaw was lucky to get off so lightly. He could have broken his neck!"

Cloudstar nodded. "It's too dangerous to try to hunt there anymore. From now on, no cat must go anywhere near the new border, not even if all the squirrels in the forest are sitting on the other side."

Nightfur looked at him in surprise. "But we have to eat!"

"More importantly, we have to stay alive," Cloudstar pointed out. "That territory no longer belongs to SkyClan. The Twolegs have stolen it from us, and there is nothing we can do. We will have to look for some other way to find enough food."

CHAPTER 8

❧

"*Weaselwhisker, you take Fernpelt, Stoatfur, and* Acornpaw and hunt along the river. You might get lucky and find a vole's nest, if you don't mind getting your paws wet. Mousefang, your patrol can hunt—"

"Buzzardtail, wait!" Cloudstar ordered, striding out of his den. He dipped his head to the deputy, apologizing for interrupting him. "No cats will hunt today. I want all of them—warriors as well as apprentices—to do battle training."

Buzzardtail stared at him in surprise. "But the fresh-kill pile is almost empty! With so little prey in the forest, we have to hunt as much as we can!"

"No," meowed Cloudstar, his heart as heavy as stone. His eyes burned from his sleepless night, thrashing in his nest as he realized there was only one chance left to find enough food for his Clan. "We have to fight."

"We can't take on the Twolegs!" Weaselwhisker protested.

Cloudstar shook his head. "Not the Twolegs. Thunder-Clan. We need to take back the territory that Duskstar gave to them. Without it, we don't have enough hunting grounds to support the Clan."

Buzzardtail gave Cloudstar a long, thoughtful look. "Dusk-star would have done the same," he mewed quietly. "You're not breaking the warrior code."

Cloudstar wasn't even sure that Duskstar—or any StarClan cats—were watching SkyClan anymore. His dreams had been empty since that night the former leaders had reassured him of how strong SkyClan was, how they would live in the forest forever.

Buzzardtail started reorganizing the patrols. The appren-tices looked excited about the change in routine. "We've been hunting for days!" Acornpaw meowed. "I can't wait to try the sky-drop again!"

"I want to practice the reverse branch swing," Mintpaw mewed. "I kept falling off the branch last time, but I'm defi-nitely strong enough to hold on now."

The warriors were quieter, and Cloudstar wondered if they had realized how desperate he was, that he was prepared to go back on Duskstar's word. He stood in the center of the clearing and watched the patrols vanish into the bushes. SkyClan war-riors fought by leaping out of trees, swinging from branches, using height and weight to overpower their enemies. It had been moons since they had gone into battle against another Clan, beyond a mere border skirmish. Every bone in Cloud-star's body ached at the thought of leading his Clanmates into a fight when they were weakened by hunger and sleepless from fear of what the Twolegs were doing in their territory. But he could not see any choice. They had to expand their territory somehow.

* * *

At sunrise the following day, Cloudstar gathered the Clan beneath the gnarled thorn tree. He balanced on the spindly branches at the top of the gorse bush and gazed down at them in the soft dawn light.

"Clanmates, it is time to take back what is rightfully ours. I will be at the head of the attack, with Buzzardtail behind me. You will all get the chance to fight—except for you, Snailpaw and Mintpaw." The two apprentices let out wails of disappointment.

"But we want to fight!" Mintpaw protested. "We practiced really hard yesterday, and I only fell off the branch three times!"

"We're not scared," Snailpaw added, puffing out his soft brown fur.

"No cat doubts your courage," Cloudstar promised. "But I need strong, brave cats to stay behind and guard the queens and elders. Will you two do that for me? I know Tansypaw will help you as much as she can."

Their cream-colored littermate straightened up. She still walked with a limp where she had wrenched her shoulder, and hadn't been able to join in with the training the day before. Cloudstar prayed that these brave young cats wouldn't be called upon to defend their Clanmates while the others were away. But they were too small to take into battle, and he had to find some way of easing the frustration of being left behind.

Cloudstar looked at his warriors. They all looked thin and tired, their fur matted and their eyes sunk in their heads as if they were ready to join the elders. *Somehow, we must find strength to fight for this territory.* "Cats of SkyClan!" he declared. "Today is a glorious day! Today we have the chance to reset our border marks, to make ThunderClan realize that we will no longer tolerate their trespassing on what was SkyClan's hunting ground long before theirs."

"Yes!" cheered the warriors at the foot of the hazel bush. "We'll drive out those mangy intruders and show them that SkyClan deserves to hunt here instead!"

Buzzardtail caught Cloudstar's eye and nodded. It was time to leave. The deputy started to divide the warriors into three attack patrols, while Cloudstar jumped down from the tree. Birdflight was waiting for him. Her amber eyes were full of fear. For a moment Cloudstar was afraid she was going to tell him not to fight, to save his life for the sake of their kits.

"Even though I cannot fight alongside you," Birdflight meowed solemnly, "I will always be with you in your heart. Let me be your courage and your strength." She rested her muzzle against his shoulder, and Cloudstar breathed in her scent one more time.

He lifted his head to meet her gaze and whispered, "We have to win this battle. If we don't, everything is lost."

"Remember, I am in your heart," she whispered back.

Cloudstar straightened up and stalked across the clearing to lead his warriors out of the camp.

"To ThunderClan!" he yowled, and raced into the brambles.

* * *

The SkyClan cats launched themselves across the Thunder-Clan boundary and started pushing through the undergrowth to set new border marks on the far side of the oak trees. Cloud-star and Buzzardtail had made it clear what their plan was: set new marks, resist all challenges, and let ThunderClan know that SkyClan would no longer tolerate trespassers in this part of the forest. Cloudstar's patrol was only a few strides over the boundary when they crashed into a ThunderClan border patrol.

Startled faces whirled to look at them. "What in the name of StarClan . . . ?" yowled the ThunderClan warrior in the lead.

"We're being attacked!" snarled his Clanmate, unsheathing his claws.

"Trespassers!" hissed a third.

"No, you're the trespassers!" Cloudstar growled. "This is SkyClan's territory once more."

The first warrior let out a yelp of amusement. "Oh, really? Prove it!" He sprang at Cloudstar, landing squarely on his tender spine and sinking his teeth into Cloudstar's scruff.

Weaselwhisker leaped forward and hauled the Thunder-Clan warrior off, holding him down and pummeling him with his hind paws. Another ThunderClan jumped onto Weasel-whisker, and his brown-and-ginger pelt vanished in a flurry of fur and kicked-up leaves. Cloudstar launched himself into the tangled heap of warriors, claws out, just as more ThunderClan cats burst out of the ferns. The forest was split with shrieks and hisses as ThunderClan realized it was under attack and raced to defend its borders.

Cloudstar managed to haul Weaselwhisker out of the throng and held off one of the ThunderClan warriors while the brown-and-ginger tom caught his breath. Cloudstar risked a glance around and saw that the SkyClan cats were scrambling up into the trees. *Yes! Fight to your strengths!* he urged. The ThunderClan warriors watched, frustrated, as their enemies vanished among the branches.

"Come back and fight!" snarled one of them, flicking specks of blood from her muzzle. "Cowards!"

There was a moment's silence, then the trees exploded with cats leaping into the air. Nightfur, Weaselwhisker, and Acornpaw plunged onto a sturdy gray tom called Nettleclaw. Cloudstar felt a surge of satisfaction, then stared in dismay as the warrior shook the cats off as if they were thistledown and pounced on Acornpaw before the apprentice could find his paws. Cloudstar raced over to help, but claws seared his pelt from behind and he staggered backward, feeling hot stinking breath on his neck fur.

He whipped around and saw Seedpelt snarling at him. "SkyClan needs to learn to respect our borders," she hissed, lunging at him and raking her claws across his muzzle. Cloudstar shook blood from his nose and reared up to scratch the ThunderClan deputy's ears, but she dodged away, well fed and strong.

With a start, Cloudstar saw that even Redstar had joined the fight. He was nose to nose with Fernpelt, who had clawed a patch of fur from his flank as she swung from a branch into his hindquarters. Now she was on the ground, swiping at the dark ginger tom with alternate paws. Redstar looked down at her, then knocked her sideways with one mighty blow. Fernpelt spun away into the bracken and lay in an unmoving heap. Cloudstar was about to go to her when she scrambled up, shook herself, and raced back into the throng.

Cloudstar focused instead on an orange ThunderClan warrior named Amberclaw. The cat was looking the other way, so Cloudstar crouched down and steadied himself for a leap onto Amberclaw's haunches. Just before he sprang, a voice from above called, "Watch out!"

In the next heartbeat, Mousefang hurled herself out of the tree and plummeted through the air. But the warning she had given to Cloudstar had been heard by Amberclaw too, and the ThunderClan warrior leaped sideways. Mousefang crashed into the earth with a sickening thud. She screeched in agony. Amberclaw's eyes gleamed and he reared up on his hind legs, ready to claw her exposed belly. Cloudstar pushed down with his hind paws and sprang over Mousefang's body, slamming into Amberclaw and shoving him backward. The Thunder-Clan cat writhed underneath him, and Cloudstar realized there was no way he was going to hold the warrior still. He rolled off before Amberclaw could sink his teeth into his neck.

At least it had given Mousefang a chance to crawl away, dragging her hind leg behind her. Cloudstar caught sight of her vanishing into the ferns, and he could tell from the angle of her paw that her leg was broken. He looked around at his warriors, their rage driven by fear and hunger, and he knew they were too weak and too thin to fight the sturdy, glossy-pelted ThunderClan cats. His Clanmates were making foolish mistakes out of desperation, and too often the ThunderClan warriors were simply waiting for their attackers to stumble over their own paws. The oak trees were still drenched in ThunderClan scent, even though their trunks and the fallen leaves were spattered with SkyClan blood. Cloudstar knew this was a battle he could not win. If he let his warriors fight any longer, there would be worse injuries than Mousefang's broken leg.

Weary beyond measure, burning with pain from more than the scratches on his pelt, Cloudstar raised his head. "SkyClan, retreat!"

CHAPTER 9

❧

"Clanmates, we lost."

Cloudstar dragged his aching paws into the clearing. Every scratch on his pelt burned like fire, and his paws were numb from leaping onto the hard, dusty ground. "I'm so sorry," he murmured.

Birdflight trotted up to him, her eyes dark with horror. "You . . . you *lost*? But you said we had to win this battle!"

"Yes, we had to. But we didn't!" Cloudstar snapped. He saw Birdflight flinch, and he softened his tone. "I'm sorry. You're right, we should have won. We need that piece of territory to feed us."

Buzzardtail squeezed under the brambles, one eye closed and swollen, his pelt sticky with blood. "Go straight to Fawnstep," Cloudstar ordered.

All around the clearing, queens and elders huddled around the returning warriors. They spoke so quietly, Cloudstar could hear a thrush warbling somewhere in the territory. *Brave, foolish bird*, he thought. *If you stay here, you'll be prey tomorrow.* There were so few birds left, he wondered if he should send a warrior now to catch it. But every cat fit enough to hunt had fought in the battle, and all had come back with injuries, from ripped ears to Mousefang's broken leg.

Cloudstar wondered if StarClan had watched their humiliating defeat. It certainly hadn't felt as if any of SkyClan's warrior ancestors were on their side.

"You need to get that cut on your flank seen to," Birdflight told him.

"Not yet," Cloudstar replied. "I must speak to the Clan first, tell them that we're not giving up after one defeat."

He clawed his way up to the branch in the gnarled thorn tree. The branch seemed higher than usual, and his hind leg exploded with pain when he tried to push himself up. Cloudstar hauled himself up with his front paws instead and balanced on the swaying twigs. Once he could stare into the trees from here and only guess where his territory ended. Now the half-built Twoleg nests loomed beyond the thin screen of branches, red and hard and threatening.

A cough below him brought his attention back to the cats below. The cats who had fought alongside him looked empty and battered beyond recovery; the only signs of hope were in the eyes of the cats who had stayed behind.

"Cats of SkyClan!" Cloudstar raised his voice, trying to sound like a leader his cats could have faith in to save their Clan. "The reason we lost today is that ThunderClan fought harder and better. They wanted victory more than us."

There were a few looks of surprise from his exhausted warriors, but others nodded and twitched their tails as if they were feeling guilty for letting their Clanmates down.

Something stabbed deep inside Cloudstar's heart. He knew his warriors had given everything they could, but they were outnumbered, hungry, and exhausted from too many fruitless hunting patrols.

"I don't blame any of you. All I ask is that you look at what you did today and see if you could have done any more. If the answer is yes, then there will be other battles, other chances to prove what it means to be a SkyClan warrior."

The cats below stirred, lifting their heads as if already contemplating future clashes with their neighbors. Cloudstar winced at their defiance. *I can't bear the thought of making you fight again, yet we will have to. I'm so sorry.*

He finished: "SkyClan will take back what is rightfully ours. We will seize that territory from those ThunderClan thieves!"

There were a few thin cheers. Cloudstar let out a sigh. His cats were so brave, so loyal. He could ask for no better warriors; but could they ask for a better leader? He jumped carefully down from the thorn tree and limped to Fawnstep's den. He needed cobwebs and something to ease his bruises—but not poppy seed. He had to stay awake tonight and figure out a better way to attack ThunderClan, a different strategy that would give his warriors the best—perhaps the only—chance of winning.

"Cloudstar! Cloudstar, wake up!"

A wet muzzle was thrust into Cloudstar's ear. Grunting, he swatted it aside and sat up. Through the branches of his den, he could see the sky turning milky with dawn, but it was dark enough that the stars still glittered overhead. *Are you still watching, StarClan? Any words of wisdom now?*

"Cloudstar, I have to talk to you!"

"What is it?" Cloudstar demanded, recognizing Fawnstep's grassy scent. "Is Birdflight having her kits?" He jumped up, wide awake. "Is she all right? Do you need me to fetch herbs?"

"Sit down," hissed Fawnstep, "or you'll wake every cat in the Clan. Birdflight is fine. Her kits will be here in the next quarter moon, but not tonight. She's sleeping peacefully in the nursery." She shuffled farther into the den and sat down. Her pale brown fur was just visible against the leaves, and her eyes gleamed when she turned her head toward him.

"I've had a dream," she began. Her voice was higher pitched than usual, and Cloudstar recognized another scent beneath the herb-dust clinging to her pelt: fear.

"I'm sure StarClan was showing me the future. Not far off—Birdflight was there with your kits, and they were still very small—"

"But strong?" Cloudstar interrupted. "There's nothing wrong with them, is there?"

Fawnstep shook her head. "No, your kits looked . . . healthy." She took a deep breath. "SkyClan was leaving the forest. We were at a Gathering, all of us. We . . . we had asked to stay, but the other Clans refused. We couldn't stay here any longer."

"What? That's absurd!" Cloudstar lashed his tail. "It's not up to the other Clans whether we stay here or not. This is our territory!"

Fawnstep gazed at him, and Cloudstar winced at the sorrow in her eyes. "You don't understand," she meowed gently. "There was no territory left. Not for us. The Twolegs had taken it all, and we had nowhere else to go."

Cloudstar stared at her in dismay. Was this really how it was going to end, with SkyClan hounded out of their home like a fox?

Fawnstep rested her tail on his shoulder. "I'm so sorry, Cloudstar. You should not have lost that battle. It is a defeat that we cannot survive."

CHAPTER 10

❧

A *pale half moon cast a* beam of light into the nursery. Birdflight opened her mouth to let out a thin wail. Cloudstar crouched over her.

"You're doing really well," he urged. "Just one more push, and our first kit will be here!"

Birdflight's eyes rolled around to fix him with a furious glare. "Don't make it sound so easy!" she hissed between clenched teeth. "You have no idea what this is like!"

"Ah, but it's the same for all toms," Fawnstep mewed. "Cloudstar's doing the best he can. Focus on your breathing, Birdflight."

Cloudstar grimaced as Birdflight sank her claws into his front leg. He reminded himself that it was nothing compared to the pain his mate was in. A spasm rippled along Birdflight's belly and a tiny shape slithered onto the moss. Fawnstep leaned over and nipped the birth sac with her teeth. The little shape started wriggling, and Birdflight twisted around to lick its wet fur.

"A tom!" Fawnstep announced, nudging the kit closer to Birdflight's belly. Cloudstar gazed down at his son in delight.

His dark fur was spiked all over from Birdflight's tongue, and his eyes were tightly shut, yet he still found his way to the source of the milk scent.

Birdflight stiffened. "There's another one coming," she gasped.

"Good!" Cloudstar meowed. "We want four, remember?"

Birdflight just glared at him. One more heave, and a second shape appeared, even smaller than the first. Fawnstep freed the kit's muzzle from the birth sac and pushed it toward Birdflight's head. The kit was much less wriggly than the first one.

"Is it all right?" Cloudstar asked.

Birdflight started licking the kit with vigorous strokes of her tongue. The kit lifted its head and let out a tiny wail.

"She's fine," Fawnstep purred. "A lovely little she-cat to join her brother." The medicine cat ran her paw along Birdflight's belly. "That's all, I think. I'll bring you some soaked moss, Birdflight. Try to get some sleep while they suckle." Fawnstep slipped out of the nursery, and Cloudstar heard Hazelwing, who was waiting just outside, ask about the kits.

He bent down and rubbed his muzzle gently over Birdflight's ears. "I'm so proud of you," he murmured. "A son and a daughter!"

Birdflight looked up at him. "I'm sorry I couldn't give you two more."

"Don't be mouse-brained. These two are perfect. They'll keep us busy enough for the moons to come!" Cloudstar studied the tiny, squirming shapes beside Birdflight's belly. "What should we call them?"

Birdflight raised her head to look at them. "The spiky-furred tom looks like a tuft of gorse! How about Gorsekit?"

"Perfect," Cloudstar mewed. He ran his paw softly over the she-kit. "Look, her fur is turning dappled as it dries, like the sun shining through leaves. Spottedkit for this one?"

"Spottedkit and Gorsekit," Birdflight murmured, settling back in her nest. "Our precious kits . . ." Her voice trailed off and she closed her eyes.

Cloudstar padded out of the den and took a deep breath. This should have been the most joyful night of his life, but nothing could shift the heavy stone of sorrow that was lodged in his belly. He raised his head and looked at the silhouettes that loomed around the Clan. Where once they had been circled by trees, now yellow monsters surrounded them on all sides. The rest of the forest had gone, cut down and hauled away to make room for more rows of gray and blood-red stones. Only the densest part of the woods remained—the part where SkyClan had made their home.

Cloudstar pushed through the brambles and walked into the empty, churned-up space where the glade of birch trees had once stood. He stared up at the claw-pricks of silver light glimmering in the purple sky. *Warriors of StarClan, do you see that I have new kits? Are you going to watch over them, or abandon them like you have abandoned the rest of us?*

Suddenly a wave of tiredness swept over Cloudstar. He had spent all day hunting in the reeds by the river, the only place left where there was any hope of finding prey. Some of the warriors had even tried to hook fish out of the water like

RiverClan cats, but had received only scraped claws and wet fur for their efforts. Every cat had started to loathe the taste of water vole, even Hazelwing's kits, who complained loudest of being hungry.

Cloudstar closed his eyes and tucked his nose under his tail. He slipped into sleep, and found himself walking in StarClan, through the lofty, whispering trees where he had met his ancestors before. He looked around, sniffing the air, searching for those cats who had told him how strong and safe SkyClan was, how it would survive in the forest forever. But the forest was empty, with only the scent of leaves and tree bark on his tongue.

"Cowards!" Cloudstar yowled. "Where are you? Come and face me, and tell me now that SkyClan is safe!" He began to run through the trees, ferns whipping at his ears and snagging his tail. Had the whole of StarClan vanished into the night? Or were his ancestors watching him in secret, avoiding him because they had realized they were powerless to help?

Cloudstar halted in a clearing, his sides heaving. "Give me a sign that there is still some hope," he begged. "Show me that you haven't given up on us! You are all we have left!"

But there was nothing except the rustling of the leaves, which grew louder and louder until Cloudstar's ear fur quivered. He put his paws over his ears, trying to block out the terrible noise, but it drew steadily nearer. With a gasp, he lifted his head and saw a yellow monster bearing down on him, huge and menacing against the milky dawn sky. With a shriek, Cloudstar raced back to the edge of the empty ground and watched as the monster rumbled past, growling.

"I doubt our ancestors even recognize their old home," rasped a voice beside him.

Cloudstar turned, startled, to see Starlingfeather crouched in the dirt, his pelt ruffled and his eyes cloudy from age. "I have come here every day to watch the Twolegs destroy our territory," the old cat went on. "Tail-length by tail-length, they have taken our trees, our prey, and our shelter. And worst of all, they have taken our hope."

Cloudstar lashed his tail. "Don't say that! We will fight on! We have to!"

Starlingfeather fixed his rheumy gaze on him. "Cloudstar, look at what lies around you. There can be nobility in admitting defeat and seeking another path. You have always led this Clan well, and that will not change, even though everything else might."

"Our only hope lies in finding more territory," Cloudstar meowed. He looked down at his paws, smeared with mud. "At the next Gathering, I shall ask the other Clans to help by giving us some of theirs, just as Duskstar did once."

"And if they refuse?" Starlingfeather prompted.

Cloudstar stared bleakly at the old cat. "Then I don't know what else I can do," he confessed.

The full moon hung heavily in the cloudless sky, turning the forest to silver and the pelt of every cat to a pale, washed-out gray. Cloudstar slipped through the bushes at the top of the hollow and led his Clanmates down over the edge. The scents on the warm air told him that the other Clans had already arrived. Cats circled beneath the four great oak trees, and the leaders waited on the Great Rock. They were staring in astonishment at the SkyClan cats stumbling down the side of the hollow.

"Cloudstar!" Swiftstar called. "What kept you?"

Cloudstar didn't answer at once. Instead, he pushed his way through the cats below the rock and scrambled up to join the other leaders. He looked down at the rest of his Clan-mates emerging from the bushes that grew on the slopes of the hollow. The apprentices were bunched together, wide-eyed and nervous beneath the stares of the other cats. Next came Starlingfeather and Hawksnow, looking far too frail to be at a Gathering. Cloudstar heard hisses of disapproval from elders belonging to the other Clans; they all expected to be left in peace once they reached such a great age.

There was a short gap, then Hazelwing and Birdflight appeared. Hazelwing carried Gorsekit, whose mouth gaped wide as he protested about being dragged through the thorns. Birdflight held Spottedkit, looking even tinier as she dangled from her mother's jaws. Webkit, Hatchkit, Emberkit, and Mistlekit stumbled behind the queens, too tired from the trek along the river to be excited anymore about attending a Gathering. The warriors circled the queens and elders protectively, bushing up their tails and pressing close as if they wanted to save their Clanmates from the gasps of alarm around them.

"Great StarClan!" Swiftstar exclaimed. "Cloudstar, any

cat would think you'd brought your whole Clan to the Gathering."

Cloudstar forced himself to meet the WindClan leader's gaze. "Yes," he mewed, "that's exactly what I've done."

"Why in the name of StarClan have you done that?" Birchstar demanded.

Cloudstar took a deep breath. *This is the moment I have to beg the other Clans for help. Oh StarClan, is this really what you wanted?* "Because we can no longer live in our territory," he announced. "Twolegs have destroyed it."

"What?" Redstar stepped forward. "My patrols have reported more Twolegs in your territory, and noise from monsters, but they can't possibly have destroyed it all."

"They have." Cloudstar stared through the dark trees, as if he might be able to see all the way to SkyClan's ravaged home. "They came with huge monsters that pushed over our trees and churned up the earth. All our prey is dead or frightened off. The monsters are crouched around our camp now, waiting to pounce. SkyClan's home has gone." He turned back to the other leaders. "I have brought my Clan here to ask your help. You must give us some of your territories."

Yowls of protest rose from the cats below the rock. Cloudstar's heart ached as he saw his Clanmates stiffen, as if they were bracing themselves for an attack. *We are only asking for help!*

Swiftstar was the first to reply. "You can't just walk in here and demand part of our territory. We can barely feed our own Clans as it is."

Redstar scraped one forepaw over the hard gray stone.

"The prey is running well now in greenleaf, but what's going to happen when leaf-fall comes? ThunderClan won't be able to spare any then."

"Nor will ShadowClan," Dawnstar meowed, standing up and meeting Cloudstar's gaze. "My Clan is bigger than any other. We need every paw step of ground to feed our own cats."

Cloudstar looked at the fourth leader. "Birchstar? What do you think?"

"I'd like to help," she mewed. "I really would. But the river is very low and it's harder than ever to catch enough fish. Besides, SkyClan cats don't know *how* to fish."

"Exactly," Swiftstar added. "And only WindClan cats are fast enough to catch rabbits and birds on the moors. There's certainly nowhere in our territory where you could make a camp. You'd soon get tired of sleeping under gorse bushes."

Cloudstar looked at them for a long moment. "Then what is my Clan supposed to do?"

Every cat in the hollow was silent. Cloudstar felt his heart pounding beneath his fur. *Please help us! Without StarClan, you are our only help!*

Redstar spoke first. "Leave."

Cloudstar blinked. *What?*

"That's right." There was a hint of a snarl in Swiftstar's meow. "Leave the forest and find yourselves another place, far enough away that you can't steal our prey."

At the foot of the rock, Larkwing, the WindClan medicine cat, stood up. "Swiftstar," she called, "as your medicine cat, I can tell you that StarClan won't be pleased if the rest of us drive out SkyClan. There have always been five Clans in the forest."

Swiftstar looked down at her with a hint of impatience in his eyes. "Larkwing, you say you know the will of StarClan, but can you tell me why the moon is still shining? If StarClan didn't agree that SkyClan should leave the forest, they would send clouds to cover the sky."

Larkwing shook her head and sat down again, looking troubled.

Cloudstar felt a wave of panic rising in his chest. "Five Clans have lived in this forest for longer than any cat can remember," he reminded the other leaders. "Doesn't that mean anything to you?"

"Things change," Redstar replied. "Is it possible that the will of StarClan has changed also? StarClan gave each Clan the skills they need to survive in their own territory. River-Clan cats swim well. ThunderClan cats are good at stalking prey in the undergrowth. SkyClan cats can leap into trees because there's not much cover in their territory. Doesn't this mean that each Clan couldn't live in another Clan's territory?"

Molepelt, ShadowClan's scrawny and rumpled medicine cat, tipped his head back to look directly at Cloudstar. "You keep saying that StarClan wants five Clans in the forest, but are you sure that's true? There are four oaks here at Fourtrees. That could be a sign that there should be only four Clans."

"SkyClan doesn't belong here," hissed a WindClan silver tabby in the middle of the hollow. "Let's drive them out now."

Cloudstar saw his warriors bristle and unsheathe their claws, ready to fight in spite of their hunger and exhaustion. *Oh my brave Clanmates! I am so sorry it has come to this. Abandoned by StarClan, and now by the only cats who could have helped us.*

"Stop!" he called. "Warriors of SkyClan, we are not cowards, but this is a battle we cannot win. We have seen tonight what the warrior code is worth. From now on we will be alone, and we will depend on no cat but ourselves." He closed his eyes for a moment, feeling his heart break in two. Without territory, SkyClan had no food and no shelter. Without StarClan, they had no hope. *There is nothing left for us here. I am the leader who could not save his Clan.*

Cloudstar jumped down from the Great Rock and pushed through the cats until he was standing next to Birdflight. His kits mewled at her paws, staring up at him with huge, frightened eyes. They looked as fragile as hatchlings. Cloudstar met Birdflight's gaze, and knew at once what she was going to say.

"Cloudstar." Birdflight's voice trembled. "Our kits are too small to make a long journey. I'll stay here with them, if any Clan will have us."

For a heartbeat Cloudstar cursed the night that StarClan had given him nine lives. If he wasn't SkyClan's leader, he could stay here as well, or live with Birdflight as rogues, beyond the wretched warrior code. Now his nine lives stretched ahead of him, cold and lonely and endless. *Oh Birdflight. Do I have to lose you, too?*

Kestrelwing, the ThunderClan medicine cat, pushed his way between two SkyClan warriors, ignoring their snarls, and bent his head to sniff the kits. "You will all be welcome in ThunderClan."

Cloudstar spun around to face him. "Are you sure?" he demanded. "After what your leader said to us today?"

Kestrelwing's eyes darkened. "I believe my leader was wrong," he meowed. "But he won't condemn helpless kits to die. They will have a future in ThunderClan, and so will you, Birdflight."

Birdflight dipped her head. "Thank you." She turned to Cloudstar, sorrow brimming in her green eyes. "Then this is good-bye."

"Birdflight, no." Suddenly, Cloudstar couldn't be brave any longer. "How can I leave you?"

"You must." Birdflight's voice shook. "Our Clan needs you, but our kits need me just now."

Cloudstar bowed his head. "I'll wait for you," he whispered. "I'll wait for you forever." He pressed his muzzle against Birdflight's side. "Stay with Kestrelwing. He'll find warriors to help carry the kits back to ThunderClan's camp." To the ThunderClan medicine cat, he added, "Take care of them."

Kestrelwing nodded. "Of course."

Cloudstar nuzzled each of his kits in turn, first Gorsekit, then Spottedkit. He inhaled their sweet milky scent, knowing he would carry it with him until his last breath. He wondered if they would ever remember him. Then he looked at Birdflight, drinking in the sight of her as if it were the only thing he would see for the rest of his life. *I'm so sorry.*

Birdflight gave a tiny nod, and Cloudstar knew what she

was thinking. She was reminding him that he was still the leader of their Clan. Without their home, without food, without StarClan, their Clanmates depended on him alone. Cloudstar lifted his head and signaled with his tail to the rest of his Clan. "Follow me."

He led the way toward the slope, but before he could plunge into the bushes Redstar called from the top of the Great Rock. "May StarClan go with you!"

Cloudstar turned and fixed a cold gaze on the Thunder-Clan leader. "StarClan may go where they please," he hissed. "They have *betrayed* SkyClan. From this day on, I will have nothing more to do with our warrior ancestors." He ignored the gasps of shock around him, some from his own Clan. "StarClan allowed the Twolegs to destroy our home. They look down on us now, and let the moon go on shining while you drive us out. They said there would always be five Clans in the forest, but they *lied*. SkyClan will never look to the stars again."

With a last flick of his tail he plunged into the bushes. His Clanmates poured in after him, and they were swallowed up in leafy shadows. Cloudstar had no idea where they were going, or where they would end up. At that moment, all that mattered to him had been left behind beneath the four giant oaks.

Farewell, Birdflight, Gorsekit, Spottedkit. I will find you again one day, I promise.

ERIN
HUNTER

is inspired by a love of cats and a
fascination with the ferocity of the
natural world. As well as having great
respect for nature in all its forms,
Erin enjoys creating rich mythical
explanations for animal behavior.
She is also the author of the bestsell-
ing Seekers and Survivors series.

Download the free Warriors app
and chat on the Warriors message
boards at www.warriorcats.com.

For exclusive information on your
favorite authors and artists, visit
www.authortracker.com.

KEEP WATCH FOR

DAWN OF THE CLANS

WARRIORS

BOOK 1:
THE SUN TRAIL

Gray Wing toiled up the snow-covered slope toward a ridge that bit into the sky like a row of snaggly teeth. He set each paw down carefully, to avoid breaking through the frozen surface and sinking into the powdery drifts underneath. Light flakes were falling, dappling his dark gray pelt. He was so cold that he couldn't feel his pads anymore, and his belly yowled with hunger.

I can't remember the last time I felt warm or full-fed.

In the last sunny season he had still been a kit, playing with his littermate, Clear Sky, around the edge of the pool outside the cave. Now that seemed like a lifetime ago. Gray Wing only had the vaguest memories of green leaves on the stubby mountain trees, and the sunshine bathing the rocks.

Pausing to taste the air for prey, he gazed across the

snowbound mountains, peak after peak stretching away into the distance. The heavy gray sky overhead promised yet more snow to come.

But the air carried no scent of his quarry, and Gray Wing plodded on. Clear Sky appeared from behind an outcrop of rock, his pale gray fur barely visible against the snow. His jaws were empty, and as he spotted Gray Wing he shook his head.

"Not a sniff of prey anywhere!" he called. "Why don't we—"

A raucous cry from above cut off his words. A shadow flashed over Gray Wing. Looking up, he saw a hawk swoop low across the slope, its talons hooked and cruel.

As the hawk passed, Clear Sky leaped high into the air, his forepaws outstretched. His claws snagged the bird's feathers and he fell back, dragging it from the sky. It let out another harsh cry as it landed on the snow in a flurry of beating wings.

Gray Wing charged up the slope, his paws throwing up a fine spray of snow. Reaching his brother, he planted both forepaws on one thrashing wing. The hawk glared at him with hatred in its yellow eyes, and Gray Wing had to duck to avoid its slashing talons.

Clear Sky thrust his head forward and sank his teeth into the hawk's neck. It jerked once and went limp, its gaze growing instantly dull as blood seeped from its wound and stained the snow.

Panting, Gray Wing looked at his brother. "That was a great catch!" he exclaimed, warm triumph flooding through him.

Clear Sky shook his head. "But look how scrawny it is.

There's nothing in these mountains fit to eat, and won't be until the snow clears."

He crouched beside his prey, ready to take the first bite. Gray Wing settled next to him, his jaws flooding as he thought of sinking his teeth into the hawk.

But then he remembered the starving cats back in the cave, squabbling over scraps. "We should take this prey back to the others," he meowed. "They need it to give them strength for their hunting."

"We need strength too," Clear Sky mumbled, tearing away a mouthful of the hawk's flesh.

"We'll be fine." Gray Wing gave him a prod in the side. "We're the best hunters in the Tribe. Nothing escapes us when we hunt together. We can catch something else easier than the others can."

Clear Sky rolled his eyes as he swallowed the prey. "Why must you always be so unselfish?" he grumbled. "Okay, let's go."

Together the two cats dragged the hawk down the slope and over the boulders at the bottom of a narrow gully until they reached the pool where the waterfall roared. Though it wasn't heavy, the bird was awkward to manage. Its flopping wings and claws caught on every hidden rock and buried thornbush.

"We wouldn't have to do this if you'd let us eat it," Clear Sky muttered as he struggled to maneuver the hawk along the path that led behind the waterfall. "I hope the others appreciate this."

Clear Sky grumbles, Gray Wing thought, *but he knows this is the right thing to do.*

Yowls of surprise greeted the brothers when they returned to the cave. Several cats ran to meet them, gathering around to gaze at the prey.

"It's *huge*!" Turtle Tail exclaimed, her green eyes shining as she bounded up to Gray Wing. "I can't believe you brought it back for us."

Gray Wing dipped his head, feeling slightly embarrassed at her enthusiasm. "It won't feed every cat," he mewed.

Shattered Ice, a gray-and-white tom, shouldered his way to the front of the crowd. "Which cats are going out to hunt?" he asked. "They should be the first ones to eat."

Murmurs came from among the assembled cats, broken by a shrill wail: "But I'm *hungry*! Why can't I have some? I could go out and hunt."

Gray Wing recognized the voice as being his younger brother, Jagged Peak's. Their mother, Quiet Rain, padded up and gently nudged her kit back toward the sleeping hollows. "You're too young to hunt," she murmured. "And if the older cats don't eat, there'll be no prey for any cat."

"Not fair!" Jagged Peak muttered as his mother guided him away.

Meanwhile the hunters, including Shattered Ice and Turtle Tail, lined up beside the body of the hawk. Each of them took one mouthful, then stepped back for the next cat to take their turn. By the time they had finished, and filed out along the path behind the waterfall, there was very little meat left.

Clear Sky, watching beside Gray Wing, let out an irritated snort. "I still wish *we* could have eaten it."

Privately Gray Wing agreed with him, but he knew there was no point in complaining. *There isn't enough food. Every cat is weak, hungry—just clinging on until the sun comes back.*

The pattering of paws sounded behind him; he glanced around to see Bright Stream trotting over to Clear Sky. "Is it true that you caught that huge hawk all by yourself?"

Clear Sky hesitated, basking in the pretty tabby she-cat's admiration. Gray Wing gave a meaningful purr.

"No," Clear Sky admitted. "Gray Wing helped."

Bright Stream gave Gray Wing a nod, but her gaze immediately returned to Clear Sky. Gray Wing took a couple of paces back and left them alone.

"They look good together." A voice spoke at his shoulder; Gray Wing turned to see the elder Silver Frost standing beside him. "There'll be kits come the warmest moon."

Gray Wing nodded. Any cat with half an eye could see how friendly his brother and Bright Stream had become as they stood with their heads together murmuring to each other.

"More than one litter, maybe," Silver Frost went on, giving Gray Wing a nudge. "That Turtle Tail is certainly a beautiful cat."

Hot embarrassment flooded through Gray Wing from ears to tail-tip. He had no idea what to say, and was grateful when he saw Stoneteller approaching them. She took a winding path among her cats, pausing to talk to each one. Though Stoneteller's paws were unsteady because of her great age,

Gray Wing could see the depth of experience in her green gaze and the care she felt for every one of her Tribe.

"There's still a bit of the hawk left," Gray Wing heard her murmur to Snow Hare, who was stretched out in one of the sleeping hollows, washing her belly. "You should eat something."

Snow Hare paused in her tongue-strokes. "I'm leaving the food for the young ones," she replied. "They need their strength for hunting."

Stoneteller bent her head and touched the elder's ear with her nose. "You have earned your food many times over."

"Perhaps the mountains have fed us for long enough." It was Lion's Roar who had spoken from where he sat, a tail-length away.

Stoneteller gave him a swift glance, full of meaning.

What's that all about? Gray Wing asked himself.

His thoughts were interrupted by Quiet Rain, who came to sit beside him. "Have you eaten anything?" she asked.

All we ever talk about is food. Or the lack of it. Trying to curb his impatience, Gray Wing replied, "I'll have something before I go out again."

To his relief, his mother didn't insist. "You did very well to catch that hawk," she meowed.

"It wasn't only me," Gray Wing told her. "Clear Sky made this amazing leap to bring it down."

"You *both* did well," Quiet Rain purred. She turned to look at her young kits, who were scuffling together close by. "I hope that Jagged Peak and Fluttering Bird will be just as skillful when they're old enough to hunt."

At that moment, Jagged Peak swiped his sister's paws out from underneath her. Fluttering Bird let out a wail as she fell over, hitting her head on a rock. Instead of getting up again, she lay still, whimpering.

"You're such a silly kit!" Jagged Peak exclaimed.

As Quiet Rain padded over to give her daughter a comforting lick, Gray Wing noticed how small and fragile Fluttering Bird looked. Her head seemed too big for her body, and when she scrambled to her paws again her legs wobbled. Jagged Peak, on the other hand, was strong and well muscled, his gray tabby fur thick and healthy.

While Quiet Rain took care of his sister, Jagged Peak scampered to Gray Wing. "Tell me about the hawk," he demanded. "How did you catch it? I bet I could catch one if I was allowed out of this stupid cave!"

Gray Wing purred excitedly. "You should have seen Clear Sky's leap—"

A loud yowl cut off Gray Wing's story. "Let all cats be silent! Stoneteller will speak!"

The cat who had made the announcement was Shaded Moss, a black-and-white tom who was one of the strongest and most respected cats of the Tribe. He stood on a boulder at the far end of the cavern, with Stoneteller beside him. The old cat looked even more fragile next to his powerful figure.

As he wriggled his way toward the front of the crowd gathered around the boulder, Gray Wing heard murmurs of curiosity from the others.

"Maybe Stoneteller is going to appoint Shaded Moss as her replacement," Silver Frost suggested.

"It's time she appointed some cat," Snow Hare agreed. "It's what we've all been expecting for moons."

Gray Wing found himself a place to sit next to Clear Sky and Bright Stream, and looked up at Stoneteller and Shaded Moss. Stoneteller rose to her paws and let her gaze travel over her Tribe until the murmuring died away into silence.

"I am grateful to all of you for working so hard to survive here," she began, her voice so faint that it could scarcely be heard above the sound of the waterfall. "I am proud to be your Healer, but I have to accept that there are things even I cannot put right. Lack of space and lack of food are beyond my control."

"It's not your fault!" Silver Frost called out. "Don't give up!"

Stoneteller dipped her head in acknowledgment of the elder's support. "Our home cannot support us all," she continued. "But there is another place for some of us, full of sunlight and warmth and prey for all seasons. I have seen it . . . in my dreams."

Utter silence greeted her announcement. Gray Wing couldn't make sense of what the Healer had just said. *Dreams? What's the point of that? I dreamed I killed a huge eagle and ate it all myself, but I was still hungry when I woke up!*

He noticed that Lion's Roar sat bolt upright as Stoneteller spoke, and was staring at her, his eyes wide with astonishment.

"I believe in my heart that the other place is waiting for those of you who are brave enough to make the journey,"

Stoneteller went on. "Shaded Moss will lead you there, with my blessing."

The old white cat glanced once more around her Tribe, her gaze full of sadness and pain. Then she slid down from the top of the boulder and vanished into the tunnel at the back of the cave, which led to her own den.

A flood of shocked speculation passed through the rest of the cats. After a couple of heartbeats, Shaded Moss stepped forward and raised his tail for silence.

"This has been my home all my life," he began when he could make himself heard. His voice was solemn. "I always expected to die here. But if Stoneteller believes that some of us must leave to find the place of her dream, then I will go, and do my best to keep you safe."

Dappled Pelt sprang to her paws, her golden eyes shining. "I'll go!"

"So will I!" Tall Shadow added, her sleek black figure tense with excitement.

"Are you flea-brained?" Twisted Branch, a scraggy brown tom, stared incredulously at the two she-cats. "Wandering off with no idea where you're heading?"

Gray Wing remained silent, but he couldn't help agreeing with Twisted Branch. The mountains were his home: He knew every rock, every bush, every trickling stream. *It would tear my heart in two if I had to leave just because Stoneteller had a dream.*

Turning to Clear Sky, he was amazed to see excitement gleaming in his brother's eyes. "You're not seriously considering this?" he asked.

"Why not?" Clear Sky demanded in return. "This could be the answer to all our problems. What's the point of struggling to feed every mouth if there's an alternative?" His whiskers quivered eagerly. "It will be an adventure!" He called out to Shaded Moss: "I'll go!" Glancing at Bright Stream, he added, "You'll come too, won't you?"

Bright Stream leaned closer to Clear Sky. "I don't know . . . would you really go without me?"

Before Clear Sky could reply, little Jagged Peak wormed his way forward between his two older brothers, followed by Fluttering Bird. "I want to go!" he announced loudly.

Fluttering Bird nodded enthusiastically. "Me too!" she squeaked.

Quiet Rain followed them, and drew both kits closer to her with a sweep of her tail. "Certainly not!" she meowed. "You two are staying right here."

"You could come with us," Jagged Peak suggested.

His mother shook her head. "This is my home," she said. "We've survived before. When the warm season returns, we'll have enough to eat."

Gray Wing dipped his head in agreement. *How can they forget what Quiet Rain told me when I was a kit? This place was promised to us by a cat who led us here from a faraway lake. How can we think of leaving?*

Shaded Moss's powerful voice rose up again over the clamor. "No cat needs to decide yet," he announced. "Give some thought to what you want to do. The half-moon is just past; I will leave at the next full-moon along with any—"

He broke off, his gaze fixed on the far end of the cave.

Turning his head, Gray Wing saw the hunting party making their way inside. Their pelts were clotted with snow and their heads drooped.

Not one was carrying prey.

"We're sorry," Shattered Ice called out. "The snow is heavier than ever, and there wasn't a single—"

"We're leaving!" some cat yowled from the crowd around Shaded Moss.

The hunting party stood still for a moment, glancing at one another in confusion and dismay. Then they pelted down the length of the cavern to listen as their Tribemates explained what Stoneteller had told them, and what Shaded Moss intended to do.

Turtle Tail made her way to where Gray Wing was sitting and plopped down beside him, beginning to clean the melting snow from her pelt. "Isn't this great?" she asked between licks. "A warm place, where there's plenty of prey, just waiting for us? Are you going, Gray Wing?"

"I am," Clear Sky responded, before Gray Wing could answer. "And so is Bright Stream." The young she-cat gave him an uncertain look, but Clear Sky didn't notice. "It'll be a hard journey, but I think it'll be worth it."

"It'll be *wonderful*!" Turtle Tail blinked happily. "Come on, Gray Wing! How about it?"

Gray Wing couldn't give her the answer she wanted. As he looked around the cave at the cats he had known all his life, he couldn't imagine abandoning them for a place that might only exist in Stoneteller's dreams.

DON'T MISS

SURVIVORS

BOOK 1:
THE EMPTY CITY

Lucky startled awake, fear prickling in his bones and fur. He leaped to his feet, growling.

For an instant he'd thought he was tiny once more, safe in his Pup Pack and protected, but the comforting dream had already vanished. The air shivered with menace, tingling Lucky's skin. If only he could see what was coming, he could face it down—but the monster was invisible, scentless. He whined in terror. This was no sleep-time story: This fear was *real*.

The urge to run was almost unbearable; but he could only scrabble, snarl, and scratch in panic. There was nowhere to go: The wire of his cage hemmed him in on every side. His muzzle hurt when he tried to shove it through the gaps; when he backed away, snarling, the same wire bit into his haunches.

Others were close . . . familiar bodies, familiar scents. Those dogs were enclosed in this terrible place just as he was. Lucky raised his head and barked, over and over, high and desperate, but it was clear no dog could help him. His voice was drowned out by the chorus of frantic calls.

They were all *trapped*.

Dark panic overwhelmed him. His claws scrabbled at the earth floor, even though he knew it was hopeless.

He could smell the female swift-dog in the next cage, a friendly, comforting scent, overlaid now with the bitter tang of danger and fear. Yipping, he pressed closer to her, feeling the shivers in her muscles—but the wire still separated them.

"Sweet? Sweet, something's on its way. Something bad!"

"Yes, I feel it! What's happening?"

The longpaws—where were they? The longpaws held them captive in this Trap House but they had always seemed to care about the dogs. They brought food and water, they laid bedding, cleared the mess . . .

Surely the longpaws would come for them now.

The others barked and howled as one, and Lucky raised his voice with theirs.

Longpaws! Longpaws, it's COMING. . . .

Something shifted beneath him, making his cage tremble. In a sudden, terrible silence, Lucky crouched, frozen with horror.

Then, around and above him, chaos erupted.

The unseen monster was here . . . and its paws were right on the Trap House.

Lucky was flung back against the wire as the world

heaved and tilted. For agonizing moments he didn't know which way was up or down. The monster tumbled him around, deafening him with the racket of falling rock and shattering clear-stone. His vision went dark as clouds of filth blinded him. The screaming, yelping howls of terrified dogs seemed to fill his skull. A great chunk of wall crashed off the wire in front of his nose, and Lucky leaped back. Was it the Earth-Dog, trying to take him?

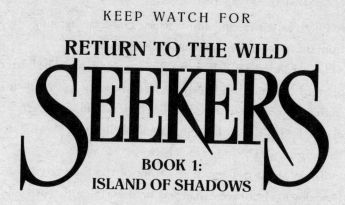

RETURN TO THE WILD

SEEKERS

BOOK 1:
ISLAND OF SHADOWS

Lusa

Excitement tingled through Lusa's paws as she padded down the snow-covered beach. Ice stretched ahead of her, flat, sparkly white, unchanging as far as the horizon. She didn't belong here—no black bears did—yet here she was, walking confidently onto the frozen ocean beside a brown bear and two white bears. Ujurak had gone, but Yakone, a white bear from Star Island, had joined Lusa, Kallik, and Toklo. They were still four. And a new journey lay ahead: a journey that would take them back home.

Glancing over her shoulder, Lusa saw the low hills of Star Island looming dark beneath the mauve clouds. The outlines of the white bears who lived there were growing smaller with each pawstep. *Good-bye,* she thought, with a twinge of regret that she would never see them again. Her home lay among

1

trees, green leaves, and sun-warmed grass, a long, long way from this place of ice and wind as sharp as claws.

Lusa wondered if Yakone was feeling regret, too. The bears of Star Island were his family, yet he had chosen to leave them so that he could be with Kallik. But he was striding along resolutely beside Kallik, his unusual red-shaded pelt glowing in the sunrise, and he didn't look back.

Toklo plodded along at the front of the little group, his head down. He looked exhausted, but Lusa knew that exhaustion was not what made his steps drag and kept his eyes on his paws and his shoulders hunched.

He's grieving for Ujurak.

Their friend had died saving them from an avalanche. Lusa grieved for him, too, but she clung to the certainty that it hadn't been the end of Ujurak's life, not really. The achingly familiar shape of the bear who had led them all the way to Star Island had returned with stars in his fur, skimming over the snow and soaring up into the sky with his mother, Silaluk. Two starry bears making patterns in the sky forever, following the endless circle of Arcturus, the constant star. Lusa knew that Ujurak would be with them always. But she wasn't sure if Toklo felt the same. A cold claw of pain seemed to close around her heart, and she wished that she could do something to help him.

Maybe if I distracted him. . . .

"Hey, Toklo!" Lusa called, bounding forward past Kallik and Yakone until she reached the grizzly's side. "Do you think we should hunt now?"

Toklo started, as if Lusa's voice had dragged him back from somewhere far away. "What?"

"I said, should we hunt now?" This close to shore, they might pick up a seal above the ice, or even a young walrus.

Toklo gave her a brief glance before trudging on. "No. It'll be dark soon. We need to travel while we can."

Then it'll be too dark to hunt. Lusa bit the words back. It wasn't the time to start arguing. But she wanted to help Toklo wrench his thoughts away from the friend he was convinced he had lost.

"Do you think geese ever come down to rest on the ice?" she asked.

This time Toklo didn't even look at her. "Don't be bee-brained," he said scathingly. "Why would they do that? Geese find their food on *land*." He quickened his pace to leave her behind.

Lusa gazed sadly after him. Most times when Toklo was in a grouchy mood, she would give as good as she got, or tease him out of his bad temper. But this time his pain was too deep to deal with lightly.

Best to leave him alone, she decided. *For now, anyway.*

Warriors: Power of Three

Firestar's grandchildren begin their training as warrior cats.
Prophecy foretells that they will hold more power than any cats before them.

Warriors: Omen of the Stars

Which ThunderClan apprentice will complete the prophecy that
foretells that three Clanmates hold the future of the Clans in their paws?

Warriors: Dawn of the Clans

Discover how the warrior cat Clans came to be.

HARPER
An Imprint of HarperCollinsPublishers

 Also available unabridged from
HarperChildren's*Audio*

Visit www.warriorcats.com for the free Warriors app, games, Clan lore, and much more

Warrior Stories

Download the separate ebook novellas or read them all together in the paperback bind-up!

Don't Miss the Stand-Alone Adventures

Delve Deeper into the Clans

Warrior Cats Come to Life in Manga!